BEYOND THE RUBY VEIL

Mara Fitzgerald

LITTLE, BROWN AND COMPANY

New York Boston

Copyright © 2020 by Mara Fitzgerald
Excerpt from *Into the Midnight Void* copyright © 2021 by Mara Fitzgerald

Cover art copyright © 2020 by I Love Dust
Cover copyright © 2020 by Hachette Book Group, Inc.

Little, Brown and Company
Hachette Book Group
1290 Avenue of the Americas, New York, NY 10104
Visit us at LBYR.com

Originally published in hardcover and ebook by Little, Brown and Company in October 2020
First Trade Paperback Edition: December 2021

Little, Brown and Company is a division of Hachette Book Group, Inc.
The Little, Brown name and logo are trademarks of Hachette Book Group, Inc.

The publisher is not responsible for websites (or their content) that are not owned by the publisher.

The Library of Congress has cataloged the hardcover edition as follows:
Names: Fitzgerald, Mara, author.
Title: Beyond the ruby veil / Mara Fitzgerald.
Description: First edition. | New York : Hyperion, 2020. | Series: Beyond the ruby veil ; 1 | Audience: Ages 12 and up. | Audience: Grades 10-12. | Summary: "After Emanuela Ragno kills the one person in Occhia who can create water, she must find a way to save her city from dying of thirst"— Provided by publisher.
Identifiers: LCCN 2020017687 (print) | LCCN 2020017688 (ebook) | ISBN 9781368052139 (hardcover) | ISBN 9781368053662 (ebook)
Subjects: CYAC: Fantasy.
Classification: LCC PZ7.1.F5732 Bey 2020 (print) | LCC PZ7.1.F5732 (ebook) | DDC [Fic]—dc23
LC record available at https://lccn.loc.gov/2020017687
LC ebook record available at https://lccn.loc.gov/2020017688

ISBNs: 978-0-7595-5770-3 (pbk.), 978-1-368-05366-2 (ebook)

Printed in the United States of America

LSC-C

Printing 1, 2021

By Mara Fitzgerald

BEYOND THE RUBY VEIL

Beyond the Ruby Veil
Into the Midnight Void

To those who just want to be seen

ONE

I'VE FINALLY BROKEN HER. TODAY REALLY IS MY SPECIAL DAY.

My nursemaid brought it on herself, of course. If she'd had any sense, she'd have gotten rid of me when I was a helpless infant who couldn't fight back. Instead, the poor sap tended to me, letting me grow and flourish and outmatch her. That's why she's standing in the middle of my bedroom, clutching at her face, realizing that she's never going to bludgeon me into the shape of a docile young lady and that she's wasted her life trying.

"It's hideous, Paola," I inform her as I tear the silk rose in my hands to pieces. "I'm doing us all a favor."

"Emanuela Ragno." She barely breathes my name, like the words are cursed. "This gown has been in your mamma's family for over a hundred years."

"Yes, and it looks it," I say. "Smells it, too. Did you really think I was going to walk down the aisle in some musty pile of lace?"

"Musty pile of lace?" she echoes in disbelief. "Musty pile

of— So help me, Emanuela, if there's one day you should wear a musty pile of lace, it's your wedding day!"

There's no time I should ever wear this monstrosity. The black skirts are so heavy I can barely move. The sleeves are enormous and puffy. The train stretches out of my bedroom and into the hall. The first time I laid eyes on the gown, I told my mamma it was the ugliest thing I'd ever seen. She sighed and opined about how it's been passed down on her side, the House of Rosa, for generations—hence the red silk roses tastelessly stuck to every surface. She rhapsodized about my spiritual connection to the women of our family and how wonderful it would be to see me in traditional clothing, for once. Occhian people love tradition. They love doing the exact same things every other person has done since the city began.

I tried the gown on. I didn't feel a spiritual connection to the women of my family. I felt like a little girl buried in hideous fabric. I also felt itchy, due to the gigantic silk rose smack in the middle of my chest. But I agreed to wear the gown, and my mamma shed a few tears, and we carried on as usual.

Then I bided my time until this very moment. Just as my nursemaid was putting the finishing touches on my outfit, I grabbed the offending rose and ripped it off. Now the fragile silk of my bodice is a ragged mess.

And just down the street, the cathedral bells are ringing. Everyone in the city is already inside, waiting for me, but I'm here, and Paola is in front of me, spiraling into hysterics.

"Your mamma got married in this!" she says. "And her mamma, and her mamma's mamma—you're her only daughter, and she's spent her whole life praying that she would live to see you married, and you just—"

"Calm down, old woman," I say, tearing another petal off the rose and dropping it onto the very satisfying pile at my feet. "You're going to hurt yourself."

"Calm down?" she screeches. "We're—"

"Late to the wedding? Then why are we just standing around?"

"Because there's a—"

"A massive hole in my bodice?" I say. "This is an improvement. Look how flattering my corset is."

Paola leaps to block the doorway, fists clenched. "Emanuela, don't you dare— I suppose you think you can talk me into this, just like you talked me into the gown with the slit. Not this time, young lady. Weddings are sacred, and you are not parading in front of the whole city with your fruits on display like—"

"Oh?" I drop the last of the rose onto the carpet. "How are you going to stop me?"

We stare each other down. Paola's nostrils are flaring and her dark eyes are burning. On paper, she's a servant, and I'm the first and only daughter of the House of Ragno. I could be rid of her with a few choice words to my papá. But I have my reasons for keeping her around, and she knows it, and every so often, we have moments like this—moments where I briefly, genuinely wonder which one of us will crack first.

She unclenches her fists. "All right, you little devil. Just tell me what your scheme is."

Paola is always the one who cracks. Just like everyone else.

I pick up my skirts and cross the room to my wardrobe.

"I should've known," Paola says to my back. "You haven't given me a moment's peace in seventeen years, so why start today? Why have mercy on an old woman for once in her miserable life? Do you know, I still remember when they first put you in my arms...."

This is the hundredth time I've heard this story.

"You were so small," she rambles on. "And so quiet. And for half a second, I thought you were a peaceful angel. But then you looked at me with those black eyes, and I swear, I heard a voice in my head say, *Hello. I'm going to ruin you.* And you opened your mouth and spewed all over my—"

"I remember it fondly, too," I say, reaching into the back of the wardrobe. "But enough about how I'm the only good thing that's ever happened to you—look what I just found. Another black gown just happens to be sitting around in here, begging to be worn. Isn't it beautiful?"

Of course it's beautiful. I designed it, and I spent months secretly stitching it to perfection. My creation is made of flowing black silk, with a tasteful rose pattern winding its way up the skirt. It has lace sleeves that look like spiderwebs and a scandalously low neckline, and when I walk down the aisle in it, the people of my city aren't going to see every other Rosa woman who came before. They're going to see me.

Outside, the peal of the cathedral bells dies off. I'm officially late. When I turn around, Paola is still across the room. She's folded her hands over her plain gray apron, and her eyes are searching me in a way I don't particularly like.

"Are you sure this is a good idea?" she says.

"Paola, I have the best fashion sense in the city," I say. "Everything I wear is a good idea."

"That's not what I mean," she says, quieter.

I know it's not what she means.

Paola glances at the bedroom door, even though we both know the rest of the house has already emptied out.

"You don't have to have a ceremony in front of God and—and everyone," she says. "The marriage will still be real if it's done in private—if you just asked Alessandro, he would be more than happy to—"

"No," I say, sharply.

I'm not going to let her talk me out of this now. Not when I spent all of last night talking myself into it.

Paola presses her mouth into a thin line. She knows the discussion is over, but she waits, like she's hoping otherwise. I hold my ground until she gives in and unfolds her hands. No one can withstand my forbidding stare for long.

"Well, then," Paola says, all familiar exasperation again. "Let's find out just how unholy this creation of yours is."

She wrestles me out of the old and into the new. Even with the unwieldy lace skirts and my excessive layers of underthings, it's a quick transformation. I know exactly how to shift and wiggle, and she knows my body better than her own. When we're willing to cooperate, my nursemaid and I are the most efficient team in Occhia.

Paola does up the last button and peers over my shoulder at the two of us in the mirror. She makes a small noise of disbelief. "God help your husband. That boy isn't ready."

I tug down my neckline. "He never will be. One final touch."

"Oh no," she says.

I open the drawer of my dressing table and fetch a tub of scarlet rouge from the back. Paola turns white as I brush it onto my cheeks.

"You are the daughter of a duke, you know," she says. "Surely some part of you understands that this wedding is about the joining of two families and not how good you— God and all his saints—"

I've moved on to dusting the rouge between my breasts. Paola grabs the brush out of my hands.

"Are you quite done?" she says.

I'm never done.

It's a short walk to the cathedral. The cobblestone road has been lined with rose petals, but the windows of the black manors are dark and silent. After the ceremony, we'll parade back this way to my husband's house, where there'll be a ten-course meal and an outrageous number of toasts, but right now, the people are waiting in the pews, praying. In Occhia, nothing is more momentous than a wedding. Everyone will be here, dressed in their finest and bearing handcrafted gifts. People I've never met are going to cry. The fact that my husband and I both made it to our wedding day is a blessing for us, and our families, and the city.

To that end, I'm supposed to spend this walk solemnly and reflect with gratitude. But I don't have the time. I pick up my skirts and march, and Paola makes a harassed noise, trotting to catch up. The towering black cathedral is waiting for us at the heart of Occhia. I crane my neck to look up at one of its enormous spires and past that to the veil overhead. And for a moment, I hesitate.

The veil is glowing a deep, rich red, like it does every day when evening is gathering. When I was a child, I asked a lot of questions about the veil. I wanted to know what it's made of. I wanted to know why it turns red in the day and black at night. I wanted to know what's inside it. Everybody had the same answer for everything—God. A thousand years ago, God created our little city. Then he created the first Occhians. He pulled their souls out of the veil and dropped them here, and they brought Occhia to life, claiming the manors and starting Houses that have stayed the same for centuries.

When we die, our souls go back to the veil. Everyone tells me that like it's as matter-of-fact as breathing and eating. No one seems bothered by the knowledge that we're encased by a mysterious entity that could swallow us up at any moment. They say that the important thing is that we spend the time we're given dedicated to our family and our traditions.

I . . . don't ask questions anymore.

We slip into the cathedral through a side entrance, where Padre Busto is waiting, looking impatient and dour. Padre Busto had the privilege of counseling me in preparation for my marriage. He loved every second of it.

"Good evening, Donna Emanuela." He dips his head politely, but his eyes linger on my gown. "I'm glad to see you took ample time to reflect on your walk over. My blessings on this most . . . holy of days. It is sure to be a . . . beautiful ceremony."

The judgmental pauses are not lost on me.

"Thank you, Padre," I say, curtsying. "You'll be baptizing our first child before you know it. My family is known for our vigorous wombs."

"For God's sake, Emanuela," Paola mutters, then remembers she's in God's house and cups her hands in apologetic prayer.

Padre Busto gives me the look of polite hatred he gives me whenever I speak crassly of my womb. I'm supposed talk about it with reverence, but if it wants to be respected, it shouldn't cramp and revolt the way it did last week.

"When you're ready, we'll move to the prayer room," he says, extending a very reluctant arm.

Paola starts to walk away. But then she doubles back and, faster than a blink, kisses me on the cheek.

"I know it's time for you to become a lady and leave your old nursemaid behind," she whispers. "But—"

"Yes, yes, I turned out wonderful in spite of you," I say. "Don't embarrass yourself, Paola."

I talk over her before I can hear the end, because suddenly, I don't want to hear the end. I pull away and take Padre Busto's arm. As he leads me off, I tell myself not to look back. At the last second, I do. Paola is disappearing around the corner. Her hands are folded tightly over her apron and her head is bent toward the floor.

She's nervous.

She has nothing to be nervous about. We have nothing to be nervous about.

The priest wordlessly brings me to the prayer room. I step inside, and he shuts the door at my back, leaving me in a tiny, dim space hazy with perfume. In front of me is a small altar smothered in burning candles. A copy of the Holy Book sits in the middle, its golden-edged pages already open to the appropriate passages. I kneel down in front of it with a creak.

Everything is going to be fine. I'm going to be fine. I've been fine for seventeen years, and I'll be fine today.

I dip my fingers into the tiny glass bowl of sacred water. I'm supposed to take the smallest drop imaginable, but instead, I take several and use them to wet down the few loose hairs curling around my face. Then I turn to the gold screen at my side and attempt to peer through the tiny round holes. Now that

I've solemnly reflected alone, I'm supposed to solemnly reflect with my husband-to-be. We're meant to slog through pages and pages of prayers about our undying devotion to each other and our commitment to spawning as many small, pious Occhians as we can. The screen, of course, is to keep us from spawning any small Occhians before the ceremony is done. I rap on it.

"Alessandro, your wife is here," I call. "Stop picking your nose and show some respect."

There's a startled thump on the other side.

"I'm not—" My future husband sputters. "Did you have to say that so loudly? What if the priests are listening?"

"You really should've thought of that before you blasphemed all over our meeting," I say.

"I'm not blaspheming on anything," he insists, taking my words very personally, as usual. "I was... Well, if you must know, I was praying. Like we're supposed to."

"How adorable," I say. "You were asking God how you can someday be worthy of me, I assume?"

"I... suppose you could think of it that way. I was just—"

"Don't bother." I idly flip the tissue-thin pages of the Holy Book. "I'm beyond all human reach. Especially in my new gown. And even if you'll never *thirst* for me the way you *thirst* for Manfredo Campana—"

He sputters again. "I don't—"

"—I hope you can at least appreciate the fact that you have the most magnificent girl in Occhia on your arm."

For a moment, there's nothing on Ale's side but flustered silence.

"I don't *thirst* for Manfredo," he says finally. "I admire him. You make everything sound so unromantic."

"Ah, yes, forgive me for daring to presume I know better than you, the master of romantic gestures," I say. "Every great love story begins with a boy stealing the used handkerchief another boy left on the card table."

Ale goes deathly quiet. The stealing in question happened two nights ago at a dinner party. He thought I didn't see him. But we're best friends. I always see.

"I meant to give it back," he says feebly. "But Manfredo was talking to all the boys from his calcio club, and they're so intimidating—"

"Don't tell me I'm going to step into your bedroom and find it covered in Manfredo's snotty handkerchiefs," I say. "My fragile constitution can't take it."

"It's not about the snot, Emanuela—there was a cologne smell on it. I just like the…" His voice is rapidly dwindling. "Never mind."

Alessandro Morandi and I were betrothed seventeen years ago, when we had just emerged from our respective mothers' wombs. No one asked us how we felt about the matter, because that's not what our marriage is about. Our marriage is about the fact that we can make the heirs the House of Morandi needs. That's why, in accordance with tradition, we put this day off until my first bleeding arrived.

My first bleeding took quite a while. Some of my peers were married at thirteen. Everyone wants as much time as they can get, because after all, the oldest Occhian in history lived to fifty before her first omen appeared. Most people don't even come close to that.

Ale and I may be arriving to the altar late—late enough that it's inspired gossip—but we've arrived. In just a few minutes, I'll be a duchess with some actual power, and everyone is going to see what I can do with it. And then they're going to regret their gossiping.

"Did you actually make a new gown?" Ale says. "Of course you did. Is it decent?"

"That depends on your definition of *decent*," I say, taking a moment to admire what little cleavage I have. It's vastly improved by the rouge.

"Oh no," he whispers.

"Oh yes," I say.

He's quiet for a moment.

"Are you nervous?" he says. "At all?"

I realize I'm smoothing down my silk skirts, over and over. Even though he can't see me, I jerk my hands back to the altar.

"What could I possibly be nervous about?" I say.

"Everybody in the city staring at us. *Everybody.* What if I trip, or forget the prayers, or vomit like I did during First Rites, or—never mind." He sighs. "You don't get nervous."

"Are you really nervous about everybody staring at you?" I say. "You need to get used to the jealous looks, Signor Morandi, grand duke of Occhia. They're not going anywhere."

He makes an uncomfortable noise. In Ale's ideal life, he sits in his room all day reading novels about other people's feelings and drama and convoluted webs of romance. In his actual life, he's about to become the head of the wealthiest house in Occhia, and he'll be expected to lead Parliament and talk to a lot of people and make a lot of decisions. That's why we're a perfect match. I'm good at making decisions, and he's good at following me.

From the heart of the cathedral, the organ starts blaring.

The priests knock on both of our doors at the same time. Ale groans, and his kneeler squeaks as he stands.

"Ale, wait." I press my hand against the cold screen between us.

"You're planning something, aren't you?" he says in a panic. "I knew it. Please don't be rude to the priest in front of everyone. Please don't make jokes during the vows. I can't, Emanuela. I can't. Not today—"

"Kneel back down," I say.

"But the priests are—"

"They can wait."

He kneels back down. When I lean closer, I can feel his apprehension seeping through the barrier between us.

"All you have to do is stand there," I say softly. "Don't think about the other people in the cathedral. They don't matter. If you get too nervous, just take my hand. Nothing is going to happen to you." I consider. "And if you do vomit, I'll take all my clothes off, and then no one will be able to talk about anything but me."

He sighs. He rests his head on the screen, and little tufts of his dark hair poke through.

"All I have to do is stand there," he says, mostly to himself. "You're right. I can do that. I can do that—"

He pulls away.

The next time we're alone, we'll be husband and wife. I promised myself I'd tell him the truth before we were husband and wife. And even though I knew exactly how my wedding would play out, it still feels like this part has snuck up on me.

"Ale—" I say.

"What?" he says. He sounds much calmer than he did moments ago. He sounds like he's almost ready for what's about to happen. I have that effect on him.

This morning, I woke up so early that the veil was still black. I crept onto my balcony and leaned on the iron railing, shivering in the chilly air, and I looked down the street to the grand House of Morandi. I found Ale's bedroom window, at the very top. The candle on the sill was dark, of course. Every night, he lights his, and I light mine. He sits in his room reading, and I sit in mine scheming and sewing, and when we go to bed, we blow them out. I realized that after today, we won't need that little ritual anymore, because we'll be together. I imagined a life married to some other Occhian boy who would see me as a means to an end, not as his friend, and I was certain I was the luckiest girl in the city.

I have to tell him now. He'll understand.

I open my mouth. "I—"

Or maybe I don't. It's not like anything is going to happen. We have nothing to be nervous about.

"I was going to remind you not to lock your knees when you're standing at the altar," I say. "If you're going to faint, let it be because you're overwhelmed by my beauty."

"Don't lock my knees," he repeats. "Don't lock my knees— There's so much to remember—"

He disappears, and I wait in the heavy, perfumed silence. When Padre Busto opens my door, I flinch.

My papá is waiting for me at the front of the cathedral, poised in front of the enormous double doors that lead to the inner chamber. He's in his usual crisp black suit, and the crests of our family are pinned to his chest—a small golden rose, for the House of Rosa, and a golden spiderweb, for the House of Ragno. When he sees me, he raises his eyebrows.

"What are you wearing, my little spider?" he says.

"Not the old rag Mamma gave me," I say. "That's for certain."

Everybody says I look just like my mamma, because we have the same shiny dark hair and the same sharp features. But Paola insists the Papá in me overshadows everything else. She claims we have the same look in our eyes. It says, *I get what I want, and I don't care what it takes.*

"How clever of you," my papá says, taking my arm. "Nobody ever remembers the people in these ceremonies. They all look the same."

Our family has lived in the same manor, passing down the same low-level seat in Parliament, since the city began. But now, we have my papá. When I was a day old, he planted himself in the parlor of the richest house in Occhia and refused to leave until they betrothed their newborn son to his newborn daughter. He spent the next seventeen years preparing me—not to be a spouse, but to be the head of a household and the head of our government. My mamma doesn't understand me. She wants me to dress like her and have babies like her and spend my life quietly tending to a home. My papá wants me to have more than any other Ragno has ever had.

And I will. I'm going to walk down the aisle in front of everybody—*everybody*—in the whole city and get the life I deserve. I'm not afraid. I have nothing to hide.

My papá pulls something out of his pocket and holds it out. It's a golden spiderweb pin that matches the one on his chest.

"You're a Ragno," he says. "Make sure they remember that, too."

In spite of myself, I hesitate. I planned the rose embroidery on my skirts and the spiderweb lace on my sleeves for a reason. I want to tell people who I am in my own way.

But of course I'll make an exception for my papá. We're a team. I take the pin.

Just as I finish attaching it to my chest, the doors to the inner chamber of the cathedral swing open. And for a split second, I wonder if this was really a good idea. For a split second, I'm wishing I was still hidden in the prayer room. But it's too late to change my mind now.

The organ music hits me like a wall of sound. The pews squeal as everybody in Occhia leaps to their feet. As my papá guides me forward, I suddenly appreciate how massive this place is. It's pew after pew and arch after arch and column after column, and they all converge on the golden altar in the distance, where Ale is nothing but a dark smudge in the candlelight.

I keep my gaze fixed straight ahead as we parade past the masses. I can tell when we reach the pews where the noble families sit, because I nearly choke on the mass of perfumes. The whispering gets louder, too. Everyone is either delighted or horrified by my dress. Either one is fine with me.

My feet have grown sweaty in their silk slippers by the time we pass my family. I don't look over, but I can hear Paola trying to shush my demon little brothers and my army of tiny cousins. We pass a row of stoic guards, their red coats barely visible at the edges of my vision. And all by herself, in the very first pew, is the only person who didn't stand for me.

The watercrea.

I've seen the watercrea from a distance before. I don't have to look to know that she has startlingly white skin and sleek dark hair, and she always wears a brilliant red gown. She looks only a little older than me, but she's looked that way since the city began.

God made Occhia and everyone in it, but there's one thing even he can't make—water. The watercrea is the only person with the power to do that. Her magic lets her control blood and turn it into water, and for a thousand years, she's been using it to keep us alive.

The watercrea takes her blood from our people. Once their first omen appears, they give themselves to her, and she locks them in her tower and slowly, carefully drains their blood into our underground well. In a matter of hours, they're gone.

I don't even bother to look at her as I pass by. Today isn't about her and her tower and her prisoners with omens. It's about me.

Ale is standing at the center of the altar, fidgeting erratically. His willowy mamma is at his side, watching me approach with a wavering mouth and dread in her eyes. As my papá kisses my cheek and deposits me next to Ale, two delicious, crystalline tears run down her cheeks.

I spend every day with Ale, but I'm always a little bit alarmed by how tall and gangly he's become in the last couple of years. Ale has his mamma's pale skin and graceful features. He could be handsome if he tried, but he's too busy being gawky and utterly embarrassed by his own existence. Right now, his enormous brown eyes are taking in the crowd, and his panic is slowly growing—as if anyone is really staring at him when they have the option to stare at me. I reach over and take his hand, pointedly pulling him closer. His fingers are trembling and clammy, so maybe he won't notice that mine are, too.

The organ stops, and in the ringing silence, we turn around to face the priest. Somebody in the crowd coughs softly, and it echoes in the cavernous space. A pew creaks. Ale's mamma sniffles. Then the priest starts to sing, and his opening prayer drowns it all out.

I sneak another glance at Ale. The traditional black jacket of the House of Morandi, embroidered with gold thread and green ivy leaves, looks wide on his thin frame. His head is bent in pious concentration, but I can still feel him shaking. I squeeze his hand, and he gives me a slow sideways look and squeezes back.

Tonight, after the celebration, we'll retire to our bedroom in his family's house, officially allowed to be alone for the first time. I know exactly what's going to happen. We're going to eat chocolates and open our wedding gifts and gossip about the silly things people did at our reception. He's going to fall asleep with a book in his lap, and I'm going to stay awake and plan everything for us, because tomorrow, it all truly begins.

I knew everything would be fine. This is my life. Nobody controls it except for me.

Then the priest stops in the middle of his prayer.

I lift my head. The priest's wide eyes are fixed on something over my shoulder. Slowly, I realize that a strange hush has fallen over the crowd. No one is coughing. No one is shifting in the pews. Even Ale's mamma has stopped sniffling, and when I turn around, I see why.

The watercrea has left her pew. She's standing in the middle of the aisle, and her eyes are on me.

Two

When the watercrea stands, everyone else bows.

They don't use the kneelers in the pews, because those are for praying to God, and God can't do what the watercrea does. Everybody in the cathedral drops to the stone floor. They disappear behind the pews, and abruptly, it looks like the building is empty.

For a moment, I'm mesmerized. With one move, the woman in the red gown has the entire city at her feet.

It must be nice.

I'm vaguely aware that Ale is already on his knees, tugging on my hand, and that the watercrea is gliding toward us. She stops a few paces away. In the shadows of the candlelight, her face is unreadable.

There's a distant little voice in my head, and it's screaming at me that I'm the only one still standing. I should kneel. I should run. I should do something. Anything.

The watercrea lifts a pale hand and beckons over her

shoulder, and one of her guards crawls out of his pew and runs forward.

"The bride," the watercrea says in a soft voice.

It feels inevitable. It feels like I've been holding a fine crystal glass that's slipped out of my fingers, and all I can do is watch it fall and wait for the explosion of shards.

The guard walks toward me. In his outstretched hand is something small and glinting, and when I realize it's a knife, I take a clumsy step back. Ale's grip on my hand tightens. But the guard stops an arm's length away, and for a long moment, he just stares at me. His face is expectant.

He's waiting for me to confess, I realize dimly. At this point, in front of God and everyone, any other Occhian would confess.

I lift my chin and regard him with disdain.

He lunges forward. He grabs my arm and yanks me away from Ale.

Obviously, I know how this is supposed to go. I'm Emanuela Ragno, and this is my wedding day. If a guard dares to interrupt and pull me around like he owns me, he regrets it.

It's just that I can't seem to wrap my head around the fact that he actually came after me. I can't comprehend his hands, heavy and foreign, on my arm. On my shoulders.

I can't let this happen. I have to do something.

The cold knife touches my back. It shocks me into action, and I leap away.

Or I try to.

But everything... stops. My legs stop. My arms stop. I don't know what's happening to me. All I know is that I'm desperate for my body to move, and it's not going anywhere. I try to scream, but my throat is squeezed shut.

Then my eyes focus on the woman in front of me.

It's the watercrea. She's using her magic on me. She's taken control of my blood.

Something is roaring in my ears, but over the noise, I hear the snick of the guard's knife cutting into my gown and my corset. He starts to wrestle them off.

I try to look away from the watercrea, but I can't. She's even taken control of my eyes.

I hear my clothes hitting the floor. I feel the cold air on my skin, and then the guard is cutting off my underpants. They fall away, and nearby, Ale's mamma stifles a gasp. I know exactly what she's seeing. I know what they're all seeing.

The mark on my hip doesn't look like much. It's just a small red smudge. But to the people of Occhia, it's everything.

"Quickly," the watercrea says. "Before it spreads."

No. It's not going to spread. They have to let me go. They have to let me explain.

The guard slides off the gold engagement ring I've been wearing since I could fit it on my finger. He tries to pull the crown of roses from my head, but Paola pinned it within an inch of her life, and it doesn't budge. A moment later, I feel his knife sawing through my hair, and clumps are ghosting down my back.

He's ruining my hair. He's not allowed to do that.

And then my feet aren't on the floor anymore. They slide out of my silk slippers as I hover a breath above the carpet, and I'm gliding down the aisle toward the watercrea.

They say the watercrea's power comes from her eyes. As I

feel myself drift past her and continue toward the back of the cathedral, I know her gaze is following me.

It feels like nobody in this whole huge room is breathing. I'm not sure if I'm breathing. I can't see Ale or my family and I can't blink and all I know is that everything is happening too quickly and too quietly.

It's not like I haven't had nightmares about this. But the nightmares were different. In the nightmares, I could talk. I could fight. I was dragged to the tower kicking and screaming, defiant and alive.

But I'm already at the double doors of the cathedral. There are guards on either side of me, pushing them open, and we're descending into the night.

The veil overhead is inky black. The guards swarm around me with glowing red lanterns, their boots heavy on the cobblestone, and I just keep gliding along against my will. We round the corner of the cathedral, and when we reach the back, the watercrea's tower is there, waiting. Its spike of a roof looks like it's about to poke right through the veil. It's the only building in Occhia that's taller than the cathedral.

I've never been this close to it. The closer we get, the less real the black stone walls look.

This is where people with omens on their skin go. This is where people with omens die. I know that.

But not me. They're not just going to put me in here. Not on my wedding day. They can't pull me from the altar and leave a pile of ruined clothes where I used to be. The whole city gathered there for me. They want me there. They need me there.

The inside of the tower is pitch-black and quiet, and the heavy, sweet smell in the air fills up the back of my throat. Blood.

The blood of dying people. I know the watercrea is somewhere behind me, because I'm floating up the narrow spiral stairs. We pass a hole in the wall, then another, then another, then so many I lose track. They all have bars over them.

Finally, we slow to a stop. A guard opens the door of the nearest cell with a creak, and I feel myself climbing obediently into the dark, even as everything inside me screams in protest. It's barely big enough to hold me, but I turn around and lie down on my back on the freezing stone. The shadowy form of the watercrea leans over me. She smells like rosy perfume.

Something pricks me in the neck. A needle. So she can drain my blood. So she can turn it to water, and everyone else in Occhia can drink it while I wither away.

The cell door closes and locks.

And the magic is gone. I can move again.

I rip out the needle without even thinking. I ignore the hot blood that runs down my fingers and turn over to grab the bars. I press my face to them and peer out at the black staircase.

The guards and the watercrea have disappeared. It's so quiet.

"Wait!" I scream, and it echoes in the stairwell. "I demand an audience!"

Silence.

"Hello?" I say, as imperiously as I can.

Nothing.

There's no reason to panic. There's no reason to let her think I'm afraid, because I'm not. I'm not afraid, and I'm not weak, and I'm not about to die.

This isn't going to happen. Not to me.

I was seven years old, and Paola was undressing me for bed. More accurately, Paola was attempting to undress me for bed while repeatedly cursing my existence. I slithered out of her arms and informed her that I wasn't cooperating until she brought me another hot chocolate, which forced her to chase me around in a very undignified manner. I chucked my dolls at her feet and tipped a burning candle onto the carpet, but I had the disadvantage of tiny legs, so eventually, I lost. She grabbed me and started to wrestle me out of my clothes.

And then I felt a strange pressure on my hip. It was quick but insistent. Like an invisible finger had reached down and poked me. My gown was already off, and I reached for my underpants and pulled them aside to look at the red smudge that had just made its home on my skin. It was like a small, bloody wound. The moment Paola realized what was happening, she stopped everything and rubbed it, like it was merely dirt. But it didn't budge.

I knew exactly what it meant. Everybody says the omens are put onto our skin by the hand of God. One day, out of nowhere, a small red mark shows up on our body. In a matter of hours, they spread across our skin, and when our body is completely covered, we disappear. And that's the end.

Some people make it well into their thirties before their first omen appears. Some people get them when they're only children. Nobody can explain why. They say it's God's decision. We're born from the veil that he created, and when our time is up, the veil takes us back. It's nothing to be afraid of. It's just the way things are.

The moment an Occhian discovers their first omen, they turn themselves in to the watercrea. That's the honorable way to die. Nobody would ever dare to hide their omens. The moment we know we're dying, we have to give up our blood, or it will disappear along with the rest of us. The city needs every drop it can get, and running from that would be selfish and shameful. It would be sacrilege.

When they feel the first sign of death touch their skin, dukes run out in the middle of Parliament meetings and priests stop in the middle of sermons. There may be a lot of powerful men in Occhia, but nobody is more powerful than their omens. Nobody is more powerful than the watercrea.

I knew exactly what the mark on my hip meant. Death was coming for me. It was time to go. But I didn't move. I just stared at Paola, and she stared at me.

"Well," she said, a tremor in her voice, "maybe it won't spread. Let's wait and see."

She got up to fold my clothes, and I stared at my skin. I waited, barely breathing, because I knew how the omens worked. I knew when adults were worried about me, and Paola looked worried. I knew she was just trying to delay the inevitable.

But the omen didn't spread. And for the next ten years, it kept not spreading.

For ten years, I've been waiting to feel the hand of God again. For ten years, I've woken up in the morning and practically torn my nightgown in my desperation to look, sure that I was going to find myself covered.

Everyone else's omens spread quickly. Everyone else dies in a matter of hours.

But not me.

I have my arm outside the bars, trying to get a grip on the lock on my cell door, when I see the shadow of a man on the stairs. I withdraw my hand just as a guard in red comes stomping by. He slows down as he reaches me.

"You shouldn't take the needle out," he says. "We need that blood."

"Ah, hello at last," I say. "I think there's been a misunderstanding. My omens aren't spreading. See?"

He looks me over. His gaze feels like cold fingers. I've never been naked in front of anyone but my nursemaid, but that's certainly changed. I casually put my hand over my hip and leave the rest uncovered. I've always designed my gowns to assure people that I have plenty of unmarked skin—so much that I couldn't possibly have anything to hide.

"Now, listen—what's your name?" I say.

The guard is still studying me. He's older, around my parents' age, with broad shoulders and a bushy mustache. He probably inherited his red uniform from his father. Being a guard comes with a house and generous rations, and if he walks through any neighborhood's art market, people will hand him things for free. But they won't meet his eyes.

"My daughter works for the House of Bianchi," he says. "I've heard a lot about you."

"All good things, I assume," I say, already knowing they won't be.

"You're the one who put the spiders in Signorina Bianchi's bed," he says.

One of my finer moments. Chiara Bianchi and I have always had a lively rivalry. At a recent party, she decided to spread very creative rumors about the things my betrothed and I were doing in bed—and the number of people we were doing them with. I found it hilarious. Until I saw that Ale did not. A few days later, on what just so happened to be the morning of her wedding, Chiara woke to discover a truly alarming number of spiders under her covers. And on her pillow. The hideous purple bite on her cheek went very well with her bridal gown.

"Oh, she blames me for it, does she?" I say. "Perhaps she should ask herself why her bed was so dusty it was attracting spiders. What's your name?"

The guard doesn't answer me.

"No matter," I say. "I've seen your face. I won't forget it. Keep that in mind as you decide whether or not to help me."

A smile creeps onto his face. It's edged with condescension.

"You're not the first person to try and threaten me," he says. "But our duty in death comes for us all. Even noble brides."

He's wrong. One tiny omen on my hip doesn't mean anything. I'm obviously not like everyone else, and this obviously isn't my duty.

"Isn't it dreadful to work in the place you're going to die?" I say. "Which of these cells will be yours someday?"

"I serve my people now, and I'll serve them then," he says.

"What if your daughter gets her omens before you?" I say. "Will you be the one to strip her and lock her up?"

"When she's meant to pass on, she'll do so with honor," he says.

It's the same way every other Occhian talks about it. Nobody should be so resigned about death.

"What if she wasn't truly about to die?" I say. "What if she hadn't gotten enough time to do everything she wanted?"

His eyes flit over me again, but he's growing detached.

"Listen to the people all around you," he says. "Do you think any of them had enough time to do everything they wanted?"

"I don't hear any other people," I say.

"Stop clawing so loudly at the lock of your cell, and you will," he says.

He turns away.

"Wait—" I say. "You can't leave me here. My omens aren't going to spread. You'll see."

He's already thumping down the stairs.

"I'm going to be the head of the House of Morandi," I say. "They can give you anything you want. You know that. And once they see how you've imprisoned me for no reason—"

He's gone. I clamp my mouth shut and cross my arms. I refuse to yell after him like I'm desperate.

The silence of the tower settles around me like a thick blanket. But it doesn't last. Because now that he told me to listen, I can hear it.

In the cell next to mine, somebody is breathing, slow and ragged and horrible. Somewhere above me, there's a muffled sob that sends a shiver down my spine.

Death in the tower is supposed to be quick. The watercrea takes as much blood as she can, but she's racing against the omens. Once the omens spread, it's over.

Maybe these people are dying quickly. But it doesn't sound like they're dying painlessly.

I draw back into the shadows, trying to hide from the sounds. I'll convince the guard next time. I can't let this go on for too long. I have things to do and people who need me.

My papá needs me. He has two sons, but I'm still his favorite. He used to sit with me in the library after my lessons, teaching me his version of history and answering all the invasive questions I wasn't supposed to ask. He used to take me on tours of

Parliament and show me the offices of the House of Morandi and tell me it would be mine someday. He used to tell me about the laws we could pass and the power we could hold if we worked together. We're a team, and we have so much ahead of us.

Paola needs me. Paola is a devout Occhian who prays before every drink of water and never breaks a law, and yet, she looked the other way so that I could stay free. She became a nursemaid, forever unmarried, because she can't bear children of her own. I was never just a job to her.

And Ale needs me most of all. We've been together ever since the day our nursemaids plopped our tiny bodies side by side on my bedroom floor. Ale was clutching his favorite doll, which I immediately grabbed. Ale didn't lift a finger in protest. He just watched as I mixed his precious toy in with mine. At the time, he was so quiet his family thought he'd never learn to speak, but I started talking and, to his nursemaid's astonishment, he talked back. He's my best friend, and we're not *in love*, but I love him. He knows that.

My legs grow stiff. I'm stretching them out when two guards appear and reach for my cell door. It swings open with a creak.

I knew they would realize their mistake. I dive for the exit.

"You really want to make this hard, don't you?" one of them says.

It all happens very fast. One of the guards yanks my arms over my head and wraps a chain around my wrists. The other one gets me onto my back. And then the needle is in my neck again, and my cell door is slamming, and I try to sit up but discover that my chain is also wrapped around the bars. I'm trapped.

"They can't do this to me," I say into the dark.

I wanted to say it out loud so that I could hear the confidence in my own voice. But instead, all I hear is the tiny quiver underneath my words.

They can't do this to me.

I don't understand why they are.

THREE

I WAKE TO THE CHIMING OF THE CATHEDRAL BELLS. AGAIN.

It's incredibly rude of them to interrupt my dream. Ale and I were at our wedding reception in the courtyard of his family's manor, surrounded by a rapt crowd. I looked, somehow, even more stunning than I usually do. We were making the first cut into our massive wedding cake, and I swear I can taste the creamy frosting and the toasted pecans now.

Last night, full of pre-wedding jitters, I ventured down to my family's kitchen to check on the cake. A maid was perfecting the white frosting. I stuck my finger in it for a taste, and she went pale with horror and scrambled to fix the dent. I waited until she turned her back. Then stuck my finger in again.

The cathedral bells die off, and the noise of the watercrea's tower seeps back in. Somewhere below, someone else's chain is scraping against the bars. The person next to me is still taking long, labored breaths. I wish they would hurry up and die. The sound is rattling my bones.

I just want to be out of here and in the House of Morandi. I want to be clean and warm and sipping sugary coffee in a parlor with my best friend.

The cathedral bells chime again. I close my eyes and count. Five bells.

I wait.

Six bells.

This is getting ridiculous. I clearly don't belong in this cell. If I did, my omens would be halfway across my body by now.

Seven bells.

I need to relieve myself, but I'm not going to just do it all over my legs. That's humiliating.

Eight bells.

Well, I can't hold it any longer. This is the guards' problem now. They're the ones who will have to pick up my grimy body when they carry me to freedom.

Twelve bells.

That doesn't seem like the right number of bells.

One bell.

Three bells.

I'm thirsty.

I hear a strange clinking noise. It takes me a long moment to realize that somebody is undoing the chains around my wrists. My cell door creaks open. I try to sit up, but my head is spinning and my body is aching and the next thing I know, I'm in somebody's arms, being cradled like a child. The guard holding me smells like sweat and salty blood.

"Leaving?" I croak out.

We're moving.

"Am I leaving?" I press.

"Quiet," he says. "I'm taking you to the watercrea."

The watercrea. I remember the sharp shadows of her face in the cathedral chamber. I remember her dark, cold eyes.

"No," I whisper.

"She wants to see you," he says. "You don't have a choice."

I should have anticipated this. Of course she wants to see me. I've defied her for ten years. I've lived longer than anyone with omens should.

I struggle to take in my surroundings as we move up the stairs. We pass tiny cell after tiny cell, and in every single one, there's the shadow of a person. Most of them are slumped on the floor, and I can barely make them out.

But then I see the girls. In the cell nearby, there are two little girls crammed into the same space. They're naked and shivering, and they're sitting up, watching me.

My insides turn cold.

"Why—" My mouth is dry. "Why are they in the same cell?"

"We need more blood," the guard says.

There are so many people in here that they've run out of space. The watercrea's tower is supposed to be a quick death.

"How long will they live?" I say.

"Until we can't take any more," he says.

I wonder how long that takes. I wonder how much blood I've already lost and how much more I'm going to lose once the watercrea gets ahold of me.

I've had quite enough of this tower.

I throw myself out of the guard's arms and hit the stairs. I'm sure it hurts, but I'm too cold and numb to feel the pain. He scrambles to grab me back, and the moment his hand touches me, I grab it and shove his fingers into my mouth.

I bite down. Hard. It crunches, and he screams, and it's disgusting and satisfying all at once. I'm already on my feet. I'm snatching the keys off his belt and scrambling for the cell with the little girls. I unlock it, but when they push on the bars with their tiny hands, I push back.

"They'll come after me," I tell them, breathless. "Stay hidden and wait for your chance."

Their eyes are huge and terrified in the dark. I only have an instant to take them in, but I can see that one has an omen on her shoulder. The other has one on her wrist.

I'm sure their omens will start spreading soon. Even still, I can't let them die crushed together in a cell like they're not even human.

The guard grabs me from behind, but I twist and slip out of his grip, and then I'm running. I stumble down the spiral stairs. He's right behind me. So I let him get closer, and closer, and then I throw myself to one side and stick my leg out. He trips and goes flying down the steps. He lands in a crumpled heap, and as I run past, I kick him in the head for good measure.

I don't belong in this prison. I don't want to be in this prison. And I always get what I want.

When I reach the door to the tower, I can hear the guard far above. It sounds like he's managed to get to his feet, and he's stumbling and shouting for help. But I'm already slipping outside into the black night.

Occhia has five different neighborhoods, made up of dark manors of varying size and grandiosity. They all cluster together to form a ring around the heart of our city—the cathedral and the watercrea's tower. Off to one side of the cathedral are the Parliament buildings, and off to the other are the public gardens. It only takes me a minute to navigate back to the winding cobblestone street where my family's house sits.

All the windows are dark. I'm shivering in the chilly air and desperate to get inside. Everyone is going to be amazed to see me. My parents are going to wrap me in blankets and my aunts are going to feed me hot drinks, and they're going to help me hide from the guards.

I move toward our front door. But then my eyes fall on the enormous manor at the end of the street.

The House of Morandi has been the wealthiest, most powerful family since the city began, when they took charge of organizing our government and our entire way of life. The central manor, with its towering, ornate double doors, is flanked by two wings, five stories high. Each wing has a tall trellis with ivy creeping up the sides. It's the most flamboyant way for a family to flaunt their status. Their household is so revered that they receive enough water to keep decorative plants.

Ale's bedroom window is at the top of one of the trellises, overlooking a small iron balcony. There's a burning candle sitting in his windowsill.

Without really deciding to, I'm running down the street. I run all the way to the trellis and peer up at the bedroom window that's supposed to be mine by now, and I decide the climb probably isn't as horrible as it looks.

The climb is horrible. The only reason I make it to the top is because going back down sounds equally unappealing. By the time I drag myself over the railing of Ale's balcony, my arms are shaking and my head is spinning. I collapse onto the balcony floor with an undignified thump and catch my breath. I peek through the large glass pane of the door to make sure his meddling mother or sister isn't around, and then I push open the door, crawl inside, and stagger to my feet.

Ale is sitting in his bed with a book in his lap. His hand is frozen halfway to turning the page.

"You look surprised," I say.

He looks more than surprised. His face has gone white. He's staring at me like I'm a ghost.

"There are guards behind me, of course, so let's move," I continue. "I need a hiding place. Do you think I can still fit in that trunk in the nursery?"

He drops the page in his hand.

"Em—" He stammers. "Em-Emanuela."

"I'm glad to see you haven't forgotten my name after... what was it? A whole day?"

"Three," he whispers.

"What?"

"It's been ... three days."

"No, it—"

I start to argue with him automatically. But then it occurs to me that he would know better, seeing as he hasn't been locked up in a dark cell, having his blood and his consciousness sucked away.

Three days. I've lost three days.

"Well," I say, "in that case, food and water wouldn't hurt, either."

He just stares at me.

"What?" I say. "Is it the hair?"

For the first time, I touch what's left on my head and dis-cover that it's been hacked off all the way up to my chin. It's not a big deal, I tell myself. Yes, I spent countless hours tending to it, and yes, I was rather known for inventing intricate hairstyles that no one else could figure out how to copy. But compared to losing three days of my life, it's not a big deal.

Ale is fumbling for words. He's still dressed for the day, his dinner jacket hanging over the bedpost. His eyes jump to the omen on my hip, but he averts them, quickly. Then they drift past me to the open balcony door.

"Guards," he says, like he's never heard the word before.

"Yes, there are guards behind me. That does tend to happen when one breaks out of the watercrea's tower."

"Guards—Emanuela—"

He scrambles off his bed and runs across the room to dig in his wardrobe, then emerges with a bundle of clothes that he shoves into my hands. The shirt is entirely too big for me, and the buttons are on the wrong side.

"Emanuela, you..." He darts around me and shuts the bal-cony door. "How did you get out?"

"Oh, it wasn't that hard." I attempt to pull on the pants. "I just—"

"Shh. Don't talk so loudly— What are you doing? You have them on backward— Oh God—" He reaches over and yanks down the pants, then forces me into them the right way like a very aggressive lady-in-waiting. He has to roll up the bottoms several times.

"I bit a guard," I declare as he buttons them for me.

"Oh God, you have blood all over you," he says. "Oh God, Emanuela—"

"We have to hurry," I say. "I told you. They're right behind me."

He still looks completely bewildered. He opens his mouth to say something else, but we're both distracted by a soft noise that comes from the direction of his bed. There's a lump under his covers. And it's moving. The sheets are tossed aside, and a girl in a black nightgown sits up, rubbing her eyes and blinking around the dim room in confusion.

It's Valentina Moretti. She's a few years younger than us. She's the oldest daughter of one of the wealthiest families in Occhia, and one of my many admirers.

I laugh. It's the only possible reaction. Ale hiding a girl in his bed is the funniest thing I've seen all year.

"What could possibly bring you here, Valentina?" I say. "You're in for a serious disappointment."

At the sound of my voice, Valentina shoots to her feet. She looks utterly terrified, which I also find hilarious.

"She's supposed to be here, Emanuela," Ale says. "She's—she's my—"

Then I realize.

She's here because she's his wife.

Valentina runs for the door.

"Wait!" Ale lunges for her. "Valentina, don't—"

She's already gone. Her feet are pounding down the hall, and when Ale turns back to me, his face is all panic.

It's been three days. And he already has another wife.

"You have to go," Ale says.

"Go?" I echo, trying to make sense of it.

"Emanuela, she's the watercrea." His voice is desperate. "She controls everything. She has magic. You can't—you can't just run in here and expect—"

He grabs my wrist. I pull away.

"Expect what?" I say.

He tries to grab me again. I stumble back.

"Expect what?" I say again.

The door bangs open. It's Ale's mamma. She's in a dark green robe and her eyes are furious.

"How are you still alive?" she demands, sounding very much like she's taking it as a personal affront.

I ignore her and turn back to Ale.

"My family?" I say.

I don't know what, exactly, I'm trying to ask. But he's still giving me that helpless look, and I still don't understand it.

"The watercrea was going to kill me," I hear myself saying. "She was—the guard was taking me to her. She was going to—"

"And that's what you deserve, isn't it?" his mamma says. "You disgraced yourself already by not going to the tower the moment you got your omens. You disgraced your family. The least you can do is go away and let us all be free of you."

Ale already has another wife.

It's like I was never even here.

"Emanuela," Ale says in a cautious voice. "You got your omens."

"No," I say. "You don't understand. I just got one omen. It's not spreading. But she was going to kill me anyway."

"But—what?" he says.

"You don't know what it's like in there," I say. "There were so many people—and these girls—they—"

"Shh," he says, casting a glance at his bedroom door. "Emanuela, you can't be in here. You have to—"

He's not listening to me. He's not helping me.

I could have gone to my family's house, but I came here. I knew seeing Ale would make this all feel a little more bearable. I knew he'd do anything I asked him to. If he were in trouble, I'd help him. He's my best friend, and if he were taken away, I would never be able to just carry on like nothing had happened. He knows that.

"I'm sorry," he says. His mouth is trembling. "I'm sorry. I don't want this, either. I don't. But—"

"Don't you dare apologize to her." His mamma sweeps into the room and takes his shoulders. "We all belong to the tower in the end, and we go with honor, like Papá. Only a coward would run from that."

Ale's papá went to the tower a few months ago. Ale was very quiet about the whole thing. He never said anything to me about it, so I never said anything to him. He wore the white memorial handkerchief in his pocket for a day, as is customary, and then it was like it never even happened.

"I'm sorry," Ale says again.

No. He's not sorry. If he were sorry, he wouldn't have been lounging around in his luxurious bedroom with his books and his new wife, not thinking about me at all.

I shove him and his mamma out of my way. I run for the bedroom door.

I don't need him. I don't know why I'm even here.

"Wait!" Ale says. "Wait, don't—"

I'm halfway out the door when a woman in a red silk dress steps into my path.

I freeze. I don't want to, but it's the watercrea's magic again. She's stopped my blood in its tracks, or at least, that's what it feels like. All of a sudden, my body doesn't belong to me anymore.

"Believe it or not, I understand why you tried to run," she says. "It's not easy to realize that when you're gone, the city will carry on without you, just as it always has."

I stand there, frozen, and I imagine Ale at his new wedding. I imagine his new bride listening to the toasts meant for me and opening the gifts meant for me and sliding so easily into my place at his side.

"I knew you were hiding an omen the moment you walked past me at your wedding," the watercrea says. "Do you know how?"

My heart is pounding in my ears.

"It was your fear," she says. "The moment you looked at me, I saw it in your eyes."

I wasn't afraid of her. I'm not afraid now. She doesn't know me.

She tilts her head, examining me. "You were hiding it for a long time, weren't you? I'm sorry, little girl. You didn't stand a chance. Once I see you, I can't let you go."

I'm not just another prisoner to her. Not after what I've done. She's determined to punish me herself, and she can, because she controls everything in this city.

She steps aside, and her magic pulls me out into the hall.

No. I can't go back there. Not without a fight. It can't be this easy for her.

Behind me, there's a small, dull thwack. The magic lets me go, abruptly, and I crumple.

I look over my shoulder just in time to see that the watercrea is crumpling, too. Ale is in the doorway to his bedroom, an enormous book poised in midair, staring at the woman in the red gown like he's still trying to process what, exactly, he just did.

Occhians don't just charge at the watercrea and whack her with a book. Even I haven't done that.

Ale meets my eyes.

"Run," he says.

"You're the one who should run," I gasp out.

The watercrea is already on her feet again. Her magic grabs me and yanks me back toward the bedroom. I slam into Ale, and we both collapse onto his bedroom floor. She advances on us, and we scramble farther into the room on our hands and knees.

"Get out," the watercrea says over our heads.

She's talking to Ale's mamma, whose forehead is pressed reverently to the carpet.

I wait for Ale's mamma to start wailing and pleading for the life of her precious son. But she crawls into the hall, whimpering with terror, and the watercrea slams the door and whirls back around.

Everyone in this city is a coward. There are thousands of us, and only one watercrea. We shouldn't let her do this to us.

"So," the watercrea says, her breathing ragged and her hair mussed, "you've got your husband in on it, too. That's fine. I'll take you both to the tower."

"Why do you get to decide if we live or die?" My voice is too loud, because I have to prove that I'm not afraid. "Just because you have magic—"

She turns her gaze on Ale, and he gasps and clutches at his face. Blood is dripping between his fingers. It's pouring out of his nose.

I'm on my feet. I charge at the watercrea on pure instinct, and she stops me with her magic.

But Ale is free. He's coughing and sputtering, but he's stopped bleeding.

She can only use her magic on one person at a time. I wonder if she's ever had two Occhians disobey her at once.

"You have no idea what it takes to keep this city alive." She spits the words. "How dare you question me. What do you think you know that I don't? What makes you think you deserve anything other than the time I've allowed you? Your blood is worth more to this city than your life."

She's wrong. My life is worth something, and I control it. Not her. Not my omen.

Ale stumbles to his feet and reaches for me, which distracts her. The moment I'm free from the magic, I lunge at the watercrea. I don't even know what I'm going to do. I just know that if she's going to hurt us, I'm going to hurt her.

She turns back to me, and I'm stuck in place, my hands outstretched.

Then it's a blur of confusion. Ale is trying to grab me. She's trying to stop Ale. She's trying to stop me. She's going back and forth, back and forth—

"Enough!" she screams.

Ale flies backward. He crashes right through the glass panel of his balcony door, and I bite back a scream.

I fight other noble girls all the time. My weapons are sharp words and little jabs in the back and cruel pranks, and I always win, because I'm always willing to go the furthest. But this is nothing like a tiff with a noble girl.

The watercrea has been killing our people for a thousand years. She'll kill us without a second thought.

She stalks across the carpet and flings open the ruined balcony door. The balcony creaks as she steps out to join Ale. He tries to crawl away, but she advances, backing him into a corner.

She's turned her attention away from me.

And I know exactly what I have to do.

I run across the room and through the balcony door. I dive at the watercrea. I push her with everything I have, and she tumbles into the railing, and she goes over.

Then, from below, there's a muffled crunch.

I've never heard anything like it before, and yet, somehow, I instantly recognize the sound of breaking bones.

And the watercrea hasn't reappeared.

And she still hasn't reappeared.

And I'm just standing here, staring at the spot where she was standing a moment ago. I have the sudden urge to turn and run—to slip through the depths of the Morandi manor and disappear into the night, and then I'll never have to look over the railing and see what made that noise.

But I'm already stepping forward. I'm already peering down at the street below.

The watercrea is sprawled on the cobblestone. Her pale arms are splayed. Her neck is bent at an unnatural angle. She's not moving. She looks like a doll that somebody stepped on.

For a moment, everything is still. Then a dark stain seeps out from behind the watercrea's head and starts to grow. It creeps into the cracks of the cobblestone.

A single red smudge appears on the watercrea's cheek. Then another. And another.

The omens spread. Quickly. Silently. They cover her skin like they're eating her up, and she disappears.

Her red silk gown crumples, and the only thing left of her is a small puddle of blood.

FOUR

NEXT TO ME, ALE GRABS THE RAILING AND PULLS HIMSELF
to his feet. There's blood on his mouth and splattered on the
front of his shirt. He looks down at the street. He looks back up
at me. His face is blank and uncomprehending.

"Well," I say. "That's what she gets."

That's the only thought in my head.

"Is..." Ale's voice is a thin whisper. "Is...is she...she's
not...?"

He looks at me like he's waiting for me to say something else.

"Oh, and you're welcome," I add. "For saving your life."

I get the sense those weren't the words he expected, but they
make perfect sense to me. His eyes dart around the balcony,
then back to the street. The watercrea's gown is still lying there,
abandoned.

She's really gone. She disappeared, exactly the same way
anyone else would. Her bones cracked and her omens spread
and she looked so fragile.

I don't know what I expected. But it wasn't that.

My eyes catch on a nearby shadow, and all at once, I realize that Ale and I have drawn a crowd. The nobles are peering out of their windows and poking their heads out of their doors. Guards in red coats are scattered around the front of the Morandi manor. Everyone is still and deathly quiet, and everyone is staring at the spot that used to be the watercrea.

The shuffle of boots breaks the silence as down below, one of the guards creeps over to the red gown and kneels next to it. He stares at the tiny puddle of her blood, like he's trying to will her back into existence.

"She can't be dead," another guard ventures. His voice sounds faint from all the way up here. "She…she wouldn't… she's not like us."

"She's not like us," the first guard repeats, like a desperate prayer.

They both look up at me, and their faces are expectant.

"What?" I demand.

Everybody on the street is looking at me. I think about all these same people, crouched down in the pews of the cathedral as the watercrea's guard searched me for omens. I imagine them peering out into the aisle, watching as my naked body was dragged off.

"You saw what she did." I gesture back at the shattered glass door. "She should have known better than to come after us. After me."

Ale grabs my wrist. His fingers are cold.

"Emanuela," he whispers.

"The watercrea told so many people when they got to live and when they got to die," I say. "But she didn't get to tell me. She'll never tell anyone again."

"Emanuela," Ale says.

Nobody down below is reacting. Their silent stares are burning into my skin.

If they had seen the inside of the tower, they wouldn't be looking at me like this. They would understand.

"You don't—" I say.

I'm trying to explain. I have to explain. But I feel the watercrea's needle in my neck, and I hear the shuddering breaths of the person in the cell next to me, and the words won't come out.

"You all thought she was so important." That's what I hear myself saying instead. "You really thought she was some sort of all-powerful, untouchable being, didn't you?"

I look at the watercrea's crumpled gown once more. I feel like I have to keep checking to make sure she really isn't coming back.

She isn't.

A laugh bubbles up in my throat, sudden and uncontrollable.

"Well, look at her now," I say. "Look at her now, and then tell me—who's really untouchable?"

"Emanuela," Ale says. "The guards—"

He tugs me backward, and I whirl around just as three men in red coats burst through the bedroom doorway.

They don't scare me. I just pushed the watercrea off a balcony. Nothing scares me anymore.

"No! No, wait!"

Ale's mamma runs in behind the guards.

"Don't take him, please—" she's saying. "It wasn't him—it was all her—she did this. I saw her—she did this—"

But the guards are already lunging at us. Ale is frozen in

terror, but I'm more awake than ever. I yank him to the side, scrambling up onto his bed. I toss the sheets onto the guards, who are already being bombarded by Ale's screaming mamma, and in the chaos, we just manage to dive through the door and slip into the hall. We careen down the nearest stairs. A guard on the next floor spots us and runs, but Ale belongs to the elaborate halls of the Morandi manor. He takes over, yanking me into a nearby study that somehow leads all the way down to the kitchens. And then we're bursting out of the servants' entrance, and then he's leading me down a back street. Around the next corner, he lets go of my hand and stops short.

"What—" he gasps out. "What do we do?"

It's obvious to me. I'm free. I can go back to the being the girl I'm supposed to be.

"Wait!" Ale grabs me again as I start walking. "Where are you going?"

"My family's house," I say.

"You can't," he says.

"Of course I can," I say. "My papá will help us."

We have a lot to do. We have to get all those people out of the watercrea's prison. We have to—

"Emanuela." Ale's grip on my wrist is too tight. "You can't. The guards will catch you. They'll put you back in the tower."

"And how are they going to keep me there?" I say. "Who's going to stop me with their magic? Who's going to steal my blood?"

I'm laughing again.

I can't believe it was this easy. I've spent every day since I was seven terrified of the watercrea and her tower, but with one little shove, I made it all disappear.

I wonder if she was just as surprised as I was. I wonder if she even had time to be surprised before her neck snapped.

All at once, my vision goes black around the edges. A loud ringing noise fills my ears, and my knees wobble. The next thing I know, I'm in Ale's arms.

"You're starved," he's saying. "You're starved, and you're not in your right mind—that's why you—"

"I found them! They're over here!"

The voice comes from the end of the street. It's a guard. I catch a glimpse of his red coat, and then Ale is sprinting. Everything turns into a dark, disorienting blur. All I can hear is the pounding of Ale's feet, and abruptly, we're racing down a set of stairs. I cling to his shirt, feeling very precarious and jostled. He skids to a stop at the bottom and sets me on the cold ground. Then he turns and runs back up the steps.

"Wait—Ale—" I crawl after him and immediately find dust on my hands and in my mouth. "Where are you going? Where are we?"

His whispery footsteps are already returning. There's a decorative lantern in his grip that looks like it was stolen from somebody's window. I try to get to my feet, but everything starts spinning again.

"Stop, Emanuela," he says. "Don't try to stand up. Hold this."

He puts the lantern in my hands, then scoops me up once more. I watch as we descend down a long, narrow hall of stone. The walls are interrupted every few steps by arched doorways leading into darkness.

I've never seen this place with my own eyes, but I know what it is. It's Occhia's catacombs.

Long ago, people used the catacombs to memorialize the

dead. Everyone got a small spot where their family could visit and leave offerings. My history tutors told me that we stopped the custom because the watercrea wanted us to focus on the city, not on the people who'd already left it. My nursemaid told me that most families had started to avoid the catacombs even before that. The halls of memorials were getting crowded, stretching deeper and deeper under the city, and sometimes, people went away for quiet reflection and never came back.

Now the doors to the catacombs sit abandoned in alleys all over the city, marked with a holy symbol. A couple of months ago, my rascally little cousins got in trouble for touching the door behind the House of Conti. They never would have been brave enough—or desperate enough—to actually open it. They've heard the stories.

Ale takes us into a side hall and stumbles around a few corners before he comes to a halt, wheezing. He sets me on the ground, and I slump against the cold wall, the lantern between us. We sit there in our little bubble of light, and for a long moment, he just stares at me.

The two of us have spent our entire lives with family or chaperones a moment away. We've never been so alone with each other, and we've certainly never been so far from the rest of our city. The quiet makes my ears ring.

"The catacombs?" I say. "Really, Ale? I told you to go to my family's house. We could have snuck in the back, if we were quick."

Ale doesn't say anything.

"Well, I'm not staying here," I continue. "For one thing, I can't work in the presence of such…"

I glance over his head at the row of memorial nooks carved

into the wall. They're filled with cobwebs. My nursemaid has a lot of dramatic tales about spirits who were sinful in life and found themselves unable to return to the veil. According to her, they roam the catacombs, trapped and furious.

"Uninspired decor," I finish, turning my eyes away. "We need to know what's happening in the city. We need food. We need—"

The next word turns into a knot in my throat.

"Water?" Ale's voice is barely a whisper.

Water. We need water.

"The city has lots of water," I say. "It's stored under the tower. Haven't you ever looked at a map?"

"And what are we going to do when that runs out?" Ale says.

"We'll…"

The watercrea has been making our water since the city began. There's no other way. Everyone knows that. I know that.

"We'll just…" I try again.

The watercrea is dead. The watercrea is dead, and I killed her, and everyone saw me do it.

Occhians spend a lot of time reminding one another how precious our existence is. In the middle of the endless veil, God created a tiny pocket of life for us. The most important thing we can do is serve the city and keep it the way it's always been, because the city is fragile.

That's what the priests say. That's what my mamma says. I've always thought it was a load of nonsense. There's no point in being alive unless you're going to do more than everyone before you has done. Things should get better, not stay the same. And our city isn't so fragile that it could be destroyed by one person.

Our city can't possibly be that fragile.

I swallow hard, and I force myself to look Ale in the eyes.

"We'll find another way," I say with all the confidence I can muster. "We don't need her."

For a long moment, he's silent.

"The city is almost a thousand years old," he says finally.

"I know," I say.

"We've always had the watercrea," he says.

"I know," I say.

He's silent again.

"Don't look so grim, Ale," I say. "My papá will help. He can get us into the records of Parliament. Surely, in the past thousand years, somebody has—"

"How can you be so sure?"

Ale's voice is loud, and it startles me into silence. I can't remember the last time he raised his voice at me.

"If we can't find more water, we're all going to die," he presses on. "Our families are going to die. The whole city is going to die. And that includes you, Emanuela. You realize that, don't you?"

My heart is pounding in my ears. "Yes," I say, and I'm impressed by how calm I manage to sound.

"And does it concern you?" he says. "At all?"

I shrug. "It's not like I could have stayed in the tower."

"Well—" he says.

He cuts himself off. But he has more to say. I can see it on his face.

I narrow my eyes. "Well?"

"You—" He's floundering and avoiding my gaze. "You got your omens. Even if they weren't spreading very quickly, it still means—"

"It means nothing," I snap. "Nothing. Do you understand?"

"But the law—" he says. "You can't just—"

"I've had an omen since I was seven," I say. "I just kept it hidden, and guess what? It never spread. It still hasn't."

Ale looks stricken.

"You—" His voice is suddenly small and betrayed. "You've—had it since…"

I'm not going to apologize for keeping this secret from him for the last ten years, even if we have spent every day of those ten years together. I had my reasons.

"The watercrea tried to kill me," I say. "It wasn't some kind of noble mercy killing, or whatever it is you tell yourself she does. It was murder."

"But…" he says. "Emanuela, are you sure—"

"Am I sure about what?" I say. "The mark on my own skin? Am I sure about the things I saw her doing with my own eyes? The watercrea got what she deserved. If you disagree, then you shouldn't have attacked her and run off with me, because now you're my accomplice."

"That's not what I—" he says.

"Would you rather be back in your room with your new wife?" I say. "I'm so very sorry about that. My efforts to stop us both from getting murdered took you away from her."

The look he gives me is wary. "Emanuela—"

"How did you two get on, by the way?" I say.

"Valentina and me? We just—"

"The conversations must have been scintillating," I say. "Every conversation with you is so scintillating."

"I—she—" He's stammering hopelessly.

"Oh, and just how terrible was it?" I say.

"How terrible was what?" he says.

"Bedding her," I say.

The look he gives me is pure horror, and I find myself relishing it.

"We didn't—" he says. "Her betrothed went to the tower last week. She was— We were both—"

"You would have had to bed her eventually," I say. "And cried the whole time, no doubt. What a nightmare."

He flushes. "Why do you care? It's not like either of us wanted…that."

"I don't care," I assure him.

"Then why are we talking about it? We have more important—"

"Nobody wants that with you," I say. "Nobody wants you at all. Do you even realize how pathetic your life is without me? What did you even do while I was in the tower? Hide in your room like a child? What would you have done with the rest of your miserable days?"

He's not looking at me anymore.

"Well?" I demand.

He doesn't answer me. But he doesn't need to.

I didn't belong in the watercrea's tower. I know it. He knows it. Everybody should know it.

I get to my feet. I'm weak and shaking, but I keep myself upright through sheer force of will.

"I'm not sorry," I say.

I'm not sorry about any of it.

Then I march off into the dark.

I make it around the next corner before my legs give out.

I collapse, biting back my scream of frustration, and urge my body to crawl, but it won't. I'm too hungry. I'm too thirsty. I've lost too much blood.

Ale creeps around the corner, lantern in hand. Without a word, he sits down across from me.

I crawl away.

"Emanuela—" he says.

When I've escaped the light of his lantern, I stop, curling up on my side. Maybe, in this exact moment, I'm not capable of sprinting off. But I'm trying to make a point.

The watercrea got what she deserved. It wasn't like I killed her for no reason. It wasn't like she was a person the way the rest of us are. She didn't have family or friends. She didn't have anyone. She just had a tower and magic and prisoners, and now all those prisoners are free. I'm free.

I'm not going to think about the sound she made when she hit the ground. I'm not going to think about the way her blood seeped out of her broken body like she was an ordinary person.

But now that I'm lying here in the dark, it's all I can remember.

I curl tighter into myself. I have to stop shivering, or Ale is going to notice.

The watercrea wasn't an ordinary person. She was just a thing holding our city captive—a thing that tried to kill me and my best friend. But she failed.

She's gone. She can't touch me anymore. And that's what matters.

When I was very small, I was sick. I had fits—bad ones. I would seize up out of nowhere and black out and, apparently, thrash around and hurt myself. Paola carried me up and down the stairs to head off a fall. Ale surrounded me with pillows whenever we played on the floor. They found my sickness terrifying, but I mostly found it aggravating. I'd be in the middle of doing something important, like making an exhaustive list of Chiara Bianchi's worst qualities to read out at her next party, when I'd feel funny and warm. The next thing I knew, I was waking up on the floor with ink everywhere and my mamma standing over me, crying noisily.

I hated losing time. I hated that, no matter how much I pressed them, nobody ever properly described what my fits looked like. It was my body, and I wanted to know what it was doing without me.

When the fits got so bad I became bedridden, it didn't strike me as anything more than another bothersome obstacle. I was used to feeling terrible and exhausted, so I assumed that I would just carry on my business from bed until it subsided again. One afternoon, I was sitting under my covers with an array of dolls in my lap. They were a gift from the House of De Lucia, known for their intricate porcelain sculpting. I was prying off the dolls' beautiful heads and swapping them. It was a very involved ritual, so at first, I didn't notice the commotion in the hall. Then my door opened to reveal one of the doctors who was always rotating in and out of my room. He was one of my least favorites. His beard was distractingly ugly.

"I believe you, Signor Ragno," he was saying. "But you know how quickly they spread."

My papá ran into the room after the doctor, and I sat up

straighter. My papá was very busy. I usually didn't see him until the evening.

"She doesn't have any," my papá was saying.

"I believe you," the doctor said again, pulling on a pair of black gloves. "But it could happen at any moment—"

My papá dove in front of my bed.

"Of course you believe me," he said. "Because it's the truth, and there's nothing more to be done. She's engaged to the heir of the House of Morandi, you know."

"I know," the doctor said.

"What shall I tell them, then?" my papá said. "That you're questioning the loyalty of both our houses to the city?"

I had no idea what was going on, but I held my breath none-theless. My papá wasn't a tall man, but he'd somehow managed to draw himself up in a way that I found very intimidating. There was a power in his voice that I'd never heard before.

The doctor, on the other hand, had gone very quiet. He wavered for a moment, but then he took a small step back.

"If it gets any worse—" he said.

"It won't," my papá said.

"I know you won't hesitate to do your duty for the city," he said.

"We won't," my papá said, in a way that made it very clear the conversation was over.

Without another word, the doctor disappeared. My papá turned to face me. He looked flushed, like he'd run from the Parliament buildings in his crisp black suit.

"What's happening, Papá?" I said, and my voice came out very small.

He took up the chair at my bedside. "Nothing," he said

coolly. "Now, tell me about your dolls, my little spider. They look rather...headless."

That night, it was Paola sitting at my bedside instead, a pile of shoes to be polished in her lap. I was supposed to be sleeping, but I was just staring at the ceiling, until finally, the words tumbled out of my mouth.

"Why did the doctor want to take me away?" I said.

"He's not going to," Paola said without looking up. "Your papá made sure of that."

"I know, Paola," I said. "I saw it. But why did he want to take me away?"

She paused in her work, and she was quiet for a long moment. Too long.

"The doctors wanted to keep a closer eye on you," she said. "That's all."

"Because they think I'm going to die," I said.

Paola opened her mouth. She shut it.

The doctors thought I was going to die, which meant they also thought my first omen was about to appear. They wanted to make sure they were nearby to rush me to the watercrea's tower before my omens spread. Anybody could get their omens at any moment, but with very sick people, it was a certainty.

Everybody said that when we died, we went back into the veil. They said God was in the veil. They said everyone who had ever lived was in the veil. But they never explained it in a way I could really understand. They never explained how it would look or what it would feel like.

When I tried to imagine it for myself, I couldn't. Instead, I just pictured my family and Paola and Ale going on without me. I imagined them growing older and filling up their lives with other people and not even noticing when my birthday passed by. Now that I was thinking about it, I couldn't believe I'd ever been able to not think about it.

"Paola," I said.

"Yes?" she said slowly.

"I'm not going to die," I said. "Do you know why?"

"Why?" Her voice was quiet.

"Because I don't want to," I said.

The look on her face was impossible to read. I was terrified she was going to laugh, because sometimes I said things that were very serious, and grown-ups just laughed. She smiled, and I tensed defensively as she picked up the washcloth at my side and reached out to dab my clammy forehead.

"Fierce little Emanuela," she murmured. "I believe you. I really do."

She was right to believe me. My fits became farther and fewer between. In a few months, I was bouncing from tea party to tea party, tussling with all the other little girls, and the worst of it was a distant memory.

I was completely healthy when my omen appeared on my hip. It just showed up out of nowhere, for no reason at all.

Of course I didn't turn myself over to the tower. My sickness couldn't kill me. One little mark on my skin wasn't going to kill me, either.

Nothing is going to kill me. I won't let it.

FIVE

I DON'T REALIZE I'VE DOZED OFF UNTIL I'M WAKING UP. It's pitch-black, and there are cold fingers on my arm.

"Emanuela—shh—shhh—"

Now there's a cold hand over my mouth, suffocating me. My first thought is that I'm in the watercrea's tower. I'm certain that her guard is carrying me off to whatever terrible punishment she uses on people who defy her.

"Sorry." The voice is whispering right in my ear. "Sorry. I—I heard something. I think—"

Of course. It's Ale. I'm in the catacombs with him because the watercrea is dead. Because I killed her.

"I blew out the lantern," he says.

I sit up and look around the dark hall, which doesn't accomplish much. Then I hear the footsteps. They're soft and quick, and they're coming from...somewhere nearby. The way the sound bounces off the stone walls makes it hard to be sure about anything more than that.

Ale fumbles at me like he's trying to pick me up.

"What are you doing?" I demand.

"Shh," he says. "I'm hiding you. In one of the memorials."

He's talking about the nooks all sitting in a row, meant for dead people. I'm not going into one of those. I squirm away.

"Emanuela—"

He tries to grab me again. A brief struggle ensues, and my foot connects with something metal. Our lantern topples over and rolls, and it is, to say the least, rather loud.

Ale and I freeze.

The footsteps get louder.

I climb to my feet. I'm still shaky, but sleep has given me just enough strength to get by. I can feel Ale close behind as I run, quietly, trying to get away from the footsteps. I reach the end of the hall and duck around the corner.

I've miscalculated. Someone is there. It's a shadowy figure holding a glowing lantern of their own.

They lunge for me.

"Emanuela—" they're saying. "Don't you—augh! Don't you dare bite me, you little—"

I recognize the shrill voice and cease my attack.

"Paola?" I say. "How did you—"

"Shh." She pushes me against the wall and urges me to the ground, where she crouches in front of me. "Here."

She puts something in my lap. It's a loaf of bread, and I'm tearing into it without even deciding to.

"Where's Alessandro?" she says. "Oh—hovering, as always. Get over here, you silly thing. We don't have much time."

"How did you find us?" I say through the bread as Ale's worried face appears over Paola's shoulder.

"A rumor," she says. "Apparently, one of the maids at the

House of Serpico saw you go this way. The guards will be close behind me—although I heard them arguing over who has to search down here, the superstitious lumps."

"You're superstitious," I remind her.

"But I'm always prepared." She produces a small pouch out of her bosom and waves it around me, like she's warding off demons. I'm very familiar with Paola's protective blends. This one smells characteristically horrid—like too-spicy peppers and rotten garlic.

"So the guards know we're here," I say.

"And they've searched everywhere else," she says. "You can't make enemies in Occhia."

You can't make enemies in Occhia is one of Paola's favorite sayings. It means that even two Occhians who live in distant manors in distant neighborhoods will see each other at every worship and every party and every holiday market. This, of course, has never stopped me from making enemies before. I like being able to see them.

"We just have to find a way back up to the city," I say. "One that's not crawling with guards. Then—"

"It's not just the guards, Emanuela," she says.

"What?" I say.

"Everyone knows what you did," she says. "Everyone's looking for you, and they want to see you punished. They're desperate for it, actually. I've never seen the city like this."

Everyone is looking for me. The thought is, somehow, equal parts disconcerting and pleasing. They're not thinking of me as the girl who was stripped naked and dragged out of her own wedding. Not anymore.

"Why are they so worried about me?" I say. "If they were smart, they'd be hoarding water."

Paola's face turns grim.

"There's no water to hoard," she says.

"But the underground well—" I say.

"The underground well is nearly empty," she says. "The men from Parliament rushed there and found nothing but a few drops. Word got out, and then the panic really started."

My mouthful of bread feels like it's turned to ash.

"But..." Ale says, his face white. "But it can't be empty. It's not supposed to be empty."

"Tell that to the well, boy," Paola says impatiently. "Nobody knows where the water went. There's all kinds of talk in the streets. Most people think you took it, somehow, which is just—" She pauses, eyeing me suspiciously. "You didn't, did you? Are you hiding it somewhere to make a point? If anyone could—"

I force down my bread and cough. "Alas, even I don't know how to steal an entire well."

Paola reaches into the bag at her side and pulls out a small jug of water. She presses it into my hands, and I take a long drink.

"But, Paola—" I'm a little breathless as I lower the jug. "It doesn't make sense. We should have had lots of water. The water-crea was taking so much blood. More than we realize."

"What do you mean?" she says.

I want to explain what I saw in the tower. All those people, sobbing and wasting away. Two little girls crammed into the same cell. The watercrea wasn't squeezing out the last drops from doomed Occhians. She was meticulously draining her prisoners for everything she could get—prisoners who turned themselves in because of omens that aren't spreading.

I'm supposed to be the only one with an omen that isn't spreading. I can't quite wrap my head around what it means. I can't put it into words with her and Ale staring at me. But two things are very certain: I didn't belong in the tower, and it's good that the watercrea is dead.

Even if the underground well is empty. Even if the city is descending into chaos. Even if I have no idea how to fix it and no time to figure it out.

I take another drink, desperately.

Then, all at once, it hits me. Paola just told me that there's no more water. Only wealthy people will have enough on hand to survive. And yet, here she is, presenting me with an entire jug.

"This—this is yours—" I hold it out to her.

She pushes back. "It's yours."

She knows the guards are coming. And yet, she snuck down here. For me. I'm so used to Paola's presence—she woke me up every morning and brought me hot chocolate every night and listened to my constant monologue of very important opinions— that I hadn't even thought about what it means for her to have sought me out. No one from my family has sought me out. But I'm sure there's a good reason for that.

"My papá," I say. "He'll help us. He will. If we can just—"

"You can't get to him, Emanuela," she says. "The heads of the Houses have all locked themselves in the Parliament building. I'm telling you—it's bad up there."

"But—"

Somewhere in the distance, a door cracks open. It's followed by the thudding of dozens of pairs of feet.

Paola yanks me up and shoves me at Ale.

"You need to run," she says.

I don't want to run. I want to help her. I want to know exactly how to fix all this. But I don't. I don't even know where to start, and for a moment, I'm frozen as that fact looms in my mind, huge and terrifying.

"We're going to find a way," Ale says.

Paola and I both turn to him.

"What?" Paola says.

"We're going to find a way to get more water," he says. "Right, Emanuela?"

His voice is uncertain, but his eyes are wide and trusting. It's the way he's looked at me since the moment we met.

He's looking at me like he needs me. Because he does.

They all need me. I'm the only person in a thousand years who had what it took to best the watercrea. That means I'm the only person who has what it takes to replace her.

Of course it does. I can figure out how to do something no Occhian has ever done, because I'm not like any other Occhian.

My people may not understand that yet. But they will soon.

I stuff what little remains of the bread in my pocket and clutch the water tighter to my chest. I look at Paola.

"Yes," I say. "We're going to find a way."

She's quiet for a moment. I can't read the expression on her face. I wonder if she's thinking that I look like a starved shell of a person, not the savior of a city. I wonder if she can tell how much effort it's taking for me to lift my chin and exude confidence. I wonder if she's remembering the last time I told her I had everything under control.

She sighs. She moves closer and gently pushes my mangled

hair out of my face, and it feels like I'm back in my childhood bedroom and everything is going to be fine.

"I believe you," she says. "God help me, but I do."

She hands Ale the lantern. "Go that way," she says, pointing. "I'll send the guards in the opposite direction. There are exits closer to the edge of the city. If—if you just keep running… maybe they won't catch you."

She scurries off into the shadows. Ale and I turn to find ourselves facing a long hall and, at the end, black nothingness.

The guards' footsteps are getting louder. Ale looks at me, and I can see the fear on his face. It's one thing to step into the catacombs—ancient, unmapped, and unknown—and take a few turns here or there. It's quite another to dive into their depths.

I reach over and take his hand. It's cold.

"Let's run," I say, with the assurance of someone who knows where she's going and has the strength to get there.

And we run.

Two years ago, Ale and I were at a party at the House of Donati. I had just finished a lively round of sparring with Chiara Bianchi. She ran off to cry somewhere, and Ale and I made our way back to the refreshments table. We were surrounded, as usual, by a throng of younger nobles trying to curry my favor. The girls watched me load crostini onto my plate, then took modest amounts for themselves. They had all attempted to copy my elaborate braided hairstyle, with varying degrees of success. I eyed them again, trying to decide who I would choose to receive the small jeweled comb in my clutch. I liked to pass out rewards. It kept them on their toes.

"You're so right about Signorina Bianchi," Valentina Moretti told me. "She does look like a sad potato dressed in old bed-sheets. You're dressed much better. And you're much prettier."

"Everyone thinks so," Giulia Cassano said quickly.

"I am prettier than her, aren't I, Signor Morandi?" I said, just to torment Ale.

"What?" he said in a panic, like the question was life-or-death. "Yes. Yes? Yes."

He took a gulp of his wine. He was already on his second drink, which was strange. He usually didn't partake. I didn't drink, for a variety of reasons—my doctors discouraged it, I preferred to stay sharp, I had other ways of entertaining myself—and Ale never did anything unless I did it first.

"You're gushing. Do try to get ahold of yourself." I beckoned him, and he obediently leaned down so I could adjust his bowtie, which was dark purple to match my gown.

Valentina sighed. "The two of you look so good together. You're a perfect match."

I glowed. I agreed, just not in the way Valentina thought. The other girls were engaged to the group of man-children across the room, who were rambling on about government business they didn't understand and throwing olives into each other's wine and generally being dull. Ale was also a man-child, of course. But he was at my side, listening to me, like a true husband and business partner.

I opened my mouth to give Valentina an appropriately haughty response, but then I caught sight of Ale's face.

There were tears welling in his eyes. And now they were running down his cheeks.

Everybody followed my gaze. They stopped, crostini halfway to their mouths, and gawked.

Without a word of explanation, Ale turned away and ran out the parlor door. Giulia leaned over and whispered something to her neighbor. They both giggled.

Everyone else only knew three things about Alessandro Morandi: He was rich, he always had his nose in a book, and he'd gotten so nervous during First Rites that he'd vomited in front of the whole cathedral. They didn't know what it was like to be his best friend. They didn't know that he scrutinized the barrage of daily letters I wrote him and responded to my every inane thought. They didn't know that he made me feel so much better just by being in a room, like a cornerstone I could always return to. And somehow, they still didn't know that he belonged to me, which meant they weren't allowed to touch him.

"Signorina Cassano," I said, "your wine looks intriguing. May I try it?"

Giulia handed me her glass. I dumped it down the front of her dress and swept out of the parlor.

I found Ale in the exact sort of place where he always took shelter—the manor's library, sitting on the floor with his back to a bookshelf. I sat down next to him, tried to think of something to say, and came up empty. I hadn't seen him cry since we were children.

"Is everyone laughing at me?" he whispered.

"Of course not," I said. "They know better."

He furiously wiped his eyes. "I'm sorry."

"What, do you think you made me look bad?" I say. "That's impossible."

His mouth trembled again. "No, it's...I don't know. Sometimes I feel like everyone else is exactly who they're supposed to be, and I'm just...not."

A strange feeling, almost like foreboding, crept over me.

"What does that mean?" I said.

Another tear rolled down his cheek. "I'm going to be awful at being the grand duke—"

"But you have me," I said automatically.

His face crumpled. He shook his head. "I'm sorry."

Instantly, I was convinced this meant his parents were about to end our engagement. They were the richest family in Occhia. They could get rid of me for any reason—for being too prone to scandal, or too sickly as a child, or even too short. They were all horrendously tall. They probably wanted tall children.

"Ale." My voice was a little too harsh. "Is something going on?"

"It's— You don't deserve this. You deserve more, and I should have told you sooner. I was trying to convince myself that I could—" He paused for entirely too long. "What I'm trying to say is that I don't think I feel the way a good husband should. About you. And if you want someone who can—"

"Wait," I said. "Are you just trying to tell me that you're not in love with me? And that it's partly because you don't favor girls at all?"

He stopped short, gaping at me. A strange look, almost like betrayal, crept into his eyes, and I wondered if I should have let him fully explain himself. Ale and I never talked about the romantic part of our engagement, but I thought it was because we didn't need to.

"Dear God, Ale," I said. "I've seen the way you look at boys. You're not subtle. Do you think you're subtle?"

He kept gaping at me. He looked so stunned that I had to laugh.

"Do you think I care about that?" I said. "Do you think they're going to perform a test on us at the altar, and if they decide we're not *in love*, they'll call it off? Wait, wait—do you think I'm in love with you? Do you think I lie awake at night dreaming of kissing your drooly mouth?"

I laughed until I couldn't breathe. I had to brace myself on his shoulder.

"I—" He rubbed at his eyes. "Everyone's always saying we're so perfect together, and you always seem so pleased—"

"We are perfect together," I said. "I'm ambitious. You're rich."

And we were best friends. But I didn't say that. It felt silly.

"You can step out with boys if you want," I continued. "I don't care. People do that all the time."

"My parents don't," he said, scandalized.

"We're not your parents. We're going to do things our own way, and that means you can have the torrid affair with Manfredo Campana that you so obviously want to have."

Ale's face turned red. "I— How did you know— Manfredo could have anybody he wanted. He would never notice me."

"Oh, I could make sure he does."

His face turned purple. "No, I don't want...I mean, it's not that I don't want— I don't know. It's just that I spend every day sitting in on all these Parliament meetings and training to be like my papá and pretending this is what I want. But that's all fine, I suppose. I know I'm lucky to be born into it."

That was an understatement. I wasn't allowed into Parliament meetings. I'd tried—once in disguise as a servant bearing the coffee, even—but it was a privilege reserved for men who were the head of their House. Unless, of course, they were the House of Morandi, and then they were rich enough to do whatever they wanted.

"I just didn't want to pretend with you, too," Ale said. "I can't spend every day of our marriage lying to you. I just can't."

"You don't have to," I said.

My fingers slid discreetly to my hip.

He went quiet. I could see the wheels turning in his head, and I wondered how long he had been tormenting himself over the idea of being a *good* husband with a *good* marriage. I wondered how it was possible that we'd spent our whole lives engaged and not been on the same page about something so basic. I wondered, uneasily, if there was anything else on his mind that I didn't know about.

He turned back to me, and I quickly readjusted my hands.

"What about you?" he said.

"What about me?"

"Well...are you having torrid affairs? Secret, torrid affairs?"

"Perhaps." I tried to sound mysterious and full of experience.

He took a sip of his wine. He stared at me, and his eyes were a little too curious for my comfort.

"Chiara Bianchi is very pretty," he said.

"Chiara Bianchi is all the worst things in existence combined into one girl-shaped object. And what is a pretty girl going to do for me, anyway? If I want a pretty girl, I can just look in the mirror."

It was so obtuse of him to bring up my lifelong enemy, just because she was the only girl who was even close to being as attractive as me. He clearly understood nothing about the concept of enemies.

"That's true," he said agreeably, which was very annoying. "Well, we should probably go back before the chaperones lose their heads."

His nose was still pink, but all other evidence of his tears was gone. He climbed to his feet, helped me up, and then started for the door. But I lingered by the bookshelf, fiddling with my skirt.

"Ale," I said.

He turned back.

Nothing he'd just told me was a surprise, and yet, the fact that he'd done it had changed something between us. I could feel the relief, like we'd been wrestling with a tangled knot that had suddenly unraveled. He'd given me something, and I could give him something in return. I wanted to. But the words were stuck in the back of my throat.

"I was just teasing about Chiara," he said in response to my silence. "Because you two have that... y'know. Long-standing rivalry. For reasons that are still very confusing to me. But obviously, it all makes sense to you."

He was smiling a little.

"I—I heard something," I blurted. "This morning. From one of my family's kitchen maids. She said that when she was growing up, she had a sister who got her first omen, but instead of going to the watercrea's tower, she waited to see if they would spread, and they... they didn't. For years. I know that has nothing to do with anything, but I heard it this morning, and I just—I was thinking about us, and how if something happened to you—"

He'd stopped smiling. A little furrow appeared between his eyebrows.

"Oh," he said. "That's...I don't think you should spread that story around, Emanuela. You don't want people to think you're—"

"But if you...if you get an omen...would you really want to..." I trailed off at the blank look on his face.

"Well," he said, "God willing, that won't happen anytime soon."

Because if it did, he would follow the law and turn himself in. Because he trusted the people who had made the laws. He trusted the city that had raised us.

He drained the last of his wine. "Can we maybe not talk about my death anymore?" he said.

He was missing the point. He was preoccupied with his own business—and also, I suspected, tipsy. I could press him on it, like I pressed everyone on everything.

But then again, I didn't need to. The omen on my hip was meaningless. It had no power over me. And whether or not he knew about it, it wouldn't change how he felt about me. So if he kept on not knowing, that was fine.

I crossed the room and sank down on a nearby love seat. "I've grown bored of the party," I said. "Let's stay in here."

"What about your friends?" he said.

"It's healthy for them to miss me," I said.

"But we're not supposed to be unchaperoned," he said. "What if someone sees us—"

"Sees us doing what, Alessandro? Or did I gravely misunderstand the talk we just had?"

He turned pink. "Right. Well, I did want to take a look at these books—I think this one is a special printing—"

He was already snatching up one of his favorites. And I knew that if I stayed on the love seat for the rest of the night, I was going to have to listen to him explain the complicated inner life of the heroine for the hundredth time. I was going to miss all the other nobles' gossip, and I'd have nothing to report back to my papá, but for a moment, I didn't care.

I've lived my whole life in the same house on the same street. I thought being "lost" meant going to a party in a less familiar neighborhood and having a moment of uncertainty that I was at the right manor. I thought it meant taking a wrong turn in the cathedral and finding one of the priests in a back room, chugging the holy wine—and then, of course, using the resulting leverage to get out of the most boring religion lessons. When I was a child and I heard the stories about Occhians of the past venturing slightly too deep into the catacombs and never returning, I assumed it was their own fault. I had no intention of ever entering the catacombs, but if I did, I thought, I would simply pay attention to where I was going.

Apparently, it's a bit trickier than that. Ale and I had the brilliant idea to arrange pebbles on the ground to mark the places we've already been, but we've yet to see any of our pebbles twice. It's been hours. Maybe days. My grasp on time has become so tenuous that I'm not sure. What I am sure about are the facts that we drank all the water, and we ate all the bread, and the lantern is burning low.

I've taken the lead, sweeping the dimming lantern around the hall as I go. My feet are aching and I'm desperate to lie down, but I can't stop moving. If I stop moving, then I'll notice how quiet it is. I'll realize how thin the air feels, like it's not meant for breathing. I'll think about the footprints we're leaving in the ancient dust—proof that people don't truly belong in this place.

When Ale and I were children, our nursemaids used to blow out all the candles and compete to tell us the most terrifying ghost story. They're a prized possession in Occhia, passed down and honed over generations for maximum spookiness. I was always the one who demanded the stories, and I would get very annoyed at Ale for interrupting with his hysterical crying. Right now, I sort of wish he'd hysterically cried so much that I'd never heard the stories at all.

We reach another fork. I stop at the top of two staircases, branching away from us and extending down into the darkness. I look desperately for a sign that we've been here before. I'm not intimately familiar with the edges of the city, because it contains a whole lot of nothing, but I feel like we should have run into the conspicuously glowing red veil by now. It surrounds Occhia on all sides, so if we haven't found it, that means we're going in some sort of horrible, convoluted circle.

Something touches my shoulder. I jump, but then I realize it's just Ale.

"What?" I say. My voice is hoarse.

He looks exhausted. His hair is dusty, because he keeps bumping his head on the low doorways. Without a word, he reaches into his pocket and pulls something out.

I recognize the embroidered red wrapper instantly. It's one of the famous handcrafted chocolates from the House of Adornetto. Ale always has one on his person. If I become hungry and unpleasant, he retrieves it and nudges it in my direction in the most passive-aggressive way possible.

It's the only thing we have left. We should savor it.

"Open it." I push at him like an impatient child. "Open it, open it—"

He fumbles in his desperation. The chocolate slips out of his hands, and I catch a glimpse of it tumbling down one of the staircases.

I scramble after it like a girl possessed, Ale on my heels.

I'm on the bottom step, reaching for my grimy prize, when I feel something strange. It feels like the chill of eyes on my skin, but that can't be. We're so very alone down here.

I lift my head.

At the other end of the hall, there's a tall, slender figure in the doorway. I have a brief impression of legs and arms. I see something gauzy and white covering most of a face, making it indistinct in the shadows. But, just for a second, I meet the figure's eyes, and they're dark and glittering.

It doesn't look like one of the watercrea's guards. The problem is that I don't know what, exactly, it looks like.

I lift the lantern higher.

There's something on the figure's hands. Something red and glistening.

The lantern finally gives up. The flame goes out. And everything is black.

I throw the lantern wildly in the direction of the intruder. It's not exactly my most cunning decision, but it's not really a decision at all. It's an instinct. I'm already scrambling back up the steps, grabbing for Ale and clinging to his shirt, because if I lose him in the dark, I'll never find him again.

We run. We can't stop. I refuse to let us stop. We're stumbling around corners and going up and down staircases and then, abruptly, we hit something blocking our path. It rattles against our hands. It doesn't have the solid finality of stone. It feels like, at last, a wooden door.

I feel around for the handle, and after a few frantic moments, I manage to get it open and tumble through.

It's so bright. It's too bright. I find myself on my hands and knees, squinting and desperate for my eyes to adjust. I can't just crouch here in uncertainty. I need to know what's happening to me.

Then, finally, I can see. I look up, and I stare.

And stare.

I should know the cobblestone street winding away from me. I should know the manors with arched windows and intricate iron balconies. I should know the towering cathedral looming in the distance.

But I don't.

I'm in a place that looks like a city. It *is* a city.

It's just not my city.

Six

MY CITY IS DARK AND MUTED, PAINTED IN BLACK AND GRAY. But the city I'm looking at is bright white—the cobblestone, the houses, and even the cathedral. It's dazzling. It's foreign. It's unnatural.

White is the color of death. Everyone knows that.

I'm kneeling in an alley between two unfamiliar manors. I tentatively get to my feet and inch forward. The only thing in front of me that I recognize is the veil. It's still high above, stretched over everything. It's a bright, vivid red, like it always is during the middle of the day.

Behind me, a door slams. I whip around to see Ale. His face is as white as the scenery, and he's very, very still, his back pressed against the entrance to the catacombs like he expects something to come bursting out.

He looks around slowly, and I wait for him to tell me I'm imagining things. I wait to hear that we're back in our city, but I've simply lost my senses from hunger, and that's the reason everything looks inexplicably not-Occhian.

"We're dead," he says. "That was a ghost. And we're dead."

I open my mouth. I shut it.

"We—we were in the bottom of the catacombs," he says. "And a ghost killed us. And now we're inside the veil. And this is what the afterlife looks like."

"No," I say automatically.

"Well," he says, like he's bracing himself, "the dying part actually wasn't so awful. Yes, it was terrifying, but it didn't hurt like I thought it would, so there's that. What are we supposed to do now that we're in the afterlife? Oh—we have to go atone for all our sins. Right. This is all fine. This is—"

"Ale," I say. "We're not—"

I try to say the word *dead*, but it gets stuck in my throat.

"That wasn't a ghost," I say instead.

"What?" he says. "Then what was it?"

"It was a person," I say.

"It looked like a ghost," he says.

"It was a person," I insist. "I saw its eyes. They were... person-like."

"I didn't see any eyes," he says.

"I was closer to them than you were," I say.

"Well, it could have been a ghost with person-like eyes," he says. "Remember that awful story your nursemaid used to tell us about the ghost that wore the face of its last victim—"

"It wasn't a ghost," I say with vicious certainty.

If the ghosts of Occhian lore were real, and one had come after me, I would know. If I were dead, I would know. I would feel it.

Ale is quiet. I wait for him to admit that he's being hysterical and I'm being logical.

"So that means a person lurking in the catacombs killed us?" he says. "Is that better or worse?"

I whirl around and march to the mouth of the alley.

We're not dead, because I refuse to be dead. I'm sure that once I take a proper look around, this will all make sense.

"Emanuela, wait—"

Ale scampers after me. I duck around the corner and, before he can catch up, I pull aside my pants to look at my hip.

I still have the same omen on my skin. Just one.

They haven't spread. I'm alive.

I knew that. I was just making sure.

Ale joins me, and we both survey the street. The manors around us are towering and pristine—and absolutely smothered in plants. There are columns wrapped in vines and windowsills overflowing with white roses and flowerbeds of every color. The house just across the way has an entire wall covered in yellow blossoms. They've been meticulously placed to form an elaborate, spiraling design.

My mamma's family, the House of Rosa, has a garden of heirloom roses in our courtyard. It's our pride and joy. It's small enough to cross in three steps. We can't afford to make it any larger.

I cross the street to the house with the yellow blossoms. I rip off one of the petals.

"Emanuela," Ale says, "don't touch anything—"

It's real. I drop it and look around again. I don't know what I'm looking for. I'm just waiting for this place to make sense.

But there's no explanation leaping out at me. All I see are a lot of beautiful manors, sitting in an unnerving quiet.

I start slowly down the street, peering in the windows we

pass. The houses are empty, but they don't look abandoned. I see a parlor with tiny sandwiches sitting out on a silver platter, waiting for teatime. I see laundry hanging in alleys. I see a manor that's been terrorized by its children, who have left toys scattered all over the floor of every room.

The people of Occhia all leave their manors at the same time every day to gather for worship. For some people, worship is about the religion, and for some people, it's the place to see and be seen, but for everyone, it's an event.

I glance up at the spires of the cathedral.

This is a city. A city that looks like Occhia, but doesn't. A city that's like Occhia, but isn't.

I can think the words, but when I try to wrap my mind all the way around them, it rebels. The idea that I got lost in the catacombs and wandered into another city doesn't make any sense. Because that would mean everything I know about Occhia is wrong. My city is supposed to be all alone in the middle of the veil. My city is supposed to be everything that's ever existed.

"Emanuela." Ale whispers it directly onto the back of my neck.

I startle away. "Must you? The point of you being twice my height is that you stay out of my breathing space."

"Look." He follows me. He grabs my head and delicately turns it to direct my gaze down the street.

At the intersection of several winding lanes, there's a statue made of white marble. It has three tiers, stacked like a cake, and on top is a figure of a woman. Her arms are outstretched benevolently.

"What is it?" Ale says.

"A ghost," I say, just to be insufferable.

He stiffens. "You don't think...you don't think it followed us—"

"It's clearly a statue, Ale," I say. "A statue of a saint, probably. That's what we make statues of in Occhia, isn't it?"

"But..." he says. "We're not in Occhia."

I hesitate.

"I know," I say.

We approach the statue cautiously. Like everything else on this street, it's polished and pretty and unfamiliar. The woman's white skirts are expertly carved to billow around her, as if she's in the middle of a twirl. She has a white rose behind one ear and long, curly hair. She looks so real. I feel like if I climbed up and touched her, I'd find her skin warm and soft.

But I'm not going to do that. I don't want to get any closer.

At the end of the next street, we find another statue. It's the exact same woman, on top of the exact same tiers.

"Who is she?" Ale whispers.

He's asking like he thinks I've somehow come up with an answer. I keep walking, hoping that maybe I will. With one eye on the spires in the distance, Ale and I wind our way up staircases and across walkways and past more identical statues. It quickly becomes apparent that there's a statue at every single intersection.

Whoever this woman is, she's all over the city.

All too soon, we're at the end of a street that faces the cathedral. Just like in Occhia, it's never far away. Its looming towers are white and striking against the red veil. The enormous double doors are shut. I strain my ears for organ music, the familiar sound of worship, but I hear nothing.

"Where's..." Ale says. "Where's the—"

He cuts himself off with an uneasy look at me.

The watercrea's tower. In Occhia, it's right behind the cathedral, peeking over its shoulder, always visible. But here, I don't see anything.

I start walking again. Faster.

"Wait—" Ale runs after me.

I reach the edge of the cathedral square. Off to one side are white, columned buildings that look very much like Occhia's Parliament buildings. On the other side is a public garden, lusher and greener than any I've ever seen. There's still no sign of anyone.

There's something very unusual about this city, and I know what it is, but I'm afraid to name it, even inside my own head.

I lead Ale across the square. I try to look like I visit this cathedral every day. I try to look like I know exactly what I'm going to find inside.

I'm just past the halfway point when I feel it. Someone is watching me approach. I'm certain of it.

I stop. I survey the cathedral's closed doors and intricate white face and narrow windows. There's no sign of life.

I turn to Ale. "Did you feel...?"

"What?" he says, instantly on alert.

"Nothing," I say, and keep going.

I'm not dead, I remind myself. As long as I'm not dead, I can handle anything.

I climb the steps to reach the cathedral doors. And finally, I can hear something beyond the thick walls. It's the steady, muffled hum of voices. Of people.

I stare at the intricate wood paneling and will myself to just reach out and push my way inside. I think about the last time I was in a cathedral that looked almost, but not quite, like this one. I think about my papá's arm in mine and Ale waiting at the altar and the woman in the red gown who took one look at me and knew about my omen.

I think about the *thing* I saw in the catacombs, and the moment when its eyes met mine.

I think about my nursemaid, stuck in a city with no water, braving the guards so that I could slip away. I think about my people panicking in the streets. I think about all those prisoners in the watercrea's tower. No one else is going to help them.

I reach out and slowly, slowly push on the door.

Someone on the other side wrenches it open and ushers me inside, and all at once, Ale and I are propelled through the foyer and surrounded by people. The inner chamber is full of them. They're milling around under the enormous arched ceilings, their chatter loud as it echoes off the walls. There are no pews. There's no altar. There's a shiny floor of black-and-white tile and, in the very center, an enormous, three-tiered dais.

It looks like the statues we saw in the street. But there's no marble woman standing on top. It's empty.

For a moment, I'm frozen at the edge of the crowd. I'm waiting, instinctively, to be recognized. I've never gone anywhere in Occhia and not been recognized. I've never been so surrounded by people I don't know. I've never walked into an event and not known, more or less, everything that was going to happen.

"She's late," the man next to me says, shifting impatiently. His eyes are on the dais.

"She'll be here soon," his friend says.

They're not speaking in Occhian, but rather an oddly accented version of Culaire. In my city, Culaire is mostly confined to a neighborhood that we call the Lily. I speak it well, of course, because I'm very educated. And I like the art market in the Lily. They have the fanciest desserts.

But I'm not in the Lily. I'm in…this place.

Someone elbows me in the back as they push past, and I whip around in surprise. People in Occhia know better than to jostle me.

It's a tall girl in a maid's dress. She has a red smudge on her cheek. It's so unexpected—so very blatant—that, for a moment, I can't even comprehend what it is.

It's an omen.

No. It's not just one omen. She has two omens on her cheek.

She doesn't seem to notice. It feels like I'm the only one who can see them. And for a moment, I'm convinced that none of this is real.

Then the dais in the center of the room goes up in smoke. Huge columns of it shoot out of the center, dissolving into the high ceiling.

I grab Ale's wrist, fully prepared to run away from whatever horrifying thing is about to happen. But then I realize that nobody around me seems concerned. Instead, they're starting to sing.

At first, it's more of a murmur. But as the smoke starts to clear, it builds. The words sound like a language I've never heard, which is unnerving. I thought I was at least passably familiar with every language spoken in my city. But then, this isn't my city.

The shadow of a person appears on top of the dais, and the singing grows. People put their arms in the air, like they're reaching for the mysterious figure.

Ale and I exchange a sideways look. We're the only people

in this entire room who don't know the song. He sinks down a little, trying to make himself less tall.

The smoke dissipates to reveal a woman in a white gown. A girl, maybe. I'm very far away and she's very far above, but she looks young and slender, with brown skin and long, curly hair. There's a white rose tucked behind one of her ears. She's smiling. And even though I can barely see her face, I can tell that she's glowing, like there's nowhere else she'd ever want to be.

I know instantly who she is. She's the statue.

The singing is tremendous now. The people are beaming and jostling me in their excitement.

The girl lifts her white-gloved hands.

The singing cuts off. The crowd around me vibrates in anticipation.

And then, water.

It pours down from the platform under the girl's feet, falling from tier to tier to gather in a basin below. Two streams form an archway over her head, framing her. All around the statue, streams are coming to life, leaping from place to place to form an elaborate lattice below her.

I've never seen anything like it. Like the rest of this city, it's beautiful.

And then, it's shooting out from the fountain into the crowd.

And then, it's everywhere.

It's hitting me in the face. I think it came out of the ceiling. I'm not sure. All I know is that I'm reeling and sputtering, and it won't stop coming. No one else seems concerned. As far as I can tell, they've still got their arms up, soaking it in.

Abruptly, the deluge stops. When I've blinked it all out of my eyes, I turn to find Ale, his hair plastered to his forehead.

He's staring at the drops of water running off his fingers like he's trying to figure out if they're real.

I look back at the dais, only to find that the girl in the white gown has disappeared. The soaked crowd pushes us back out the cathedral doors, like the show is over, and I'm too baffled to resist.

At the top of the steps, I catch a brief glimpse of the city laid out below—the red veil over the shining white manors, and the branching cobblestone streets cutting it all up.

Ale grabs my arm, which is how I know he sees it, too.

The statues we saw earlier—the smaller versions of the dais inside—are all alive with water. Every statue I can see in the distance is glistening as it pours down the tiers. And it shows no signs of stopping.

I've never seen so much water in my life. I can't comprehend it. I don't even know how to start.

When we hit the cathedral square, the people splinter off, returning down the streets to their teatime, and their laundry, and their children. They pass by the water-filled statues without a second glance. Ale and I stand there, soaking wet and watching it all, until we're some of the only people left. A cluster of gossiping nobles lingers near the gardens, wringing out their fine clothes.

No one is surprised by what just happened. It's like it happens every day.

I turn back to the cathedral just in time to see the doors swing shut. It's quickly followed by the heavy sound of a deadbolt sliding into place.

The cathedral in Occhia was never locked.

"What is this place?" Ale says.

It's not like Occhia at all.

"Emanuela?" Ale presses.

"What?" I say.

"What should we do?" he says.

I don't know. I don't know how we got here. I don't know what to make of the things we just saw. I don't know the name of a single person or a single place around me, and I feel the prickling sense of not belonging in a way I've never felt it before. I'm stranded and hopelessly out of context, like a child dropped into a dinner party where the adults will never think to explain anything, because it's all so obvious to them.

There's only one thing I'm certain about. Somewhere in the veil, my city is out of water. And I've come upon a city absolutely drenched in it.

Surely I can persuade them to share.

Seven

"So..." Ale says. "What exactly are we doing?"

We're sitting against the wall of a manor at the edge of the square, stealthily positioned in the midst of an herb garden. I'm peering through the stalks at the mostly silent cathedral. We've probably been here for a couple of hours, but I'm not sure, because I haven't heard the familiar peal of the bells. Overhead, the veil has darkened to the deep red of late afternoon. I'm trying not to the think about the veil darkening in Occhia, too.

"We're waiting," I say.

"For what?" Ale says.

"For an opportunity," I say.

Ale is quiet. I pick through the plants in front of me, looking again for something I can eat. I don't recognize everything, but I do notice a familiar intruder that's sprung up next to the sage. It's called the calalla flower. Its beautiful white bulbs are incredibly rough on the stomach. I'm a gentle-mannered young lady who would never wish stomach illness on anyone, of course, so I have no reason to know that. We just happen to be very vigilant about weeds in our garden at the House of Rosa.

I pick some bulbs and put them in my pocket. I'm sure they'll be useful.

"So we're waiting for an opportunity," Ale says. "An opportunity for... what?"

"We need to know more about this cathedral," I say. "And the front door is the only way in."

I know this because we walked around for an examination, arm in arm like we were on a casual stroll. In Occhia, the cathedral has a dozen side doors for the ease of its various priests and visitors. Here, there are none.

There's also no sign of a tower. There's just empty cobblestone.

I can't shake the feeling that this whole city is playing a cruel prank on me. The longer I sit here, the more it gnaws at me.

"Alas," I continue, "the front door seems to be closed to visitors. So we need to find a way around that."

Ale glances around. "By sitting in an herb garden? How—"

I hold up a hand to shush him. I hear footsteps through the open window over our heads.

"We're listening to gossip," I whisper. "Kitchens always have the best information."

Inside, pots are clanking. Bowls are rattling. Drawers are opening and shutting. All I have to do now is wait to hear something juicy.

"Where's my good knife?" a voice says, high and melodic. "There's so many potatoes tonight. I need my good knife."

"Oh, do you mean this knife?" The second voice comes from across the room.

"Aubert! Give it back!" The first voice has gone all giggly.

"Don't you dare. If you lick it, you're the one who has to wash it again, you silly—"

So this city has incredibly tedious flirting, too. It would have been nice if it didn't.

The minutes tick on as more of the house staff appear in the kitchen. The potato-cutting maid and the dishwasher continue to poke at each other. Two cooks argue passionately about some card game they lost last night. The housekeeper comes in and scolds everyone for not arranging yesterday's cheese platter properly, and when she leaves, they all grumble about how the cheese platter isn't their job. Food starts to sizzle, and the smell of garlic and rosemary drifts out the window, and I think about how I haven't eaten since we left the catacombs. And how, before that, I hadn't eaten since the day of my wedding.

I'm deep in amorous thoughts about rosemary potatoes when Ale elbows me. He casts a significant look at the window, and I sit up straighter.

"It seems like so long ago," the maid is saying. "Things have changed so quickly."

"I'll never forget the first watering," one of the cooks says. "And to think—I'll soon be telling my grandchildren about it. I still can't believe I'll live to see them grow up."

"Your wine habit might have something to say about that," the other cook says.

"I'm only driven to wine because of your terrible strategy—"

"We're very blessed to live in such historic times," the housekeeper interrupts, because apparently she's returned. "Perhaps we should show our gratitude by doing our jobs and *arranging the cheese platter correctly.* If you lot try and serve the family this disaster, I swear I'll—"

There's a small kerfuffle during which the cheese platter is rearranged and the housekeeper leaves. For a moment, the kitchen is quiet.

"Do you think the Heart means it?" the dishwasher says. "All the things she says about how one day, everyone in Iris will have a house of their own? Not just the noble families?"

"Of course she does, Aubert," the maid says. "She's only been ruling the city for two years. She's working on it."

"The Heart keeps her promises," one of the cooks says. "She promised that Iris would always have all the water we'll ever need. She promised that the tower would come down and no one would ever die in it again. And here we are."

I'm very aware that Ale is looking at me. But I'm not brave enough to look at him. I'm just holding my breath, desperate to hear more.

"It is a bit strange, though, isn't it?" the dishwasher says.

"What is?" the maid says.

"That we only see her at the waterings," he says. "And that it's the only time we're allowed in the cathedral. When she started, she said she wasn't like ... y'know."

There's a silence that I can't quite interpret. But it doesn't seem good.

"Just to be clear," one of the cooks says, "the Heart spends every day using her mystical powers to make water for the whole city—water she creates out of nothing—and your complaint is that she's never pulled you aside after the watering and invited you upstairs for tea?"

"It's not a complaint," the dishwasher says quickly. "I just thought it might be nice if we got to see her more, that's all."

"She is very beautiful," the maid says, a jealous note in her voice. "I'd love to meet her, too. Colette and I are always saying that if she ever wants to hire maids—"

At that moment, somebody in the kitchen chooses to dump a potful of dirty water out the window. I barely manage not to scream. I had just dried off from the watering in the cathedral.

I need to move anyway. I need to think. I crawl out from the hedges and drip my way down the darkening street, trying to make sense of the swirl in my head.

"Emanuela," Ale says, "did you hear what they said about—"

Yes. I heard. They said that the ruler of this city—the girl they called the Heart—makes water from nothing. They said that their people don't have to give up their blood and die in a tower. They did, two years ago. But they don't anymore.

I near the end of the street, where one of the statues is located, and stop. Water is still flowing down from the tiers, bubbling madly as it collects in the basin below. The figure of the girl in the white gown stands on top, her slender hands outstretched, smiling in a way that looks gentle and virtuous. I study her blank eyes.

I don't know what to believe. The watercrea of Occhia was supposed to be invincible, but I pushed her over a balcony and killed her. Occhia is supposed to be everything that ever was, but I went into the catacombs and ended up in another city under the veil.

I can't believe anything. Not until I see it for myself.

I have to find a way into the cathedral. I have to know if this city is really as perfect as it seems.

"Isn't she beautiful?"

At the unfamiliar voice, I turn to see a girl in a frilly blue day gown hovering nearby. She was speaking to Ale, apparently, because she's looking at him like she's waiting for a response. This is, of course, a lost cause. Ale doesn't speak to strangers, especially not in one of his secondary languages. At least the interloper isn't a handsome boy. Ale would have died on the spot.

"Who's beautiful?" I say.

The girl looks at me. She hesitates. I assume it's because of my intimidating aura.

"The Heart," the girl says finally, like it's obvious. "I was just... I just can't help but admire her every time I pass by."

She inches over to the basin. She's holding a small glass jar that she dips into the water. She takes a drink.

So these people carry around their own jars. And they fill them up and chug them down whenever they please.

In Occhia, the watercrea controlled everything about the water. Her guards portioned out rations and brought them to each house every morning. Nobody ever got more, not even sick people in dire need of it.

This luxury is grotesque.

My people need it. *I* need it.

"I was admiring the Heart, as well," I say, with a subtle attempt at mimicking the girl's lilting accent. I'm uncomfortably aware of the way every single word differs, ever so slightly, from the way I would have said it in Occhia.

"Well," she says, curtsying briefly, "have a blessed day."

As she starts to turn away, her bag shifts, and I catch a glimpse of supplies that I recognize.

"Do you sew?" I say.

The girl pauses. She fiddles with a strand of hair that's fallen out of her hilariously puffy updo. I don't know how her delicate neck is supporting it all.

"Yes," she says. "I'm from the Circle du Brodeur."

She says it as though I'm supposed to be impressed.

"How impressive," I say.

"Actually, I..." She pauses. She glances at Ale, then back at me, and puffs up her chest a little bit. "I've been invited to sew for the Heart," she says.

"Oh?" I say.

"If you hadn't heard, she's planning a big celebration for her anniversary," she says. "And she wants to be dressed accordingly, of course."

"So you'll get to meet the Heart?" I say.

She glows. "Yes. It's such an honor."

I put my hands in my pockets. "An honor indeed. When will you meet her? Soon?"

"This evening," she says, a little jittery. "I'm just finishing my preparations. I'm getting specially made lace from the Circle du Bisset, and then some roses from—" She cuts herself off. She thinks she's said too much in her excitement, and she doesn't trust me. I can't imagine why. I think I look very wholesome and trustworthy.

"Well." I curtsy, a bit awkward in my baggy pants. "Good luck. Now we'll be able to tell everyone that we met the famous... what did you say your name was?"

She glances at Ale one more time. He attempts a smile. It's undoubtedly the least threatening thing she's ever seen.

"Tatienne," she says to him, slightly reassured. "Tatienne du Brodeur."

Somehow, when she wasn't looking, one of her tiny sketchbooks was slipped out of her bag and into my pocket. Also, a powder of crushed flower bulbs has been sprinkled into her jug of water. I hope it doesn't make her sick and cause her to miss her appointment.

She turns back to me. "Anyway, have a blessed day." She walks away, taking a sip from her jug as she goes.

Ale gives me a sideways look, his gaze flickering to the lump in my pocket.

"What?" I say. "Did you expect me to push her off a balcony?"

His face goes pale. He looks away.

All at once, I remember the watercrea's blood seeping onto the cobblestone. I remember the way her lifeless face looked right before her body disappeared.

I shake myself. The watercrea is gone, and she's never coming back. She's taken up enough space in my thoughts, and I'm not going to give her any more.

Esteemed seamstress Tatienne du Brodeur is making her way to one of the manors down the street. As she knocks on the door, she glances at us one more time. I quickly turn my attention to the statue, like I've already forgotten about our encounter, and wait for her to disappear inside.

Then I head toward the nearest manor. The door to the kitchen is propped open in the alley. Next to it is a window. I peek over the sill to find a dozen servants bustling around, preparing dinner. There's a vase of white roses sitting within arm's reach, so I knock it over in very dramatic fashion.

My little distraction works even better than I expected. Apparently, it's not the first thing that's been broken this evening. Everyone blames the same kitchen boy, despite the fact that he happened to be across the room. Said kitchen boy blames ghosts, and when the room is at its noisiest, I grab Ale and pull him inside. We're able to quietly slip through a nearby doorway into the rest of the servants' quarters.

It takes a minute to find the room where servants do laundry and mend clothes. In Occhia, I know from snooping around in my own house, clothes are carefully spot-scrubbed. But here, of course, they do it to excess. There's a massive tub of soapy water on the floor. I shut the door and lock it. I sort through the nearby piles of clothes and pick out something for Ale that's respectable and relatively clean-smelling. I spend admittedly too much time on my own outfit. I find a not-hideous green day gown, but the neckline is too high and frilly, so I have to make a few quick alterations. I also take a black handkerchief that I can tie around my hair, because I have no illusions that it looks like the hair of a renowned seamstress.

When we're both changed, I inspect Ale. His hair is damp, but more or less patted back into its aristocratic coif. His pants—the longest ones I could find—are too short. He looks extremely self-conscious about it. In other words, he's as good as he's going to get.

I pack up the sewing kit on the table, making sure it has several pairs of scissors. I slip an additional small but very sharp pair into my pocket, for good measure.

"There's a mirror out in the hall," I say. "I'll just go admire my new gown and tie on this handkerchief, and then we can—"

"Um," Ale says. He's staring at me.

"What?" I adjust my neckline. "It's not even that scandalous. It's like you've never seen anything else I've ever worn."

"Just, um…hold on." He roots around the room until he finds a washcloth. He dips it into the soapy water and comes at me.

I back up. "What are you doing? Don't get me wet."

"Just…" He won't let up. "There's just some dust from the catacombs on you. I can—"

I squirm out of his grip and snatch the washcloth away.

"Emanuela," he says.

I'm already pushing the door open. "I can do it myself. You're not my nursemaid, Ale—"

As soon as I look in the mirror, it becomes glaringly obvious why he was trying to clean me up.

My face is gaunt and my cheeks are hollow. My hair is in absolute tatters. I knew it was bad, but it's far worse than I'd imagined. There are pieces touching my collarbone and pieces so short they're sticking straight up. There's dried blood on my neck, smeared around the wound where the watercrea's needle went in. It's definitely going to leave a scar.

This isn't how I'm supposed to look. I'm supposed to look like a girl who can do anything, not a girl who's been broken and cobbled back together.

I try to wipe the dirt off my face. It barely helps.

Ale appears at my side. His fingers brush my hair, and I jerk away, sharp and defensive. Undaunted apparently, he reaches over to pull the washcloth out of my hand. "Let me try," he says.

He takes me back into the laundry room. He wipes me off again, then fusses with my hair as I clutch the sewing kit and stare at the buttons on his shirt. He smells sweaty. I can only imagine how I smell.

He ties the handkerchief on for me and steps back.

I pat my head. "Is it all covered? Do I look…normal?"

It pains me to even say. I don't want to struggle for normal. I want to look better than everyone else.

Ale smiles. The disconcerting thing about growing up with my best friend is that he's somehow every age at once. I'll spot his lanky figure down the street and think he's an actual adult man and have a moment of panic. Then he'll beam at me the way he's beaming now, and he's a little boy.

"You're the prettiest girl I know," he says.

I roll my eyes. "And I can't live without your approval."

Outside, I can hear footsteps. Cabinets are opening and plates are clinking. The servants must be starting to set the table for dinner. We open the laundry room window and quietly shimmy out.

A few minutes later, we're standing at the bottom of the cathedral steps. The veil overhead has sunk into a deep red, and the city around us has gone quiet. In Occhia, this is the time when noble families are in their parlors, having drinks before dinner. Perhaps in Iris, this is when families get a giant bowl of water and guzzle it down and splash it everywhere.

Ale casts a glance up at the dark cathedral windows. "We shouldn't be nervous, right? People in this city would be excited to meet her."

"Thrilled," I say.

But we're not from this city. We're not here for a simple dress fitting.

Before I can lose my nerve, I march up the steps and knock. The sound of my fist seems so small and insignificant against the huge wooden door.

A long moment passes. Then, from behind the doors, there's the dull click of a lock, and we push our way inside.

The foyer looks very different now. The lights are low, and the inner chamber is closed. Even still, the space feels huge, and

Ale and I are standing all alone on the black-and-white tile. I squint around in the shadows. I don't see anything.

I clear my throat and decide to address the iron chandelier hanging from the ceiling.

"I'm Tatienne du Brodeur," I say. "The seamstress." I glance at Ale. "And this is my…manservant."

Silence.

"This was a bad idea," Ale whispers. "We shouldn't have done this. We should have just—"

Off to one side, there's a loud crack. I jump at the same time that Ale seizes me around the shoulders.

A door on the far wall has swung part of the way open. Beyond it, I see the hint of a staircase. There's still no sign of a person.

I assume the Heart wants me to be impressed that she can open doors without being anywhere near them. This must be another mystical quality that the people of Iris worship.

I'm not impressed.

I march for the door. The stairwell has warm lanterns on the wall and a soft red carpet. The top of the staircase is shrouded in darkness.

Tatienne du Brodeur, the seamstress who lives in this city and attends its magical waterings every day, wouldn't be afraid to go up these stairs and meet her benevolent and powerful ruler. So I'm not, either. I touch my pocket, feeling the reassuring presence of my sewing scissors. Then I start to climb.

As Ale and I spiral up the steps, I hear the lock on the front door slide back into place.

EIGHT

AT THE TOP OF THE STAIRS, A DOOR IS WAITING FOR US, poised between two ornate statues. Each one depicts the same girl in the white gown, one hand raised, holding a decorative glass lantern with a flame burning inside.

I stop, bracing myself on the wall. It was a very long staircase, and I'm winded.

"So..." I say over my shoulder to Ale. "Do you...think..."

I have to pause to suck in air. The sound is not flattering.

"Do you think I should knock on the door?" I manage at last. "Or is she going to open it with her special connection to all of the cathedral's—"

The door swings inward to reveal the shadowy, imposing figure of a man.

"Hello." I straighten up. "I'm Tatienne du Brodeur. I'm the—"

"I know," he says.

He stands back like we're meant to come inside, so we do. We're in a long, narrow entrance hall. It's empty, except for a small table in the very center holding a vase of white roses. As the man leads us along, I give them a wide berth. We don't grow white roses in the House of Rosa. Nobody would want to decorate their home with flowers the color of death.

When we reach the far door, the strange man stops and turns toward us. He's younger than I thought, actually—close to my age. He's just very tall and broad in the shoulders. And he has a severe way about him. He looks like the sort of person who hates fun.

"You're early," he says.

"My apologies," I say. "Perhaps there is such a thing as being too punctual, after all."

He narrows his dark eyes. He has brown skin and perfect curly hair. His clothes, like the cathedral, are white and spotless, and the embroidery on his vest is finely detailed.

"The Heart won't be able to meet with you now," he says. "Surely you can appreciate how many demands she has on her time and energy."

"Of course," I say. "Is there somewhere we could wait, so we could start setting up...?"

He's silent. He surveys Ale for a moment, but then, seemingly unimpressed, he turns back to me.

"What's in your pocket?" he says.

I haven't touched my pocket since I was standing at the bottom of the very winding staircase. I wish the people I'd eavesdropped on had mentioned something about the Heart having a fancy servant who is, apparently, all-seeing.

"Oh, these?" I reach for my sewing scissors, glad I didn't bring something even more suspicious. "They're just my favorite pair of—"

"You must be Madame du Brodeur!"

The voice comes from directly behind me. I want to pretend like it doesn't scare me half to death, but it absolutely does. I scramble to collect myself and turn around with dignity.

It's her. It's the Heart. She's standing right here, within arm's reach, and the very fact of her presence is enormous—too enormous for this tiny hall. I expected her to look less immaculate up close, but her gown is pristine. Her long curls are artfully piled on top of her head, a delicate white rose still tucked behind one of her ears. I didn't realize she was quite so tall. Or quite so elegant in the face. If anything, the statues don't do her justice.

I meet her eyes. They're dark and glittering.

I know those eyes. I've seen them before.

I drop my gaze as fast as I can.

"Yes," I say. "That's me."

My voice comes out hoarse. The hall has suddenly gotten very cold.

I saw this girl in the catacombs. I saw her, and she saw me, and she had something on her hands that looked very much like blood.

"I'm so glad you could make it," she's saying, her accent light and airy and completely carefree. "I'm such an admirer. That gown you did last season, with the gigantic train and the— Theo, get out of their way, would you? We shouldn't force them to linger in the hall."

"They're early," the serious-looking boy insists from the door.

"I have time," she says.

The boy opens the door and stands aside, but he doesn't look happy about it.

I can't go into her quarters. She's going to recognize me. She's going to see through me, just like the watercrea did.

Ale is nudging me into the room, and I don't want to go, but I don't know how to stop it, either. I find myself in a parlor with a high vaulted ceiling. The most striking feature is a towering stained-glass window on the far wall. It depicts two raised, white-gloved hands shooting a cascade of water into the air. The blue glass scatters the dark red light from the veil outside, creating shards of color all over the tile floor.

The Heart shuts the door. We're alone with her.

I reach up to make sure the handkerchief on my head is in place. My ruined hair is so distinctive. If somebody only caught a glimpse of me, it's the thing they would remember.

"Please, sit down," the Heart says.

We cross the room to perch on a love seat. I'm vaguely aware that Ale is looking at me with concern.

"Is something wrong?" he whispers.

I shake my head. I can still pretend to be an ordinary seamstress. I just have to learn more about this girl and her water. That's all.

The Heart brings over a silver platter of food. I wonder why her servant didn't stay for such a job. There are no signs of any maids, either. In fact, I notice as I subtly glance around, the room looks a bit dusty. I can see it floating in the beams of light filtering through the window.

The Heart pops the cork of a bottle that was already open and pours us very generous glasses of white wine.

"I'm sorry about my brother," she says over the gurgling. "He means well. He's just tragically uptight."

I glance at the parlor door. So he wasn't a servant. Now that it's been pointed out to me, the two of them do resemble each other, all tall and dark and graceful.

Having a brother is very…nonmystical of her. The watercrea in Occhia didn't have a family. I don't know what to make of it. I don't know what to make of any of this.

"He won't—" I clear my throat. My accursed voice is still coming out raspy. "He won't be joining us?"

"Oh, he'll already be locked up in his study." She waves a white-gloved hand at the far side of the room. "He loves his work too much to sit around and engage in our chatter."

She plops down across from us in a flurry of skirts.

"But for me…" She nudges the silver tray closer to us. "Getting to know my people is my favorite part of being the Heart of Iris. It's so much more intimate than standing on top of a fountain and looking down at you, although of course, I love that, too. Cakes?"

I eye the tiny squares, frosted in delicate pastel shades. I try to convince myself to pick one up.

The girl takes a gulp of her wine.

"Anyway, Madame du Brodeur, let's talk about you." She looks at Ale. "And you, as well. Are you her assistant? What's your name?"

Ale freezes, looking mortified. There are approximately three cakes in his mouth.

"You can call me Verene, by the way." The girl realizes that he's incapacitated and jumps in to fill the silence. "Madame du Sauveterre is fine if you insist on sticking to formalities. Please tell me how you'd like to be addressed. And then tell me everything about yourselves and your work."

I glance up to see her settling back onto her love seat, like she fully expects us to regale her with hours of seamstress stories.

I can't sit here for that long. Not with her right across from me, staring at me so attentively.

"Actually, Madame du Sauveterre—" I say.

"You really can call me Verene," she says.

"V-Verene," I say. "If it's not too rude to suggest, perhaps we could talk as we begin our work? I must admit, in situations such as these, I often find that I become rather…shy."

She's quiet. Just for a moment. I resist the urge to slip a hand into my pocket and make sure my sewing scissors are still within reach.

"Of course it's not too rude!" she says. "You're the brilliant artist. We shall do whatever makes you the most comfortable. Let me just show you to my—"

She leaps to her feet and abruptly sways, like she's dizzy. Ale reaches for her, because his instinct is to be a polite gentleman. I'm halfway to my feet, because if something is happening, I have to be prepared. But she's already braced herself on the arm of the love seat and recovered.

"Oops," she says. "I think I drank that wine a little too fast."

She winks at Ale before she strides away. He blushes demurely.

"Get ahold of yourself," I mutter at him, trailing behind Verene out of the parlor.

"She's nice," he whispers. "I was so afraid. But she's nice."

That doesn't change what I saw in the catacombs.

We quietly follow Verene into a side hall. There are three doors, and Verene heads for the one at the back. She opens it—it wasn't locked, I observe—and slips through.

"Emanuela," Ale whispers, hovering for a second, "if she can really make water out of nothing, that would be amazing. It would solve everything."

For a moment, I imagine the streets of Occhia filled with beautiful, bubbling statues of Verene. I imagine my people gathering in the cathedral and singing to her as water pours down on their heads. I imagine them calling her the Heart of Occhia and worshipping her forever.

My stomach turns.

"Well—" Ale is still talking, apparently. "It would solve almost everything. We'd still have to figure out...y'know. How to get the water back home. But if she agreed to—"

We reach the doorway and stop short. Verene is waiting there for us.

"I have to ask you a very important question," she says.

She leans closer. I catch a whiff of sweet, flowery perfume, and it takes everything I have not to leap back.

"Is something wrong?" she says softly. "Do you not have enough food?"

I open my mouth.

"You ate the cakes very quickly," she says, looking at Ale. "And I'm not trying to be rude, I promise, but you both look a bit...peaky."

"Oh, that?" I'm speaking a little too quickly. "We stayed up all night preparing for this appointment. We were very nervous. That's all."

"There's no need to be nervous," Verene says. "You know that, don't you?"

"Yes," I say.

"And everything is all right at the Circle du Brodeur?" she says.

"Yes," I say.

"And you're not lying to me because you're too shy to ask for help?" she says.

"No," I say.

"If you ever need anything, you can ask me, you know," she says. "Anything at all. I won't be able to magic it up like I do the water, of course. But I'll find a way. That's what I do."

"We know," I say. "Thank you."

I come dangerously close to meeting her eyes. I quickly look away.

"Well, all right," she says, but I can tell that she's not convinced.

We're in what I assume to be her room. It's a high-ceilinged, hexagonal space, with a plush canopy bed underneath a beautiful chandelier. It's also a huge mess. There are literal piles of white gowns on the floor. I would say that it's totally unnecessary for her to be commissioning a new one, but I happen to think one can never have enough gowns.

"So." She marches into the room and quickly kicks something under the bed. Judging by the sound, it's an empty wine bottle. "Based on what I told you in my invitation, I'm sure you have ideas. Perhaps you can start by showing me your drawings?"

"Of course," I say, setting down my sewing kit. "I— Oh. Hmm. I must have left my sketchbook in the parlor. I'll go get it. But if you'd like, my assistant would love to see some of your favorite gowns. You have so many beautiful ones."

"Certainly," she says, and reaches for the heap of clothes on her bed. "So, I like this one because of the pearls. They're just very pretty in the light—"

The dress is a hideous mess of lace and bows. I glimpse that much before I slip out of the room. I shut the door most of the way and survey the empty hall, my heart pounding in my ears.

I've quickly gathered that Verene enjoys talking. If she's busy carrying on about her gowns, I can get away with a little more time than it reasonably takes to walk down to the parlor and fetch a sketchbook out from between the love seat cushions. But I still won't have long.

I don't know what, exactly, I'm looking for. I just need something else—something besides a glimpse in the catacombs that I could barely comprehend.

I try the second door in the hall and peek inside to find a dimly lit bedroom. It looks like the much neater sibling of the bedroom I've already seen.

The knob of the third door is locked. I decide that makes it the most promising avenue. I glance back at the end of the hall, where I can faintly hear Verene prattling on, and root around in my hair. There are still a couple of pins buried deep. I stick one into the lock and start jiggling. Breaking and entering wasn't a formal part of my Occhian education. I merely got tired of trying to snoop around people's houses during dinner parties and running into locked doors.

When I ease open the door and realize I'm looking at a study, I freeze. Verene said her brother spends a lot of time in his study. But after a moment, it becomes very obvious that the room is not only empty but abandoned. There are no books on the bookshelves and nothing on the desk. There's a thick layer of dust on all the furniture.

I slip inside and shut the door. There are no lanterns lit. The only light comes through two narrow windows at the back. The veil is starting to turn black as night falls, and I have to squint to see.

Hanging on the wall behind the desk is a map of the city of Iris, drawn from above. There's the cathedral, of course, and the winding streets that form an intricate ring around it. From here, it's easy to see that the neighborhoods aren't laid out in an exact copy of my home. This city is almost like Occhia. But it's not.

My eyes catch on a small dot drawn near the back corner of the cathedral. It's right where the watercrea's tower would go.

There used to be a tower here. There used to be prisoners wasting away in cells and a woman taking their blood and a city living in fear. And they tore it all down and wiped themselves clean and now they have...this. A girl and her brother, living in an empty cathedral, surrounded by more water than they'll ever need.

I wonder how a city could possibly change so quickly.

Behind me, the door creaks, and I stiffen and turn around, already working on my excuse.

It's not Verene's brother, whom I expected. It's a woman I haven't seen yet. She's small and bony, with a touch of gray in her hair. She's wearing a white apron, and she's looking at me with flat, dark eyes.

"Snooping?" she says without preamble.

"Looking for the washroom, actually," I say, curtsying. "I'm Tatienne du Brodeur. I'm a seamstress of the Circle du Brodeur. I just stopped in to work with Madame du Sauveterre on her anniversary gown. And you are...?"

"All the guests snoop," she says. "You're curious. I know."

"Well," I say, "perhaps a little."

"But most of them don't go so far as to pick the locks," she says.

I smile politely. "Could you show me to the washroom?"

Her face betrays nothing, but she stands aside to let me out. She shuts the door behind me, pulls a key out of her apron, and locks it.

"And yes," she says. "It belonged to her. That's why it was locked."

"What?" I say.

"The study belonged to the Eyes," she says.

A chill runs up my spine. From the way she says *the Eyes*, I know exactly who she's talking about. She's talking about this city's version of a woman who kept people in a tower and took their blood.

"She...she had—" I'm struggling to figure out the words. "My apologies. I just didn't know the Eyes had a...study."

"It was where she tutored them," she says. "She never hired any tutors. Always did it herself."

"Tutored who?" I say.

The woman looks at me like I'm very dense. "Her children."

My first thought is that a watercrea couldn't have had children. My second thought is that I don't know why I'm so sure about that, because apparently, I don't know anything about watercreas at all.

"Were you here?" I say, my mouth dry. "Before...before the Heart was...?"

"Before the Eyes got sick?" she says. "Yes. I was a nursemaid for the twins. Now I'm their housekeeper. So you can understand why I don't appreciate it when people pick locks to snoop around in their private quarters."

"I'm very sorry," I say with incredible humbleness, if I do say so myself. "I wish I wasn't so nosy, but I just can't seem to help myself. Anyway, I'll just be on my way to the—"

Then I see the stain on the housekeeper's white apron. It's just a smear on the corner, but it's unmistakable.

Blood.

It takes me a moment to realize that I've been staring at it for too long. The housekeeper has followed my gaze.

I wait for her to explain why there's blood on her apron. She doesn't.

"The washroom's around the corner," she says. "Off the parlor, next to the big white vase."

She makes her way out of the hall. But not before she gives me a final, watchful look over her shoulder.

I'm suddenly very aware of the fact that I left Ale alone. I grab the sketchbook as fast as possible and return to Verene's bedroom. She's sitting at the dressing table on the far side of the room, Ale hovering politely over her shoulder. She's showing him her jewelry box. There's a white rose tucked behind his ear, just like the one behind her ear.

I don't know why the rose is the thing that feels like entirely too much, but it is. This girl is hiding something. She can't just sit there with her sparkling eyes and her singsong voice and put flowers in my best friend's hair.

"Oh, there you are," Verene says as I join them. "We were just—"

I put the sketchbook on the dressing table. "The drawings."

Verene flips through the sketches. I scanned through them earlier and discovered that they're all hideously frilly.

She stops on what's undoubtedly the ugliest one. "Oh, I like this. It's so dramatic. That's what I want. I want to look… inspirational."

"You *are* inspirational," I say.

I need this to go faster. I need to learn as much as I can about the water and where it's supposedly coming from. And then I need to get out of here and plan. I can't think with her in my face.

"Oh, thank you," Verene says sweetly, like people tell her she's inspirational all the time. "I suppose I mean that I want to look more inspirational than usual. I just… well, I just love the people of Iris so much. When they see me, I want them to feel like…"

She trails off, studying herself in the mirror. For a second, I catch myself studying her, too. I take in her radiant skin and her soft hair, and I think about the way I looked right before my wedding. I looked perfect. Almost as perfect as she does.

"I want them to feel like we can do anything," she finishes. "Together."

"That's a wonderful sentiment," I say. "There is one thing about the gowns—since they are rather large, we just want to make sure that they won't get in the way of your business as the Heart. Could you just describe what sort of things you'll need to do with your magic—"

She's looking at me in the mirror. She's looking at the handkerchief over my hair, like it's the first time she's really noticing it. And then, before I can stop it, she's looking right into my eyes.

I remember what the watercrea said to me when she had me captive on Ale's bedroom floor.

Once I see you, I can't let you go.

Verene turns around.

"Wait," she says, a note of realization in her voice.

I rip off my handkerchief and fling it over Verene's face. For a split second, she's very still. I'm very still. I moved so quickly that I surprised even myself.

She reaches up and starts to pull the handkerchief off.

No. She knows who I am now. She knows what I saw.

I can't let her go.

So I lunge at her and knock her off her chair.

NINE

As soon as we hit the floor, Verene fights back. She's not particularly strong, but she's feisty. I throw myself on top of her, desperately trying to keep the handkerchief over her face, but she's screaming and flailing and she has so many long limbs.

"Ale," I say, "bring me the—"

"What are you doing, Emanuela?" Ale is hovering above us, engaged in a lot of hand-wringing. "Oh my God, what are you doing—"

"The sewing kit—" I grunt out.

"What?" he says.

"Bring me the sewing kit!" I demand. "And help me tie her up!"

"But why—"

"Ale, do it. Now." My voice makes it clear this isn't up for debate.

He brings me the sewing kit. I've managed to crush Verene's arms under my knees, but she's still kicking and screaming into her handkerchief.

"Hold her down," I instruct. "Keep her quiet."

"What?" he says. "I can't—"

I put his hands over Verene's face. He whimpers as I grab the sewing kit. In a frenzy, I dig out some ribbon that looks like it might get the job done. Together, we wrap the ribbon around Verene's eyes to hold the handkerchief in place. We wrap her mouth. We wrap her wrists and her ankles. We push her into a sitting position against one of her bedposts, and we tie her waist to it. Then, and only then, do I feel like I can let go. I sit back, and Ale and I stare at the Heart of Iris, disheveled and blindfolded and wiggling against her bonds.

"You…" Ale's voice is high and thin. "You just… Why did you…?"

"She was going to attack me," I say.

"What?" he says.

"She had to be subdued," I say.

I'm jittering. I feel like I could run across the whole of Iris right now. Simultaneously, somehow, I feel like I might need to go vomit.

I let myself get so close to her. She was looking right into my eyes.

"Emanuela," Ale says. "She's… she's the most important girl in this city."

"If you say so," I say.

"They have statues of her everywhere," he says. "They worship her. We can't—we can't just—"

"Tie her up?" I say. "It's interesting that you would say so, because we just did."

Ale is scrambling. He looks at the bedroom door. He looks out the narrow windows at the darkening veil and the roofs of the city that's not ours. He looks back at the girl tied to her bedpost.

"She was being so nice," he says, a little helplessly.

I narrow my eyes. "We'll see about that."

I crawl closer to Verene. I pull the sewing scissors out of my pocket and press them to her neck. She goes stiff.

"Don't scream," I say. I roll down the ribbon we used to gag her, fully prepared to smother her if she screams anyway.

"I know who you are," she says the moment she's able.

"What?" I say.

"*I know who you are*," she insists.

"Oh?" I say. "Who are we, then?"

"You're—" She's holding her head high, but she's also quivering, and when I realize it's with fear, I get a strange, sick thrill. "You're with them."

I glance over my shoulder at Ale, perturbed.

"With who?" I say.

"I know about it, all right?" she says. "I know about the Red Roses. I know who your leaders are and where you meet."

I, of course, have no idea what she's talking about.

"Hmm," I say noncommittally.

"I know you've been sneaking around the catacombs, trying to investigate me," she says. "Why do you think you saw me down there? I was at the underground well. I was painting, actually. And I heard noises, so I went to make sure it wasn't somebody in distress, because it's very unnerving to hear noises in the catacombs. And then you threw a lantern at me and ran off."

That's...not what I expected her to say.

"You were...painting?" I say.

"I spend all day making water for the city," she says. "I would never complain, but it is exhausting, you know. When I need a break, I work on my paintings. I'm sorry if that offends you."

"What were you painting?" I say.

"A picture!" she says. "Of scenery! Does it matter? The point is that I tried to approach you, and you reacted like I was a...bloodthirsty ghost."

"Oh my God." Ale is whispering to himself behind me. "That was her. I was so sure it was a—"

"Well," I say to Verene, "it does seem that you have more information about us than we suspected—"

"I'm not hiding anything," she says. "I don't have a secret room of prisoners, or a secret supply of blood, or whatever it is you suspect me of. I make water for the city with my magic, and I do it from nothing, and no one gets hurt. I'm the Heart of Iris. I'm different. I'm not—I'm not like—" She cuts herself off.

"You're not like...?" I echo.

She's silent.

"I'm not like her," she says, quieter. "And I can prove it."

"Really?" I say. "How?"

"I'll show you my magic," she says. "Right now."

"Right here?" I say.

"Right here," she says.

"And what exactly does that involve?" I say.

"Oh, water will go all over the room," she says. "My brother hates it when I do magic up here. But he'll live."

The little water ritual she did for the city was, admittedly, rather impressive. But I've already seen it. I need something else. I need more.

"So you spend most of your time at the underground well," I say.

"Yes," she says. "It's always full. That was my promise to the city, and I've kept it. But we don't have to go down there. I can do my magic here."

She says it all a little too quickly.

"Do it, then," I say.

"I will," she says.

There's a long moment of silence where she just sits there, and we just stare at her.

"I don't see any water," I say.

"I'm waiting for you to untie me," she says, like it's obvious. "I can't do it unless I'm free."

That's what I thought. I reach for her gag.

"Wait!" she says, squirming away. "Just wait. Don't do anything you'll regret. I know my powers seem too good to be true. When they first manifested, that's what I thought, too. But they're real. If you want me to explain where they came from, I can't. I just know that I've been given something special, and that's why I have to use it. For everyone. For you."

She sounds so very certain. She sounds like she believes in herself—in the Heart of Iris—all the way down to her bones.

For one disconcerting moment, I wonder if I've miscalculated. I wonder if it's really possible for a city to be this uncomplicated and this perfect. I wonder if I've spoiled it all by treating their leader like she's just as dangerous as the watercrea was. I have to imagine that once you've attacked a girl and tied her up and told her that you think she's a liar, it's pretty hard to convince her to share her miraculous, blood-free water with you. I barely knew anything about the watercrea's magic, and I know nothing about this city. I could be wrong.

My hand drifts, of its own accord, to my hip, and the mark

that's been on my skin since I was seven years old. That mark means that I'm not like other Occhians. I'm not like anyone. I'm a girl who can survive the watercrea's tower, and cross the veil, and do things that no one else has ever done. I'm not wrong about that.

And I'm not wrong about the girl in front of me. I can't be wrong about her.

I've hesitated for too long. Verene has sensed it, and she's barreling on.

"Just let me show you," she says. "Then you'll have no choice but to believe."

I shove the gag back over her mouth.

"I'm the only one who gets to decide what I believe," I say.

For good measure, I grab a silk pillowcase from her bed and shove it over her head. I tie it in place with a ribbon around her neck.

She looks well and truly secured, so I stand up. I beckon Ale and lead him to the far side of the room.

Tucked away on the other side of the wardrobe is a small window alcove filled with an easel and paints. A quick glance around at the works in progress tells me that Verene has painted the city streets below at least a dozen times. The light of the veil changes—from deep black in the middle of the night to the brilliant rich hue of midday—but the rest of it stays more or less the same. The paintings are, I reluctantly admit to myself, rather good. She has an eye for color. Especially the red.

I turn away, uneasy.

"Emanuela," Ale says, "were you planning this the whole time?"

No.

"Yes," I say.

"Because you knew that was her we saw in the catacombs?" he says.

"I didn't just see her," I say. "I saw blood on her hands."

He looks pointedly at the easel. "She said she was painting—"

"I know what she said," I snap. "Has it occurred to you that sometimes people lie? Sometimes they pretend to be things they aren't, because it means they can be beloved like a living saint?"

"So you think..." He shifts. "You think she's like..."

"Like the watercrea?" I say.

I can speak the word out loud, even if he can't. She's dead. Saying her title means nothing to me.

His eyes drift back to Verene's wiggling form.

"How can you be so sure?" he says.

"How can you be so sure that I'm wrong?" I say.

He's quiet.

"You can't," I say.

"I know," he says. "I know, Emanuela. I'm not that naive."

"Pfft," I say.

"I just..." Ale fiddles with the white rose behind his ear. "I don't know. I don't *feel* like she's evil."

I roll my eyes harder than I thought possible.

"Anyway." I reach up and snatch the white rose from his ear, discarding it on the floor. "If you're done wasting time with your feelings, we can discuss our plan. We need to get down to the underground well. I suspect there's something there she doesn't want us to see. And, obviously, we need to take her with us."

Ale goes a little pale. "But we have to get past her brother. He might be evil. I did get that feeling about him."

"She also has a housekeeper," I say. "I saw her when I was

sneaking around. There could be any number of surprises out there, so our approach has to be…" I look around the room. "Flawless."

That's how we end up stuffing Verene into a trunk we find at the foot of her bed. It's filled with papers, and at first, I think we've come across something very interesting, but I quickly discover they're nothing more than letters from her adoring citizens. I pick through them, hoping to find a hint of something worthwhile, as Ale tightens Verene's bonds. Some people wax on about Verene's elegance and generosity and incredible hair. More than one proposes marriage. And every single letter tells her how much better their life has been since she became the Heart. One man writes that he got his first omen the night before his daughter was born, and that he thinks every single day about how in the old Iris he would have missed his daughter's entire life.

Obviously, what the watercrea told us about omens wasn't true. They don't all spread within hours. I heard the other Occhians wasting away in the tower, taking entirely too long to die. I can see the people of Iris, walking around marked but free. But I'm sure this man's omens will spread sooner than he thinks. Not everyone is like me. Obviously.

I pick up my sewing kit, instructing Ale to drag the trunk. I peek out to make sure the hallway is empty, then lead us on.

"Do you really think anyone will believe that the Heart gave us a trunk of her gowns as an act of kindness?" Ale whispers, eyeing each door we pass.

"Only if you stop whispering to me like we're in the middle of a devious scheme," I say.

The parlor is mercifully empty, its lights low. Outside, the veil is nearly black. For a moment, I hover in the middle of the quiet room, waiting for someone to show up and regard us with the suspicion we deserve. No one does. I eye the two doorways on the far wall. I can only see shadows beyond them.

"Wait here," I tell Ale.

"What?" he says in a panic. "You can't just leave me alone with a suspicious trunk!"

"I'm just going to run over and look for an entrance to the underground well," I say. "If she spends all her time there, she might have a way down from her quarters."

"But what if somebody comes?" he says. "What am I supposed to do?"

"Act like a human being," I say. "Can you manage that?"

"No!" he says.

I run off. I don't have time for his fretting. I don't have time to think about how we're in a cathedral we don't understand, in a city we don't understand, holding captive a girl whose powers we don't understand. I'm going to understand it all soon.

Through the first doorway is a dining room. The round table hasn't been set for dinner yet, a jeweled chandelier overhead flickering gently. There are sets of arched double doors on either wall. I approach one and peer through the small round window at the top to see a balcony overlooking the cathedral square. The windows of the white manors are glowing softly beyond. It looks like a nice place for Verene to stand and wave prettily to her people. Or spy on them.

I go over to the other set of double doors. They don't have a window, so I carefully, carefully push them open. I see nothing but a staircase that descends steeply into blackness.

I hate the look of it. And I'm pretty sure it's where we need to go.

I turn back to the parlor and stop short just shy of the doorway.

Ale is no longer alone. He's hovering by the coffee table in the center of the room, looking moments away from death. Standing a few feet away is Verene's brother. I recall her addressing him as Theo.

I move forward, already working on my excuse for being in his dining room, but then I catch what Ale's saying.

"They're in her bedroom." His voice is whispery.

I hide against the wall, peering out.

"And you're not with them because...?" Theo says.

I realize the trunk is no longer at Ale's side and have a brief, overwhelming moment of panic. Then I spot it on the far side of the parlor. Ale slid it behind one of the love seats. At least he managed that much.

"I..." Ale says.

Seeing Ale with another boy is a rare sight, and I'm not sure if I find it sad or funny. Theo has a perfect posture and haughty cheekbones, all severity and aristocratic disdain. Ale is from the wealthiest house in Occhia. He should be very good at looking superior. Alas, he looks like the sort of person who has absolutely no idea what to do without something to hide behind.

"I'm just waiting out here," Ale says.

"What are they doing?" Theo says.

"Girl things," Ale says.

Theo is silent for a long moment. Somewhere, I can hear a clock ticking.

"Are you going to elaborate on that?" he says finally.

"They were just...they wanted privacy?" Ale says.

They stare at each other. I can see how desperately Ale is

trying to not lose his nerve. Theo starts to turn toward the bedroom hall.

"Can I see your study?" Ale blurts out.

More silence. It's physically painful for me to endure.

"Why?" Theo says.

"It sounds interesting," Ale whispers.

"You're...interested in how I designed the fountain system?" Theo says.

"Yes," Ale says.

"It's not magic." Theo says it like he fully expects Ale to change his mind.

"I know," Ale says. "I just...your sister mentioned— I just was curious about it."

Theo hesitates. I start to reach for the sewing scissors in my pocket.

"You can look at the maps," he says at last. "I suppose."

And then, before I can figure out how to intervene, he's leading Ale away. I run into the parlor and hover over the trunk. I don't want to leave Ale up here. But we don't have much time before somebody in these quarters figures out Verene is missing. I have a very small window of opportunity, and I can't waste it.

I drag the trunk into the dining room, very aware of the conspicuous slide of it on the tile. I push open the doors and stand poised at the top, looking down into the shadows.

I'll just quickly search the well and then come back. But I didn't expect that I'd have to go down this staircase by myself. Now, when I find out what's really happening in this city, I'll be facing it alone.

But that doesn't scare me. I was alone in the watercrea's tower, and I handled that just fine.

I try to take the first step, but my body rebels. It won't. It can't. It remembers the cold floor of my cell and the chains around my wrists. It remembers the sounds of the prisoners around me, their breath rattling as they barely clung to life.

I grit my teeth. I have this city's ruler tied up in a trunk. I'm in control now. I'll always be in control.

I pull the trunk onto the landing of the staircase, shutting the door behind me.

Last year, Ale was at my house for our usual afternoon coffee. Two of my aunts were chaperoning us and sewing in the corner, bored out of their minds, while we steadily demolished an overly generous serving of raspberry tart.

"I found out the reason Giulia was crying when we left the reception," I said. "Her new husband got drunk and told her he'd rather have married her sister."

"Oh, that's…" Ale pushed the last bit of tart in my direction. "Is she all right? That's horrible."

"It's hilarious," I insisted.

I idly tapped my fork. Giulia was two years younger than me. It's possible I was a bit grumpy about having to stand in the crowd while she got to parade around as a bride.

"Isn't it ridiculous, though?" I said.

"What?" Ale said. "Giulia's husband wanting to marry her sister? I suppose he can't help who he falls in love with, but…"

"Isn't it ridiculous that the only thing standing between us and our own marriage is my womb? And all because the cursed thing refuses to bleed."

Ale paled and gave my aunts a nervous glance, but they didn't even look up. This was nothing they hadn't heard before.

"It clearly has a mind of its own." I considered, then dropped my voice. "Do you think I should…hurry the process along?"

Ale paled even further. "You can do that?"

"I've been contemplating it. If I say I've got blood coming out of my nether regions, what man is going to stick his head down there and check? Paola will go along with it. We'll just—"

"No," Ale said.

I paused, my fork halfway to my mouth. "No? Why not?"

"You…" His eyes darted around the parlor. "You shouldn't."

"But I want to," I said.

"But—" he said.

"Yes, Ale, I know it's against the rules." I set down my fork. "But I'm bored of this juvenile lifestyle. It's time for me to be a married woman. Just because we can't have children yet doesn't mean—well."

I stumbled a bit over the words. I met Ale's eyes accidentally, and we both looked away. I noticed our feet were touching under the table. They often were, because he had no concept of where to put his absurdly long legs, but all of a sudden, it seemed very urgent that we not.

Ale and I spent quite a lot of time listening to our families talk about our future children—how pretty they would be, how numerous they would be, and how many deceased relatives we could name them after. To everyone else, the children were the entire point of our marriage. They were the entire point of our existences. But somehow, when it was just the two of us, this crucial topic never came up.

Ale fiddled with his napkin. His knee was now jiggling

and rattling the plates. All at once, I decided I was tired of this unbearable awkwardness. We were best friends. We talked about everything else, so we could talk about this, too.

I poured more sugar into my coffee and stirred. "I don't know what you're so worried about anyway."

"What?" he said.

"It will be much worse for me," I said. "I'm the one who'll have to squeeze out your enormous babies."

He went very still.

"I'm quite pretty down there, just by the way." I pressed on despite my extreme discomfort. "And it's all going to get wrecked by your—"

He set down his coffee with a loud clink. My aunts paused in their sewing.

"Don't," he said.

"Don't what?" I said.

"Don't make light of it," he said. "You know…you know I don't—" He cut himself off, glancing at our chaperones.

I leaned closer.

"Oh, and you think I do?" I said. "Do I sound like I'm giddy with anticipation? I've just decided to be mature about it. If we don't produce heirs, they'll nullify our marriage. Or did you forget?"

"Well…" he said.

"Well?" I said, uncomprehending.

He looked away. He was still jittery, his face pink and agitated.

"It's just…" he said. "It'd be nice if any of it was real."

"If any of it was *real*?" I said.

The words felt like broken glass in my mouth.

"Wouldn't it?" He looked back at me. "Does that really not matter to you?"

I didn't like the expression on his face. I didn't like the tone of his voice. It felt presumptuous. It felt like he thought he understood how this all worked better than I did.

I jumped to my feet. I grabbed the front of his vest and dragged him out of the parlor, and as soon as we were out of my aunts' sight, I pushed him against the wall.

"You want something real, do you?" I said.

"I was just—" he said.

"If that's what you want," I said, "then you can go propose to your beloved Manfredo, who doesn't even know you exist. Let's see how that goes for you. How do you think that will go for you?"

"I—" he said.

"If that's what you want, then there's nothing stopping you," I said. "You can give up your title. You can give up your house. You can give up ever doing anything with your life, because you're never going to do it without me."

He stopped trying to protest. I glanced at the doorway of the parlor just in time to see a shadow shift across its threshold. That meant my aunts were pressed against the wall, eavesdropping. Ale and I never argued. This was undoubtedly the most exciting thing they'd witnessed all day.

"If that's what you want—" I let go of him and turned away.

"Wait!" Ale said, and grabbed my wrist. "I'm sorry. I'm sorry. You're right. This is…this is the way it's supposed to be."

"Of course it is," I said.

"And it is real, in its own way," he said. "I know that. You're my best friend."

I didn't say another word. I just yanked free of him and marched pointedly back to the parlor. He joined me, of course, and we finished our coffee in silence, avoiding each other's eyes.

That night, I sat in my window, staring down the street at the House of Morandi. The candle in Ale's bedroom was still burning, a tiny pinprick of light against the blackness of the veil. After a few hours, his shadowy figure appeared at the windowsill, and he blew it out. I leaned over and blew mine out, too.

He disappeared, but I stayed there. Still watching.

I didn't have any other friends. I had a nursemaid who knew entirely too much about me. I had followers who clustered around me at parties. I had family who passed down their legacy and pushed me to do even better. They were all important, but they weren't friends the way Ale was. Ale didn't spend every day with me because there was something he wanted. The only thing Ale ever wanted from me was...me.

I didn't have any paramours. I never had. Just the other day, Chiara Bianchi and I had been alone in a garden alcove, and in the middle of sniping at each other, she'd faltered and looked at me in a strange way. And I'd felt...something. But I didn't know what to do with it. I wasn't prepared for it. So I turned away. I preferred to keep those feelings locked up. I could let them out in my bedroom, late at night, not around a real girl—a girl who could betray me or discover my omen or, worst of all, decide I was unremarkable and treat me just like everyone else.

I didn't need any of that. I had Ale. Ale didn't have any paramours. Ale didn't have any other friends. He had no romance to offer me, but he'd also never marry somebody else, and he'd never carry on a life without me. He couldn't.

He wouldn't.

Ten

I DON'T KNOW WHY I THOUGHT IT WOULD BE EASY TO GET A trunk with a girl inside it down a steep, dark staircase. My first approach is to get in front and pull, but after it nearly runs me over, I try pushing. In an instant, it's gotten away from me. I chase it down the steps, grimacing at the obnoxious noise. When I finally manage to catch it, I wrestle it down, and down, and down. Just when I start to fear the stairs will never end, I wind around a bend and find an arched doorway, two flickering lanterns on either side.

I leave the trunk for a moment. I creep to the doorway and peek into the room.

I never saw the underground well in Occhia, but I was taught how it works. The watercrea collected blood in a glass tank beneath her tower. Then she opened a hole at the bottom and let it flow down into the well. She used her magic to transform it as it went.

After ten years of nightmares about the watercrea, I have a very particular mental image of what I think it all looks like. It makes seeing the well of Iris even more jarring. It's not a small hole in the floor, like the one I imagined for Occhia. It's wide, taking up most of the space in the round room. It's full to the brim, the surface dark and glassy. And there's no glass tank holding blood above it. There's nothing above it—just endless stone walls stretching up into shadow.

Off to one side is a black doorway. It must lead to the catacombs. This place has a silence to it, ancient and total, that I would never find in the city streets above.

I move to the edge of the well and kneel down. I can't see the bottom.

Verene claims that she spends most of her day here, filling the well. But I don't see any sign of that. I don't see a chair, or a bottle of wine, or an easel and paints. I don't see any signs of… anything. The well looks like it was simply filled out of nowhere, by magic.

I touch the surface of the water, just to be sure it's real. It's cold.

Occhia could live off this water for days. Months. Years.

Behind me, there's a loud crash. I whirl around to see that the trunk has fallen onto its side, and Verene is tumbling out.

I run for her, my sewing scissors out. But she's already on her feet. She's pushing her mussed hair out of her eyes, and all at once, she's looking at me. In the dim light, her eyes look bigger. Colder.

"So?" she says.

I can't move. I can't even breathe.

She gestures to the well behind me, and I stumble back.

"Do you believe me yet?" she says. "Or are you going to tear up the catacombs, looking for whatever evidence you think you can find?"

The scissors are shaking in my grip, and I clutch them with both hands.

Verene sighs. "That's what I thought."

I jab at her. I have to. I have to do something. But she lunges at me, like she's not even afraid of getting stabbed, and grabs my wrists. And the scissors are out of my hands and in hers. I have no idea how it happened. I thought I'd be better at using a sharp thing on another person. It seems like the sort of thing I should be good at.

"This is insulting," she says. "It's really insulting. You attacked me for no reason, and then you tied me up in the most undignified way—and I'm sure you snooped around in my things, too. There's nothing I wouldn't do for this city. I give so much of myself, and I do it for you and everyone you love. Can't you see that?"

She's coming at me. The scissors are clutched in her white-gloved fingers. And her eyes are unblinking. Unrelenting.

"Just explain it," she says.

"Ex—" I'm stammering, even though I'm not the sort of person who stammers. "Explain what—"

"My magic is real!" she says. "You have to know that! You can see it all around you! So why do you and your little group of conspiracy theorists still have meetings in the greenhouses? Why do you make up these ridiculous rumors about how I'm taking blood from people in their sleep? How would I even do that? I couldn't. Things are so good in Iris. Everyone is happy. Except you."

She won't stop advancing. I stumble along the edge of the well, groping the cold wall for balance.

"I—" I say.

"I'm not like her." Her voice is too loud, echoing off the stone walls, and I swear she still hasn't blinked. "I would rather die than be like her. Do you think you had a bad time of it, with her ruling over you? Imagine being her daughter. She treated me like a prisoner, too. She never let me go anywhere. She made me watch as she stuck needles in dying people and took their blood. She—"

She cuts herself off. She's breathing hard, and the scissors are trembling in her grip. She presses a hand to her forehead, like she's suddenly dizzy.

I feel like I've been frozen inside. I haven't been thinking. I've just been backing away, instinctively, trying to get away from her eyes. But all at once, I come back to my senses.

If I was being attacked by magic, I would know. I'm terrified right now, but the sensations in my body are all my own.

The moment I realize that I'm still free to act, I do. I lift my skirts and kick Verene in the stomach, hard. It catches her off guard. She doubles over and drops the scissors. I snatch them up and back away. And I wait to see how she's going to retaliate.

"What—" She's a little breathless. "What are you going to do? Stab me? You'll regret that."

"You…" My mouth is very dry. "You don't have it. The blood magic."

"No!" she says. "I don't! That's why I've been trying to tell you the whole time! For the love of—"

"Then show it to me," I say. "Your true magic. Your water magic."

She straightens up, all defiance and pride. And for a split second, I think she's going to raise her graceful hands and shower me in water, and I'm already trying to figure out what it would mean for Occhia and me.

"No," she says.

I blink at her. "No? After all that carrying on about your miraculous powers, you're just going to—"

"No," she repeats. "I gave you the chance to see it before, and you turned me down. You stuffed me in a trunk. You threatened me with scissors—which you're still doing, by the way. I don't have to show you anything."

"But—" I fumble. "Don't you want to convince me? Because I'm still not convinced."

Her nostrils flare.

"Look at all this water." She gestures widely. "If I didn't make it, then who did?"

She says it with so much confidence. Because in her mind, she's talking to Tatienne du Brodeur, a seamstress from Iris who only knows one city and one ruler who makes water.

But she's not talking to Tatienne du Brodeur.

I glance at the doorway to the catacombs and think about Occhia, mysteriously connected to this place by the maze of tunnels. I think about the grim set of Paola's face when she told me our underground well was empty, and no one knew why. I think about two little girls crammed into the same cell of the watercrea's tower, like the watercrea had become desperate to get every last drop of blood she could.

A few feet away, Verene is hesitating. Her eyes are searching my face, and I don't want her to read what's written there, but it's all coming too fast for me to hide it. Realization. Bewilderment.

And a sudden, blinding fury.

Verene isn't like the watercrea. But she's not a miraculous saint who can create something out of nothing, either.

She's a thief.

And I'm already running at her. I'm already attacking.

She tries to fight back, but I'm angrier. In an instant, I have her on the floor, the point of my scissors in the hollow of her throat.

"You—you—" I seethe, unable to finish the sentence.

"Who—" she chokes out, disbelief in her voice. "You're not— Who are you?"

I dig the scissors deeper, and her breath catches. She's trembling underneath me. I can feel it as I try to gather myself. I swallow down my anger so that I can regard her with the coldest hatred I possess.

"My name is Emanuela," I say. "You're going to tell me how you stole my city's water."

And I'm going to steal it back.

Verene's breathing is ragged. Her gaze flits down to the scissors pressed into her throat and I notice, irrationally, how very long her dark eyelashes are. Then she looks back at me, and somehow, her eyes are even more defiant than before.

"No," she says.

My grip on the scissors tightens. "I'm not afraid to draw blood."

I'm not. I'll push these scissors in and ruin her perfect skin. It's what she deserves.

"And I'm not afraid of you," she says.

"This water was made in my city," I say. "It's mine."

"My people need it."

Her words still have an unsettling conviction to them. She may not have magic, but she really believes she's the savior of her city. I can see it on her face. I can feel it radiating off her body.

I want to destroy it. I want to destroy *her*. I want to see her lying in the ruins of this place, while I bring my people the water that they died for.

"Aren't you wondering where my accomplice is?" I say.

"I assumed he was hiding nearby," she says. "As part of some trap you thought you could set, perhaps?"

"Actually," I say, "he's with your own accomplice. I'm referring, of course, to your brother."

Something flickers in her eyes. I don't know exactly what it is, but I know that I've found a promising avenue.

"Your brother designed your so-called fountain system," I say. "The one that lets you distribute water all around your city. It's such an impressive feat. I wonder if he has any information about the way you're getting water from my city to yours."

"Even if he did, you'll never get it out of him," she says.

I smile like I know something she doesn't. "Well, my accomplice is very good at getting information out of people. You thought he was sweet and innocent, didn't you? You were practically courting him earlier."

"Courting him?" she says. "Please. I was being kind to someone I thought was my new friend. But you're obviously not familiar with that concept."

For a moment, all I can think about is the way she made courting a boy sound so ridiculous, like the thought has never occurred to her before. But it's beside the point, of course. The point is that I'm on top of her, and my scissors are making a dent in the soft hollow of her throat, and she's going to give me what I need.

"He's not sweet and innocent," I say. "He's almost as dangerous as me. If I were you, I'd start thinking about what you're going to do when he gets down here with your brother in his captivity—"

In the distance, a door cracks open. It's quickly followed by the sound of someone moving down the stairs. I freeze. I can feel Verene holding her breath. And for a second, we just wait to see what's going to happen next.

After a moment, I realize it doesn't sound like a person walking down the stairs at all. It sounds like a person falling. Falling while simultaneously attempting to juggle a variety of heavy objects that keep slipping out of their grip and thudding onto the steps.

I glance at Verene. She looks just as perturbed as I am.

Then I hear a familiar, muffled voice.

"Emanuela! He got suspicious—I'm trying to stop him—"

It distracts me. I don't even realize it's distracted me until Verene takes advantage of it. She knocks the sewing scissors out of my hand, and they clatter to the floor. We both dive for them. She gets there first, because of her long arms—I decide that I also now have a personal vendetta against how tall she is—and she tries to jab them at me. I leap up and kick her in the nose, and she falls back, dropping the scissors and clutching at her face.

I scoop up the scissors just as Theo stumbles through the door. He's breathing hard and his crisp white shirt is half-untucked. He looks, to put it mildly, displeased.

Verene is on her feet again. I catch a flash of her white gown, and I have just enough time to calculate my move. I back up to the edge of the well. She charges, and when she throws herself at me, I leap out of the way.

She hits the water hard. There's a loud smack and a splash, and then she's thrashing. Her heavy skirts are already pulling her down.

All of a sudden, she looks helpless. And after what she did to my city, that's how she deserves to feel. It's as simple as that.

Theo curses under his breath and runs for the edge of the well. I block his path and point my sewing scissors at him.

"If you stay very still and answer my questions, maybe I'll let you save her," I say.

If she can even be saved, that is. She's sinking so quickly.

I know, obviously, that Verene could die. The thought is occurring to me as I stare at the desperate blur of her under the water. But I don't care if she dies. She's not magical. She's not special. And she's certainly not important to me.

Theo considers me. Then, with one precise movement, he whacks the scissors out of my hand.

I should have brought a bigger weapon.

Just as Theo is about to push me aside, too, Ale bursts through the door. He's holding an enormous kitchen knife.

I've never been so glad to see him.

What happens next is a blur. Ale dives at Theo. There's a sharp, wet sound and a very undignified yelp. A second later, the knife clatters to the floor, and Ale leaps away from it like it's on fire.

There's blood all over it. And Theo is on the floor at the edge of the well, clutching at his side.

I look at Ale. "You... you stabbed him."

Ale is still staring at Theo. He looks like he hasn't processed it. He looks like he's not going to process it any time soon. His face is all horror, but I mostly feel a strange sense of pride. For once, I didn't have to do absolutely everything myself.

I march over to Theo. I kick him onto his back, and he grunts in pain as I put my foot on his chest. There's blood all over his white gloves and smeared on the floor next to him. It's actually quite a lot. I can even smell it, and for a moment, I feel a little nauseated. But I don't feel any sympathy.

"I know that you're stealing this water," I say. "And I know who you're stealing it from."

"Em-Emanuela," Ale stammers behind me.

In the well, Verene has stopped splashing.

I've been in this city for less than a day, and I've already reduced its leader and her accomplice to this. It's almost pathetic, how quickly I broke down their little act of being more perfect and more powerful than everyone else. They look so ordinary now. Ordinary and broken. Just like the watercrea.

I lean harder on Theo's chest, and he winces. He must know how close Verene is to dying, too, but he doesn't look panicked. Maybe he's too distracted by the pain. Maybe they didn't even care about each other. Maybe he's glad that he doesn't have to design her fountains anymore.

"I know there's no magic in this city," I say. "You can't control my blood. You can't scare me with..." I trail off.

I don't like how quiet he's being. I don't like the look on his face. He's looking at me like he knows something I don't.

"Emanuela!" Ale grabs me and pulls me back.

Only then do I see it.

On the floor beside Theo, something is...happening.

There's a shadow forming. It doesn't have a shape. It's just a smudge. But Theo's blood is disappearing. Like the shadow is consuming it.

The shadow moves abruptly, and Ale and I leap back, pressing ourselves against the wall. But it's not moving in our direction. It slides over the edge of the well and disappears.

Theo sits up. He's clutching at the wound in his side, and his breathing is ragged, but he doesn't look the least bit afraid. He just looks grim.

"Did you really think there was no blood?" he says. "There's always blood."

The shadow flies out of the well, and all of a sudden, water sprays all over the room, cold and heavy. I duck. When I can see again, Verene is lying on the floor, soaking wet. She rolls onto her side and retches, water spewing out of her mouth.

And then the shadow is coming for us.

I don't think. I just run. I push Ale back toward the stairs, and we throw ourselves up the steps. I don't know how we make it to the top. It must be out of sheer desperation. We fling open the door and then, suddenly, we're back in the peaceful dining room of the cathedral. The chandelier is still flickering softly.

I slam the door behind us and look around, searching the shiny tile floor and the white walls.

The shadow is nowhere to be found.

"What—" Ale is dripping wet and shaking. There's blood on his hands. "What was that...thing?"

I don't know. All I know is that we need to get out of here.

I run through the parlor, down the stairs, and into the foyer of the cathedral. The double doors are dead-bolted shut, and I'm certain that when I try to push the lock aside, they're going to magically slam back into place. But they don't. A moment later, Ale and I are stumbling out into the night.

For a moment, I just stand in the cathedral square, looking around wildly. It must be quite late. The veil has already deepened to black, and some of the windows in the manors around us have gone dark. I spot a few distant figures loitering on the steps of a manor, passing around a bottle of wine, and off to the side, I can hear the sound of revelry coming from the public gardens. Of course someone is having a garden party. This is a beautiful, perfect city, and its people can enjoy all the parties they want.

Everyone here thinks Verene is a saint. They don't know about my people. They don't know what she's taking from us. They don't know that we're dying.

I turn to Ale. "We can't get back to Occhia."

"What?" he says.

"We can't get back to Occhia," I repeat, more forcefully. "That thing...it lives in the catacombs. It moves around in the catacombs. It's what they're using to steal the water from us. It has to be. If we try to go back down there, it could—"

"They're stealing water from us?" he says. "With that thing? But, Emanuela, what *was* it?"

"I don't know." My voice is too loud.

"It can swallow water," he says, like he's realizing it as he speaks. "And people. But...where did it come from?"

"They're the children of this city's last ruler," I say. "The ruler with blood magic. Maybe it was some sort of power they got from her."

"What?" he says. "She had children? But why didn't she just pass down the exact same magic—"

"I don't know, Ale! I don't know what's going on in this city. But I was so sure I could figure it out. I was so sure—and we can't get back to Occhia—and—"

And I almost killed Verene back there. I almost killed another person. And I didn't even really think about what I was doing until it was too late.

My papá always says that I never stop until I get what I want, and that it's the best thing about me. And it is. It's never scared me before. Not the way it's scaring me now.

Ale puts a hand on my back.

"I…" I say. "We should…"

I want to tell him that I have a plan. I want to tell him that we're closer to getting this city's water. But we're not. And I can't.

He glances back at the towering face of the cathedral.

"We should hide," he finishes for me.

ELEVEN

WE REACH THE EDGE OF THE CATHEDRAL SQUARE. ALE moves in the direction of a quiet, unassuming street, but I grab his wrist.

"Let's go to the gardens," I say.

He gives them a nervous glance. "It sounds like there's a party."

"Which means they'll expect us to hide somewhere quieter," I say.

And I can't go sit in an empty alley. Not after the darkness of the underground well. It doesn't seem like the blood-eating shadow we just encountered can venture into the city above—if it could, surely it would still be chasing us—but I'm finding it harder and harder to trust my own instincts.

We head for the gardens and push through an ornate iron gate at the entrance. In Occhia, the name "gardens" is a bit of a misnomer. They're more of a stone plaza, with plenty of statues of saints and the occasional plant. Everyone crowds the prettiest path that's lined with tall, skinny cypress trees. There are always, at minimum, three couples trying to have romantic moments. It's impossible for anyone to enjoy it.

My people would probably faint if they could see the gardens of Iris. They're so green and so very alive. Ale and I are instantly lost in a maze of hedges. We wind around sharp corners and through ivy-covered tunnels, and I look for a hiding place that feels secure enough.

"So," Ale says. "You're…you're absolutely certain that Verene doesn't have blood magic?"

"We were fighting," I say. "I was besting her. If she had it, she would have used it on me the moment she escaped from the trunk—"

I stop short.

"You loosened her bonds," I say.

"What?" Ale whispers very delicately.

I round on him. "She escaped the trunk on her own. And I couldn't figure out how. When we were in her bedroom, I told you to tie her up even tighter while I searched her things. But you didn't. You loosened her bonds."

The guilt is all over his face.

"I was afraid she wouldn't be able to breathe," he says. "And I didn't—I really didn't think she was dangerous. I just—"

"And were you right?" I say.

He's not looking at me anymore.

"You useless piece of garbage." My ears are very hot. "This is why you're supposed to do exactly what I tell you. She attacked me. She could have killed me."

"You left me with her brother," he whispers. "He could have—"

"You left yourself," I say. "That was your own incompetent floundering. And it was mortifying to watch, by the way."

"I'm sorry," he says. "I just—I thought maybe, if we didn't treat her like an enemy—"

"She is our enemy," I say. "She's taking Occhia's water, Ale. That water belongs to us. I was right about what's happening in this city—I was more right than you, at least. These people are a danger to us, and they need to be stopped. Am I wrong about that? Tell me I'm wrong."

He's quiet. He's looking at the blood that's still smeared on his fingers.

"You're not wrong," he says.

I whirl around and march off. I find a gap in the hedges and slip through it. Now that I'm hidden in the narrow, dark space between two walls of hedges, I should feel a little safer. I should feel a little better. But I don't.

"Emanuela." Ale squeezes in after me. "Please don't run."

"I didn't want us to get separated," I hear myself say. "I didn't— When things started to go wrong, I didn't know what was happening to you."

I pause, suddenly aware of how hard my voice is wavering. I can't look at him, because I know he heard it, too.

For a long moment, he's quiet.

"Well," he says, "we won't be separated again."

He sits down, his back against a wall of hedges. He rubs at the blood on his fingers, then sighs.

"This city was too good to be true," he says. "I should have known."

I sit down next to him, closer than I normally do. I'm cold

and wet and I'm craving the warmth of another person at my side. He idly rests his knee against mine.

If we were still in Occhia, and we were married, we would be doing whatever we wanted right now. We would be throwing a party, or holding meetings, or just sitting together in the parlor we owned. That was the way things were supposed to be. Things will be that way again, once I fix my city.

"I took something from him."

Ale says it so quietly that for a moment, I think I imagined it. I give him a sideways look and find that he's hunched and shamefaced.

"What did you just say?" I say.

"The brother," he says. "When he was showing me his study—he had all these diagrams of the fountains on the wall. There was a lot of math. I didn't understand any of it. But I noticed that there was a piece of paper on his desk that he had folded and slipped under some books, like it was a secret. The books were very boring, by the way. They were also about math. I was so disappointed. I was thinking about how this city must have so much beautiful art and so many novels that I've never read. Isn't it amazing that they've been over here for a thousand years, making their own—"

"What's your point, Ale?" I say.

"Oh," he says. "I, um, I waited until he turned his back and I took the secret paper."

"You stabbed him and stole his private documents?" I say. "What has this city done to my wholesome Alessandro?"

He squirms. "I'm not proud of it. It was terrible of me. But maybe it will have something useful. I hope it didn't get too wet..."

He reaches into his shirt pocket and pulls out the paper, unfolding it on the grass between us. I shift to get a better look. For a long moment, we're both still, trying to figure out what we're seeing.

It's a drawing in red ink. There are eight circles arranged in a ring, just barely touching. In the middle of each circle is a tiny drawing of a familiar building. A cathedral. Surrounding the cathedrals are webs of painstakingly rendered streets.

One of the circles catches my eye. It's labeled with the word *Occhia.*

I touch it, delicately. The drawing looks like it's supposed to be a map, but I don't recognize the path of the streets. I can't find my family's house. But after a moment of searching, I realize that maybe it's not a map of the city above. Maybe it's a map of the city below.

My eyes drift to one of the neighboring circles. It's labeled as Iris. The others are labeled, too, with names I've never seen before.

"Ale," I say.

"There's—" he says.

"There's more," I say.

There are other cities. Six other cities.

"We're all connected by the catacombs," I say. "Everything around us—that's the veil. But inside it, we're connected. That's how we got here."

I trace the path between Occhia and Iris.

"Does no one know about this?" Ale's voice is hushed. "Do the other watercreas know?"

There's a tiny dot behind the cathedral—a tower—in every city. Except Iris.

There are six other cities. I can't quite wrap my head around what it means. I can't quite comprehend the fact that for my entire life, I thought Occhia was all alone, a tiny bubble inside the veil, and I was so wrong.

There are six other cities, and no one in them knows my name. No one in them knows what I have to offer. But they could.

"What do you think these marks mean?" Ale touches the outside of one of the circles.

Somebody—Theo, I would assume—has been making small tick marks next to each city. Again, Iris is the only exception. I consider.

"The water," I guess. "He marks it off every time they steal. And they go in a circle. So each city takes a turn, and each city has time to recover."

"They have so much water here," Ale says. "They're taking more than they need. Why?"

"Because they can," I say.

"Don't they ever think about what it does to us?" he says.

"Obviously not," I say.

This is the reason why Occhia's underground well is empty. Verene and Theo must have stolen the last of our water right before our watercrea disappeared. She didn't have time to replace it. My people are panicking and rioting and afraid so that the people here can splash around in happiness and comfort.

"The rulers of these other cities..." Ale says. "The other... watercreas. They must notice when their water gets stolen. Why haven't they stopped it?"

"They must not know how," I say.

"Maybe they've tried, but they can't," Ale says. "If Verene

and Theo were born with this, like their mamma was born with her magic..."

A cold dread is creeping down my spine. There are six other rulers out there who have a thousand years' worth of power and knowledge. If they knew how to get their water back, they would have done it already.

I know how to fight against people. I know how to look for weaknesses in humans. But that thing we saw in the catacombs wasn't human. It wasn't like anything I've ever seen before.

"But we have to figure out a way," Ale says.

"What?" I say.

"We have to figure out a way to stop them," he says. "To stop that thing. If we stop it, then we can use the catacombs to get home. And we'll have helped the other six cities. They'll be free again. So maybe, in return, we could ask them each to give us a little bit of their water..."

And Occhia will be saved.

And Verene will be destroyed. And I'll be the savior of my city. I'll be the one with the power.

"Emanuela." Ale is eyeing me nervously. "What are you thinking?"

"I'm thinking that you're brilliant for finding this," I say.

He beams.

We slip out of the hedges, and I lead us in a winding path, following the noise to the garden party. We find everyone in a large clearing. At the center—of course—is a statue of Verene. This one has been lovingly draped in chains of white roses. Below her, water is spilling out into an enormous pool. It's as wide as a manor and filled with people, and looking at it makes my stomach churn.

"Emanuela," Ale whispers as we peer in. "Why are we here?"

"We need food," I say. "They must have food. And…"

I trail off as I take another look around the clearing. I've just comprehended the fact that most of the people lolling on the grass and playing around in the fountain are rather… undressed.

I straighten out my wet skirts, undaunted. I grab Ale's hand and pull him into the party, to his obvious distress. We meander through the din of shrieking and splashing like we belong.

"Everyone is going to notice us—" he says.

"If you're confident enough, people only notice what you want them to notice. How many times do I have to tell you this, Alessandro? Besides, they're all drunk. Can't you smell it?"

I've already casually bent down and scooped up a basket someone was kind enough to leave on the grass. It contains a bundle of neatly cut fruits with a jar of chocolate spread and loaves of savory cakes studded with olives. I hand a cake to Ale. I spot a promising pile of clothes near the edge of the fountain and approach, because some disguises could come in handy. I bend down and quickly shove it all into my basket. As I close it up, I accidentally make eye contact with a girl in a chemise who's sitting on the edge of the fountain. I continue to look confident. Extraordinarily confident. She turns away, unconcerned.

I've never seen another girl in nothing but a chemise before. I'm used to being the most scandalously dressed one in the room.

I stand up. It's very hot in this garden. "Let's go, Ale. Ale? Where did you—"

He's hovering behind me. He's eating his cake, slowly, and gaping at something in the fountain. I follow his gaze to see two boys getting very intimate with each other's faces. They're not the only people in the pool engaging in such…activities.

I mean, we have debauchery in Occhia. It's not this extravagant, but we have it. Occhians who follow the rules—accepting the spouse their family chooses and promising to bear children—are given some unspoken freedom in that regard. I knew about it. I had followers who told me who was sneaking off to wine cellars together after a few too many drinks at a dinner party.

No one ever asked me to sneak off to a wine cellar. They were intimidated, of course.

I wave my hand pointedly in front of Ale's face. He jumps.

"I wasn't—" he says.

"Of course not," I say. "You don't sound guilty at all. Let's go before someone notices that I'm stealing their basket."

"Mmm-hmm," he says.

He's staring at the boys again.

I sidle closer. "If you ask nicely, they might let you smell their handkerchiefs."

"I—" He startles again. "I don't want to smell every single boy's handkerchief, Emanuela! Just because—"

The boys glance over at us. In true Ale fashion, Ale drops his cake and flees. I catch up to him at the entrance to the clearing, where he's withering away from embarrassment.

"Here, you absolute fiasco." I give him another cake. "Now we need to—"

Then the cathedral bells ring out.

Ale and I both go still. The entire party goes still.

The bells chime again.

And again.

And again.

And then, everyone is running. They abandon their wine and clamber out of the fountain, dripping wet, and they charge at the entrance to the clearing—at us.

"Don't just stand there!" A girl stumbling over the bottom of her soaked gown reaches us first and shoves at me. "Remember the last time we were summoned like this?"

The cathedral bells are still chiming.

So the Heart of Iris wants to speak to her people. I wonder what this could possibly be about.

Ale and I melt into the crowd that's pushing into the cathedral square, which is already full. It's impressive how quickly the city has assembled. Manor doors have been left open. People are in their nightclothes. The air is tense, and everyone is whispering, their eyes on the cathedral.

Ale and I find a spot in a back corner. I take a moment to quietly shove down an olive cake, very aware that everyone else is too nervous to eat. A young girl nearby is in tears, and her friend is holding her around the shoulders.

"I'm sure the Heart is fine," she's saying, her voice trembling. "I'm sure it's nothing bad."

"What if—" The other girl is choking on her tears. "What if something happened to her? What if she got sick, too? What if—"

Up above, the balcony doors of the cathedral open. Instantly, the crowd stops breathing. And I wonder if anyone else is imagining a woman in a red dress, sweeping out and expecting us all to bow and saying that this fever dream is over—that it's time to go back to the way things used to be.

When the people see Verene, I feel their collective sigh of relief. But as she staggers forward to grip the balcony, that relief starts to fade.

She's still wearing the same disheveled, wet gown. Her hair is hanging limply in her face, and when she pushes it aside to reveal a bruise on her nose, dried blood crusted below it, a gasp rips through the crowd.

It's all very theatrical. Verene certainly looked worse for the wear after what I did to her, but she didn't look this bad. I don't know why, but it makes me smile. I suppose I appreciate some dramatics from my enemies.

"People of Iris," she says. Her voice is hilariously ragged, but the square is so silent that it carries anyway. "You all remember the last time I called you outside of a watering. Two years ago, when I announced that I would become your Heart and showed you my powers, it was a joyous occasion."

She pauses.

"This is not," she says.

The girl next to me sobs even harder.

"Earlier this evening, I had some visitors," Verene says. "I welcomed two citizens of Iris into my House, hoping to learn more about their lives. And they attacked me. I was able to get free, but only after I almost—"

She cuts herself off, like she can't bear to say it.

"As they were beating me, there was only one thought that kept me going," she continues, quieter. "I thought of you. My people. I thought of what would happen to you if I was gone."

The people all around me are trembling.

"I managed to get to safety," she says. "I went to my brother, and he helped me fight the attackers off. But unfortunately…"

they escaped. I don't know where they are now. And I'm terrified of what else they might try to do."

In an instant, her people are terrified, too. The ones on the edge of the square look around at the dark streets. In spite of myself, I shiver a little.

"I don't know who they are or what they want," Verene says. "There was only one thing they told me. One clue to their motivations. They said... they said that they don't believe my powers are real. They said that they think I'm just like my mother."

I didn't think it was possible for the crowd to get any quieter. But it has.

"How could they say that?" Verene says it softly, almost like she's talking to herself. "Do they not see everything I've done? Everything that we've done?"

She turns her eyes back to us, suddenly.

"We tore down the tower," she says, and her voice is fiercer. "We changed the rules. We gave our city new life."

I know that Verene is a liar and a thief, and yet, in this moment, it's so hard to believe. Her voice has a fervent sincerity to it. She's so utterly gripped by her own righteous indignation. I can see exactly how someone weaker-minded than myself would never even think to question her.

"Do they want to take us backward?" she says. "Do they really think we were better off before? Our city changed because it needed to be changed."

It did need to be changed. If nothing else, she's right about that.

"Just because things were the same for a thousand years doesn't mean they have to be the same forever," she says.

She's right about that, too.

"We saved ourselves," she says. "And no one has the right to take that away from us."

The crowd rustles in agreement. Even the girl next to me has stopped crying. Her wide eyes are on the balcony, transfixed.

"So," Verene says. "Are we going to let these attackers spread their lies and hatred, or are we going to protect our home?"

Verene leans toward us, and everyone around me leans toward her.

"These are the attackers," she says. "You know what to do."

She reaches down and unrolls a banner tied to the balcony.

Oh. Right. I don't know why I was waiting with bated breath to see the terrible miscreants who attacked Iris's leader. I already know their faces. Rather well, in fact.

It's a quick, sloppy painting, but the likeness is unmistakable. Ale is fine-boned and wide-eyed, and I'm...striking. My hair is a mess, but my face is razor sharp and my eyes are dark and knowing. I look so alive.

I've never seen a painting of myself. It's not something we do in Occhia. Only saints get paintings.

My heart is pounding. I have the brief, ridiculous thought that this is the most exciting thing anyone has ever done for me.

And then Ale dives on me, pushing me to the ground.

"This is bad," he whispers. He has his jacket over both of us, trying to hide our faces. "This is so bad—oh God—what's happening—"

The crowd has started to run. They're leaving the square in a stampede. They all seem to be suddenly filled with purpose.

"We have to move with them, or we'll be crushed." I urge Ale up. "Stay low—but not in a suspicious way—"

It's chaos. Ale and I are swept onto one of the streets without even really trying. We cling to each other as, all around us, people shout and scramble into their houses. The doors to the manors slam shut, one by one. I can hear the click of locking doors up and down the street. A woman nearby gives a final, anxious peek out her window before she pulls it closed and shuts the curtains.

I yank Ale into the nearest alley. On my hands and knees, I crawl to the mouth and peer out.

For a long moment, the street is totally empty. Then, I see the glow of lantern light at the far end, and a group of people turns the corner. They're holding all sorts of things—wine bottles and fire irons and, in one case, a rock that appears to have just been pried off the street. They huddle together, like they're receiving instructions.

Footsteps on the other side of the street draw my attention. There's another group. They, too, have an uncomfortable amount of weapons in their possession.

Both groups break apart. They race in every direction, in twos and threes. They check each alley they pass, weapons poised.

We're being hunted. Again.

TWELVE

TWO WOMEN WIELDING WINE BOTTLES STALK CLOSER TO US. Silently, I push Ale in the other direction. We emerge onto a street that, for the time being, is mercifully empty. We press ourselves against the wall of a shuttered manor.

"So," I whisper, "Verene doesn't have guards, but she can turn her people into a mob on a moment's notice. That's a fun trick."

I wish I could do that. One day I'll be able to do that.

"Where are we going to go?" Ale's face is very white in the dark. "We can't go into the catacombs, because of the ghost."

"The ghost?" I say.

"I've decided that the blood-eating creature in the catacombs was a ghost," he says. "Since the catacombs are obviously haunted. I knew it all along."

"If that makes you feel better," I say.

"It doesn't," he says.

"So we can't go into the catacombs," I muse. "Or any of the manors."

And we obviously can't go back to the cathedral.

There's only one thing I can think to do. With another look around, I get to my feet and gesture for Ale to follow.

It takes a long time to sneak through the winding streets. It takes much longer than I wish it would. We have to stick to the shadows, our eyes constantly peeled for the glow of lantern light. The city feels tense, and the manors are all unnaturally quiet. Once or twice, I see a curtain flick aside as someone peeks out.

But at last, I see the vaulted roofs of the greenhouses up ahead. They surround the edge of the city. I've visited the ones in Occhia before, when my papá took me. He showed me that some families have their own, passed down since the city began. Other families, like ours, rely on the limited rations from the public food supply. My papá wanted me to understand that, no matter how much I thought I had, I could always have more. He told me that the people who have the most hold on to it the tightest, and if I wanted it, I'd have to take it for myself.

"Are those the greenhouses?" Ale whispers. "Maybe we should turn back."

Ale's family owns five greenhouses, because of course they do. If our wedding had gone through, I would own five greenhouses.

"That's where we're going," I say.

"What?" he says. "Why?"

Because Verene said that there's a group of people in Iris who don't believe in her powers, and they meet here in secret. She said that they've been snooping around the catacombs, trying to spy on her. Maybe I can find them. And maybe they know something about her that I don't.

"Because I'm still feeling peckish," I say, which is also true.

Unfortunately for my peckishness, the first greenhouse we enter has nothing but lettuce, arranged in neat rows under the glass ceiling. The next one is more promising. The ceiling and the walls are covered in lush grapevines, with two trellises running down the middle. I make my way to the far side, then start munching. I try to think about how I would go about organizing a secret group in this network of glass buildings. Ale watches me anxiously.

"Emanuela," he says, "the mob is going to search here eventually. If they trap us, and we still have no idea how to get past the ghost—"

The door opens. In a scramble, Ale and I dive for the nearest trellis. There's a wheelbarrow full of gardening supplies sitting there, and we crouch behind it for extra cover.

Soft footsteps make their way across the stone floor. I peek through the leaves of the grapevines, and my heart leaps uncomfortably into my throat. It's the last person I expected—Verene. She's almost unrecognizable in nondescript clothes, a handkerchief over her face and her hair stuffed underneath a cap. After her ridiculous, frilly gown, it's odd seeing her in pants. I feel like I'm being bombarded with the fact that she has legs.

"Oh, look," she says, brushing the grapes with a gloved hand. "My favorite."

Theo trudges in behind her. He's also changed into a drab ensemble. He doesn't look like he's having a good time. I'm not sure what, exactly, would prompt him to have a good time, but it's definitely not this.

"Anyway." Verene turns back to him. "They saw the vide with their own eyes. They saw how we summon it. If they tell the Red Roses, well...it's more information than any of them need to have."

It's strangely thrilling that she's figured out my plan already. Now I have to plan faster.

"Vee." Theo rubs his eyes. "There's fifteen people in the Red Roses, and everyone else thinks they're paranoid. They're not our problem. Our problem is the intruders from the other city who are loose—"

"That's fifteen people too many," she snaps.

The subject of people who don't believe in her magic and aren't exuberant about her rule strikes such a nerve with her. It's fascinating.

She rips a couple of grapes off their stems and pops them into her mouth, surveying the greenhouse in front of her. Then she starts walking again, and Theo follows her. He's eyeing each and every single leaf with distaste.

"The intruders will come here," she says. "They're trapped, and they know it. They're going to get desperate. They're going to start trying to use anything they can against us."

She stops. Her eyes flit to the trellis Ale and I are hiding behind. I hold very still.

"And then," she says, "they're going to find out what happens to people who threaten our city. They're going to be sorry they ever— Wait."

I tense, but she's looking over her shoulder now.

"You're bleeding again," she says, reaching for Theo.

"Am I?" He sighs. "Maybe I should just go ahead and die."

"Oh, stop it. Let me see." She rolls up his shirt to look at the knife wound on his side and wrinkles her nose. "The stitches ripped. Sit down."

He resists her tugging. "Not right there. It's dirty."

"You know what else is dirty?" she says. "Dripping your blood all over the floor to summon a—"

"I still have standards," he says.

She forces him down, his back against the trellis opposite ours. She kneels at his side, pulls fresh gauze out of her pocket, and wraps him up quickly, like she's always prepared for this exact situation.

"Marie will have to fix it properly later," she says.

"I just knew they were bad news," Theo mutters. "I knew from the moment I saw them at the door. I never should have let them in."

"We're going to stop them," Verene says.

"She had that insufferable face," he says. "And he had those giant, creepy eyes. And he was in my study...looking at all my things...."

"You mean your boring diagrams of fountain pipes?" Verene says. "What could he have found to use against us there?"

"I don't know," Theo says darkly. "But he was trying."

I glance at Ale. His hand is pressed anxiously against his shirt pocket.

If they knew we had the map of the eight cities, they wouldn't be happy. Anyone who saw it would start to ask questions. Even someone completely devoted to Verene.

Verene pushes a loose curl back under her cap. "This is exactly why we destroyed all her information. So no one can find it and use it for their own purposes."

"I know," Theo says.

"Even if they did see the vide, they haven't seen the rest," she says. "The cities. The...the source of the magic. They don't know everything, and they never will."

"I know," he says. "It's just..."

He hesitates. He has the look of someone who's about to have an emotion and is desperately trying to fight it off.

"They almost killed you," he says finally, and I hear the tiniest crack in his voice.

Verene's face softens. "You would have liked that, wouldn't you? I know it's your dream to be the Heart of Iris. I know you secretly wish all the fountains had pretty statues of you."

"I am prettier," he says.

She punches him in the arm. Then, abruptly, she sighs and leans into him. She puts her chin on his shoulder and closes her eyes and for a moment, she just rests there. He sits patiently, like he'd let her stay for hours if she needed.

But he's also quietly fiddling with his gloves. There's something strange and agitated about it.

Verene pulls away and stands up. "We need to search faster. I'm not letting anyone else get the satisfaction of catching *her*."

Me. She's talking about me. It's obvious, of course, but the knowledge gives me a little thrill.

Her gaze goes, one more time, to the trellis that I'm hiding behind. It lingers for a little too long, like maybe the shadows look different to her than they did before. I hold my breath.

But she turns away. We stay crouched between the wheelbarrow as the greenhouse door opens and shuts. I listen to their footsteps fade away.

"He knows I took it," Ale whispers.

"What?" I say.

"He knows I took the map," he says. "That was when we started fighting. He was trying to get it back." He hesitates. "Why isn't he telling her?"

I don't know. My eyes go back to the trellis where the twins were sitting.

"And did you hear anything that will get us closer to figuring out how to stop the ghost?" Ale continues.

"The vide, you mean?" I say. "That's what they called it."

"The vide, then," he says. "Did you hear anything…useful?"

I heard a lot of things that could be useful. I don't fully understand them yet. But I want to. I need to.

"Give me the map," I say. If it's even more important than we thought, it's obvious which one of us should be carrying it.

Ale fiddles with his shirt pocket. I don't know why he looks so reluctant. It's not like it's his personal map.

"Are you willing to stab someone again to protect it?" I say. "Because I am."

He hands it over. I unfold it and examine it once more. I study the maze of tunnels between Occhia and Iris, and for the first time, I notice that one path has been gone over several more times, emphasized in red ink. It connects the center of Iris to the watercrea's tower in Occhia. And then, it connects every other tower in every other city. From underground well to underground well, forming a ring of water.

For a moment, I survey the six other cities. I try to imagine what their rulers are like. I try to imagine what these mysterious people I've never met are doing right now, as night turns to early morning. There's so much else out there. There's so much to see and so much to do.

"What are you looking at?" Ale says. "Is there something else—"

I fold the map up and shove it in my pocket. Ale starts to stand up.

"Wait." I grab his sleeve and pull him back down.

"What?" he says. "Didn't you hear them walk away?"

But I saw the way Verene studied our trellis. If she really wanted to find me, she should have ventured back here and searched more thoroughly. And she looked like she really wanted to find me.

I open up the basket I've been lugging around. "It's time for a change of clothes."

As it turns out, the disguises I hastily stole from a garden party leave something to be desired. There's only enough for me. I refuse to part with my green dress, in case I need to look fabulous later, so I tuck the skirts around my hips and stuff myself into a pair of pants. I pull a cap low over my eyes. As a finishing touch, I take some of the chocolate spread from the basket and smear it on my lip.

"What?" I say as Ale eyes me. "Are you jealous of my mustache?"

He's always wanted a mustache.

"What am I supposed to do?" he says.

"Get in the wheelbarrow," I say. "I'll hide you and take us to the next greenhouse so we can keep searching. Would Verene dare attack a lone worker going about their business?"

"I'm not going to fit in the wheelbarrow," he says.

"I'll make you fit," I say.

"But—" he says.

I make him fit. When I cover him with a tarp, he looks like a pile of anxious bones.

"Don't fidget," I tell him, and start pushing.

The door to the greenhouse, like the rest of it, is made of glass. I don't see any signs of life on the dark street outside, so I head toward it with all the confidence I possess.

Then I discover that the door has been locked from the outside.

"Oh," I say. "I see."

"What?" Ale says, muffled.

I don't know why Verene thinks she can lock me in a room made of glass. I have no qualms about breaking one of Iris's pretty little buildings.

I back up.

"Stay under the tarp, Ale," I say.

"What?" he says, squeakier.

I'm bracing myself for the charge when everything goes dark. I try to breathe and find that I can't.

There's a bag over my head. Somebody is grabbing my wrists. They're tying me up.

"This is my city," Verene's voice says in my ear. "I know it better than you ever will. I even know how to climb through a greenhouse window without being—"

There's a loud crash that sounds very much like the wheelbarrow falling over.

"Theo!" Verene says. "What are you doing? You can't let him get away—"

"Oh, I can't?" Theo says. "Thanks for reminding me. I definitely forgot after he *stabbed me*—"

I hear scampering feet and breaking glass. But I can't tell what's happening to Ale, and I can't help him, because I'm too busy fighting Verene. When I try to break free, she tightens her grip. We hit the floor and struggle viciously. I do a lot of kicking, because the rest of me is rather restrained, but before I know it, she's sitting on my feet, pinning me down.

She pulls the bag off my head. She's managed to get me behind one of the trellises, and even in the dark, the triumph on her face is clear.

Ale is nowhere to be found.

"Well?" Verene sits back. "How does it feel to be someone else's captive? It's not fun, is it?"

I shrug. "I've had better."

Instantly, her triumph turns to irritation. Her eyes flicker over me, just for a moment, and I realize that during the fight, my new pants ended up down to my ankles. It exposes the fact that my skirts are ridden up awkwardly around my thighs. With my hands tied, of course, there's nothing I can do about it.

She grabs my skirts and yanks them down, covering me up hastily, like one would cover a disgusting wound. It's rather offensive. But, I have to admit, it's also a relief.

"Nice disguise," she says. "It wouldn't have worked."

"Tragically, we'll never know for sure," I say.

"It's your eyes," she says. "You can't disguise eyes that soulless." She pauses. "It's also your height. Anyway, I know why you're out here."

"Do you?" I say.

"You were looking for the Red Roses," she says. "And eavesdropping on us."

"Why would we do that?" I say innocently.

"You're trapped in our city," she says. "You can't scheme against us. Nothing you do will work."

"Oh," I say. "How unfortunate."

She eyes me. She's very unhappy about the eavesdropping.

I can tell. She looks like she's trying to remember every word she said to her brother.

"So…the vide?" I say. "Is that what you call it? Your little shadow pet?"

"Oh, it's not a pet," she says.

"What is it?" I say.

"Wouldn't you like to know?" she says. "Also, since it obviously isn't clear—I'm asking the questions. We're not sitting around having cake in my parlor."

"Having experienced both, I still prefer this," I say.

"My people love having cake with me," she says, indignant. "I make them happy."

"And you make me nauseated," I mutter in Occhian.

"What?" she says.

I remain pointedly silent. She looks like she's seriously considering putting the bag over my head again.

"I saw the painting you did of us," I say. "I liked it."

"I was trying to make you look evil," she says.

"Well, I look fantastic. Can I take it back to hang in my parlor?"

She puts the bag over my head again. She shifts, and I think she's looking around for her brother. I wait patiently in the dark. I don't know very much about Verene, but I know that she won't be able to sit quietly for very long.

A minute later, she pulls the bag back off.

"Why?" she says.

"Why what?" I say.

"Why did you even end up here? In Iris?"

I can tell the question has been bothering her since she found out where I'm really from. I'm a mystery. I like that.

"We got lost in the catacombs," I say.

"But why?" she says. "What were you trying to do?"

I stay quiet.

"Did you already know there were other cities when you set out?" she says.

I don't answer. I'm just going to let her decide all of this for herself.

Her dark eyes linger on my face and the chocolate smeared all over it. Then they go to my ruined hair. I wonder suddenly if she thinks I style it this way on purpose. I don't care what she thinks of me. But also, the thought is mortifying.

"You're not just someone who got lost," she says. "You want something."

I tilt my head as gracefully as I can while lying on the floor. "What do you think I want?"

She gestures to herself. "This."

I scoff. "I don't want *you*."

I'm not one of her people. I'm not besotted with her just because she's my ruler who also happens to have very good bone structure.

"I think you want what I have," she says. "I think you'd like being worshipped by a whole city. I think, maybe, there was a reason you left your old city. Maybe you thought you could come into a new city and…what? Take over? Are you regretting that yet? Have you realized just how much you underestimated me?"

The back of my neck is very warm. I don't trust myself to say anything, so I just look at her imperiously.

She plants her hands on either side of me and leans forward. I can see straight down the front of her shirt. Not that it matters.

"Let me tell you a secret," she says. "I can rule Iris the way

I do because I'm a good person. I have principles. I do what's right for my people. They can see that, and that's why they love me."

"You're stealing from my city," I say.

"I'm helping Iris," she says.

"And in the process, my people are getting hurt," I say.

"Well—" She falters, just for a moment. "I'm pursuing the greater good. Sometimes, sacrifices have to be—"

"That's the most absurd thing I've ever heard," I say.

"What?" She bristles. "That I have something I believe in?"

"I have something I believe in, too," I say. "I believe in myself. I believe that I can change things no one else has ever been able to change, and do things no one else has ever been able to do. I don't care if people love me, or if they think what I do is *good*. But rest assured, they're going to know I was here."

She draws back. She's looking at me with revulsion.

"So all you care about is whether or not you come out on top," she says.

I shrug. "It's where I deserve to be."

"I bet he's terrified of you," she says.

"Who?" I say.

"Your accomplice," she says.

I swallow hard. Ale's not terrified of me. He respects me. It's not my fault if she can't tell the difference.

"He obeys me," I say, with forced carelessness. "That's all that matters."

"Don't tell me he's your paramour, too," she says.

"I have better taste than that," I say.

She raises her eyebrows. "Oh really?"

I feel the sudden urge to clear my throat. "So, let's talk about your brother. Do you both give your blood to the vide? Or do you make him give up more of his, for the greater good?"

"I don't make him—" She cuts herself off, pressing her mouth into a thin line. "I know what you're trying to do. You're trying to find out more about the vide. You think that if you stop it, you can escape Iris."

I don't say anything. I wait to see what she thinks about this particular plan of mine.

"Well, you can't stop it," she continues. "But I'll tell you this much—Theo and I are working together. I would never make him do something he doesn't agree with. I couldn't, actually. We're both very stubborn."

"So you two are on the same page about everything?" I say.

"Everything that matters," she says. "We did recently stay up half the night arguing over a card game, but I was right, and he'll realize it eventually."

"You're not both the leader of Iris, though," I say. "And that works just fine?"

"Here's some more advice," she says. "Don't try and turn me against my brother. We're...well, I can't explain it to you."

"You could at least try," I say. "I'm such a good listener."

"You don't know what it's like to have someone at your side," she says. "Not the way I do."

I roll my eyes. "Yes, it was very special of you two to be born at the same time."

I'm not going to tell her anything, but if I were, I could tell her that I know exactly how it feels to have someone at my side. I could tell her that Ale has been with me for every day of my life.

Almost every day.

"It's not just that we were born together," Verene says, clearly annoyed. "No one else in the whole city was raised the way we were raised, and being alone in that would have been— You know what? You don't deserve to know anything else about me."

She turns around impatiently, trying to get a look at the greenhouse door.

"What was it like?" I hear myself say. "Being raised by her?"

She goes very still, and when she speaks, her voice is low. "What do you think it was like?"

I can't even begin to imagine. It's so hard for me to picture the watercrea doing anything ordinary people do, let alone raising two children. I just think about her impassive stare and the feeling of her magic invading my body. I think about her throwing Ale through a glass door like he was a rag doll.

I think about the way her broken body looked after I was done with her.

"Did you have…another parent?" I say. "Or was it just—"

Verene whips around, and all at once, the bag is back over my head.

"Get up," she says. "I'm tired of waiting for the boys to get their acts together. And I'm tired of you."

Thirteen

APPARENTLY, VERENE HAS A KNIFE. SHE DRAGS ME TO MY feet and presses it into my back, then forces me out of the greenhouse. We're sneaking somewhere. I can tell from the erratic way she keeps pressing me up against walls and then making me run. When we hit a staircase, she doesn't see fit to warn me first, so I tumble to the bottom, my ankle twisting painfully.

The ground is cold and dusty and familiar. As soon as I hit it, my skin starts crawling.

I wish I knew what was happening to Ale. I wasn't supposed to have to do anything else alone. Especially not anything involving the catacombs.

"Keep going." Verene is right behind me, nudging my rear end with her foot.

"If only your people could see all your generosity and compassion on display right now," I say, fumbling to crawl.

"No more—" She's still nudging me. "Talking—I'm so tired of your—voice—here. Stop."

I stop. I wiggle the bonds on my wrists, trying to subtly loosen them.

"Can't you at least take the bag off my head?" I say.

"No," she says.

"Why?" I say. "Because when you can't see my face, you can tell yourself that you're not really killing a person?"

She pulls the bag off my head. I sit up, enjoying my small victory. We're in the middle of a narrow hall. The only light is a lantern on the ground at her feet, and the shadows on her face are startlingly sharp.

"I know you're a person," she says. "A terrible person. A person who tried to kill me. A person who needs to be stopped."

"Must you declare everything so dramatically?" I say.

She glares at me. "I must."

"You think that I deserve to die, then?" I say.

"The vide isn't going to kill you," she says. "It will swallow you and carry you to our prison. And maybe, while you're there, you'll think about the morality of coming into a new city and trying to kill its ruler. Maybe you'll have a change of heart. It could happen, I suppose."

"Where's the prison?" I say. "In your cathedral?"

"No," she says. "At the very bottom of the catacombs. And I do mean the very bottom. It's incredibly dark and isolated. But don't worry. We'll send you food."

My heart thuds in my ears. I can find a way out of this. I always find a way out.

Verene pulls off one of her gloves to reveal a bandage around her hand, then starts to unwind it. On her palm, there's a long gash, barely healed. She slices it open with the knife in one quick motion. She turns back to me, squeezing her hand into a fist, and pointedly lets the blood fall onto the ground by my feet.

"So it's not just your brother," I say. "You feed the vide, too."

"I would do anything for my people," she says.

I remember her random dizzy spells that I saw in the cathedral. I know how dizzying it is to lose your blood. It seems she's doing quite a lot for her people.

At my feet, a shadow is starting to form. The air is getting colder. I shiver.

I don't have much time. I have to get her to tell me something I can use. Anything.

"You know," I say, "in a way, you're even worse than your mother was."

Verene goes very still. Her eyes are fixed on me, dark and intent and, suddenly, unblinking.

"What?" she says.

The shadow has eaten up her blood.

"You think your powers are noble, don't you?" I say. "Instead of the people of Iris bleeding for you, you bleed for them. But what you conveniently neglect to realize is that when you steal water from the other cities, that's still water that somebody had to bleed for—"

In an instant, she's on the ground and in my face. I flinch away automatically, and she grabs a fistful of my hair, forcing me back.

"Don't—" she says. "Don't you ever—"

I feel something cold against my neck. It's the blade of her knife. It's shaking in her hands. It's digging in a little too hard.

"Don't pretend that you know me," she says. "Don't pretend

that you understand me. I did this for my city. No one will ever hurt them again, and it's because of me."

"Am I supposed to be impressed?" I say. "You were born into this life. You were born into this magic. Your power obviously doesn't look like your mother's, but that doesn't make you—"

I falter. Because, just for a moment, I felt her falter, too.

I meet her gaze. We're close. Too close. I can feel the warmth of her breath and I can smell her sweet hair. And I can see something deep in her eyes. Something that she's trying to hide. It looks almost like fear. Like she's afraid of what I'm saying. Like I'm getting too close to asking a question she doesn't want to answer.

She believes in her power so strongly. She believes in it like it was something she chose.

People don't choose to have magic. Our rulers are born with magic, and that's why they're our rulers. That's what I've always been told. That's what I've always believed.

But so many other things I've believed are turning out to be wrong.

I know that I only have a split second to act, so I do the last thing she would expect me to do. Instead of trying to throw myself away from her, I throw myself forward.

The knife cuts into my neck with a sting. Before it can go too deep, she flings herself back. The knife lands in my lap, and I twist around in my bonds until it falls to the ground. A drop of blood flies off it and lands in the dust.

Verene and I both used the knife to cut ourselves. I don't know if the blood is hers or mine.

Either way, the dark shadow is already underneath it. I scoot away and watch as the vide swallows it up.

It pauses. Like it's considering.

I look at Verene. Her eyes are wide. She looks like she doesn't know what's going to happen now, either.

"What are you so worried about?" I say. "Surely you don't think a terrible person like me could just...use your magic?"

And then I feel...something. There's a cold, tingling sensation in my neck.

Experimentally, I look at the vide, and I will it to go after Verene.

It does.

The rush is unbelievable. Verene is scrambling away on her hands and knees, and I've never felt so powerful.

I'm so caught up in the euphoria that it takes me a long moment to realize the vide has turned around. It's coming for me again.

Down the hall, Verene is squeezing her wounded palm. It's still dripping.

Of course. She gave it more blood than I did. She must have more control than I do.

I throw myself at the knife. I rub frantically at it with the bindings around my wrist, and right as the vide is almost upon me, I manage to saw through and break free.

I seize the knife and cut my hand. I don't even feel the pain. I splatter my blood on the floor and silently tell the vide to swallow Verene up and take her to her own prison.

She's already unwinding the bandage on her other hand. The wound there is only semi-healed, too, and when she presses them both into the floor, the vide comes back at me.

I meet Verene's eyes. They're burning with pain and righteous fury in equal measure.

She's not going to stop.

That's...perfect. I don't want her to stop. I want her to fight me the way I deserve to be fought.

I back up, leaving a trail of blood for the vide. From the tingling in my hand, I know that it's swallowing up my offering. Verene hunts around on the ground. She finds a sharp rock and slashes at her hand, gritting her teeth.

It's unsettling to watch. It makes me wonder just how far I can get her to go.

The vide comes for me again, and I steel myself and slice the one place on my palm that's not already shredded.

Verene gets to her feet. She's breathing hard and trembling. She's all passion and rage and a burning desire to be rid of me, and I can't take my eyes off her.

She presses the sharp rock into her wrist. The first drops of blood well up.

And then, abruptly, she sways. I see a flash of panic on her face, but it's too late. She's already crumpling. She hits the ground with a dull thump, sending up dust.

I tell the vide to stop. I don't even really think about it. I crawl down the hall, picking up the lantern as I go.

Verene is collapsed on her side. Her eyes are closed and her bloodied hands are limp, but she's breathing, slow and soft. I wait to see if she's just faking it to lure me closer to her. But she doesn't move.

I set the lantern down. A moment ago, she was ready to cut off her own hand to defeat me. Now, she just looks like a vulnerable girl lying all alone.

So Verene wasn't born with this power. She wasn't born with any power at all. She went into the catacombs and somehow found this creature she could bargain with. And now she gives her people a life more perfect than they could have ever dreamed.

She shouldn't pretend to be a saint. She shouldn't care if they think she's perfect. She should let them see just how far she would go for them. Because it's real, and it's a little extraordinary.

A drop of blood rolls off Verene's hand and hits the ground. Immediately, the vide is there.

"Don't—" I say.

I realize I'm reaching for Verene's hands, and I stop myself. I don't know what I think I'm doing. I don't know why I'm just sitting here, staring at her like I don't have anything better to do.

I have so much to do. I know how to control the vide now. I've beaten her. I can go back to Occhia and steal all her water for myself. I can kill her. I can let this city crumble, just as it deserves.

But for some reason, I can't get myself to do anything.

I hear the footsteps in the dark, but I can't quite piece together what they mean. And then someone is walking around the corner. When they see me, they stop short.

It's a young man. He's holding a lantern. He's dressed in dark clothes, a handkerchief around the bottom of his face.

"You shouldn't be down here," he says in a rush.

"Well, why are you down here?" I say.

He's quiet, but his eyes are on the bloody slash on my neck. When they drift to Verene, they widen.

"Is..." he says, and I hear the note of fear in his voice. "Is that...?"

I look at Verene's long, dark eyelashes. One of her curls has fallen over her face, and it's stuck to her mouth. Her mouth looks so soft. Unimaginably soft.

I tear my gaze away.

I'm not just going to kill her while she's already unconscious. That would be too easy for her.

She stole from my city for two years. She's going to suffer.

I clutch at my throat.

"Run," I tell the boy. "Run, before she gets you, too."

He doesn't need telling twice. In an instant, he's disappeared into the shadows.

I grab the lantern. Then I grab Verene's ankle, and I drag her down the hall. When she's on her feet, she looks so light and graceful. When I have to pull her through the darkness with one hand, she's the heaviest person in all the cities.

With a rush of relief, I finally find the staircase that leads up to the city. I pause at the bottom, trying to catch my breath.

I have to drag Verene just a little farther. I want to make sure all her people see her like this.

I set the lantern on the steps. I grab Verene's ankles with both hands and heave.

My vision goes gray. For the first time, I notice that the cuts on my hand are still bleeding. My palm is absolutely sliced to pieces. And now, all of a sudden, I can feel the pain.

No, I tell myself firmly. I didn't lose that much blood. Surely I lost more than this in the watercrea's tower. I'm not going to faint. Not now.

I try to pull Verene again. I drag us up the stairs through sheer force of will. We're almost at the top.

But then my knees give out. I reach for the street, but everything is spinning out of control before my eyes.

And then, nothing.

It's my wedding day.

I'm lying in my bed, snug and warm. In a moment, I'll hear the door open and smell the coffee Paola brings me with breakfast. I'll eat in bed as we go over the final plans for the reception, and tonight, everything will be perfect. Nothing will go wrong. I refuse to let it go wrong, so it won't. The thought is reassuring. It's all so simple.

"Emanuela. Emanuela."

I recognize the voice and frown. Ale and I do spend a lot of time together, but he usually isn't in my bedroom when I wake up. He must be very nervous about the wedding. Even more nervous than I expected, which is saying a lot.

"Emanuela," he says again.

I open my eyes. I see Ale's face, pale and worried. I feel his cold fingers on my hair.

And then it all comes back to me.

I sit bolt upright.

"Don't." Ale grabs me. "Don't. Shh."

I look around wildly. It's dark. I have no idea where I am.

"Verene," I say. "She—she was—"

"She's right out there," he says. "Shh, Emanuela."

We're in an alley between two manors. For a bewildered moment, I just take in the laundry strung up overhead. Then I turn around and see lantern light. I crawl to the mouth of the alley and look out.

There's a small group of people in the street. They're all staring at something on the cobblestone. Someone. Verene is lying there, limp and unconscious. Theo is standing over her stiffly.

He looks very much like he's trying to get rid of the bystanders, but they're not moving.

I turn back to Ale. "What happened?" I say. "You were—"

"I came back to the greenhouse, but you were gone," he says. "He tried to chase me into the catacombs, and that was when we found you. You and her, lying at the entrance." He pauses. "Bleeding."

I notice dimly that there's a strip of fabric wrapped around my injured hand. Ale tore off the bottom of his shirt.

"We have to—" I'm still fumbling to get my thoughts in order. "We're too close to them. He's going to send the mob after us—"

"He was trying to come after us himself," Ale says. "But then he got interrupted. When he saw all the blood on you, he looked...I don't know. I don't think he wants the people of Iris to see you."

He looks at me expectantly. Like he wants me to explain how, exactly, all this blood came about.

"So we have the advantage right now," I say.

"We could escape," Ale says. "If...if we knew how to stop the vide."

It comes back in a rush. I want to tell him everything I just learned. I want to share the thrill of the magic. The thrill of the control. The thrill of not having to be afraid of something anymore.

But then the last piece of my memory falls into place.

I fainted. I barely even did any magic with the vide, and I fainted.

Verene has been using this magic to bring water to her city, but there's a price. She's weakened. She spends all her time in the cathedral, dizzy and resting. She gives up entirely too much of herself just to keep things the way they are.

The disappointment is bitter. Magic isn't supposed to cost this much. Magic didn't seem to cost the watercrea anything.

If magic can be chosen, I want to choose the most powerful magic there is. I want the kind of magic that can bring water to a city that has none. I want the kind of magic that will let me go everywhere and change everything.

I want the kind of magic that belongs to me, and only me.

I want more.

But I don't know how to get more.

I look back at the street just as a man tries to duck around Theo, reaching for Verene. Theo shoves the man in the chest, hard.

It startles everyone. For a moment, I think Theo looks a little startled, too. But then he doubles down, bracing himself in front of Verene like he's daring someone else to try.

"Emanuela," Ale whispers. "What...what should we do?"

The people on the street look so unsettled. They don't know what's happening to their Heart. They don't know why she would have been attacked in such a strange way—ending up with blood on her hands, and nowhere else.

They don't know why her brother is suddenly acting like he's hiding something.

I stand up. I'm a little woozy, and Ale reaches for me, but I brace myself on the white wall of the alley.

"Quickly," I say. "We have to get back to the cathedral before they do."

FOURTEEN

I DON'T KNOCK ON THE FRONT DOOR OF THE CATHEDRAL.
I find a narrow window around the back and shatter it with a
rock, because we don't have the time to bother with subtlety.

I pick the lock to get back into Verene and Theo's quarters. We
make our way down the hall and into the dark parlor. I survey the
fluffy white love seats arranged under the beautiful stained-glass
window, and I wait for someone to leap out and try to stop us.

No one does. So I lead Ale down the hall and into the stu-
diously clean bedroom that I ignored the last time I was here.

"Shut the door," I say. "Look around."

"That was a long walk," he says. "Are you sure you don't
need to sit down—"

"Just start looking," I say.

"What are we looking for?" he says.

"Haven't you always wanted the chance to snoop around in
a boy's bedroom?" I say.

Ale flushes. "Not this boy. Do you know what he told me,

when he was trying to catch me back there? He told me that I'm ruining *his* life. What a selfish thing to say."

"He also said your eyes were giant and creepy," I say, opening the nightstand drawers.

"Oh, I remember," he says.

"And look at the books all over his bed," I say. "What kind of sad person keeps books on his bed? It's like admitting that you'll never have any suitors."

"And—" Ale says. "Well, I—I do that."

I know. I couldn't resist.

"But my books are good," Ale insists, rifling through the ones on the bed. "They're imaginative and romantic, not... math."

"Shake them out and make sure there's nothing hidden in the pages," I say.

"Do you think he's hiding something about the vide in here?" he says. "But why in his bedroom? We could look in his study again. I wasn't able to properly search it with him glowering at me the whole time."

I look beneath the pillows and run my hands under the mattress.

"Do you think he's hiding something...from her?" Ale says.

I wish he would stop asking questions and just help me. Verene and Theo are probably sneaking through the catacombs or the streets right now.

"Anything is possible," I say. "He seemed to be hiding that map of the eight cities."

"I don't know, Emanuela," he says. "Maybe...maybe there's another explanation for that. Maybe he just didn't want her to worry about it being stolen. What they're doing is terrible, but they're in it together. They have to trust each other."

I turn around. "Everybody hides things."

I'm not really thinking about the fact that I'm talking to the boy who found about my secret omen on our wedding day. As soon as I realize it, I regret the words.

For a long moment, Ale just looks at me. I can't quite read his face, which is disconcerting.

"Everybody hides small things," he says. "Things that don't really matter."

"Fine," I say. "Everybody hides *small* things."

I turn away quickly to search the dresser. For a moment, we both work in a profound silence. I pick through a truly astounding assortment of colognes.

"Emanuela," Ale says. "I found something. Under the bed—"

I whip around. Ale is kneeling on the floor, holding a large painting.

It's a family portrait. It takes me a moment to recognize the children. Theo and Verene are sitting with their tiny hands folded, dressed in a startling shade of red. Verene's voluminous hair is pulled back and stifled, and her high-necked dress looks like it's choking her. There's a dark-skinned man standing behind her with his hand on her shoulder. He has a perfectly groomed beard and a regal face. A single rose is pinned to his chest.

Next to him is a pale woman in a vivid red gown. The woman they called the Eyes. Her face has been destroyed by an angry streak of white paint.

I touch it, so carefully that I hold my breath. I'm suddenly desperate to know what she looked like.

"So they had a papá," Ale says. "It's so strange. Why would a watercrea have children?"

I look at the woman's slender hand on Theo's shoulder. Something about her grip seems possessive.

"And what really happened to her?" I mutter.

Ale shifts. He gives me an uneasy look.

"Put that back," I say. "Go search his underwear drawer."

Ale turns purple. "I'm not doing that."

"There's no better hiding spot," I say, pushing him.

I make my way over to the armoire and rifle through perfectly pressed white clothes. I reach all the way inside, running my hands along the back panel, then crouch down and grope behind the shoes to search the deepest corners.

I touch something that is decidedly not a shoe. It feels rectangular and leather.

I pull it out. It's a small red book.

A journal.

I peek around the armoire door to glance at Ale. He's searching the dresser. He's become very occupied with the colognes.

I flip open the journal. One corner of it looks rather burned.

It's like someone else tried to destroy this. And someone else saved it. My hands start to shake with excitement.

On the first page, there's a date at the top—five years ago, assuming Iris keeps dates the same way Occhia does—and below it, writing in a narrow script:

He got his first omen today. It appeared on his face in the middle of dinner. They begged him not to go to the tower, and they begged me not to send him. But it wasn't their decision to make.

They think I've betrayed them. They don't realize that I loved their father more than they ever could. I waited a thousand years to find someone worthy enough to help me raise my heirs. But now I'll just have to raise them alone. Nothing is more important than keeping the city in balance.

My mind is reading the words in the voice of Occhia's watercrea, even though I know they're not the same person. It feels wrong to imagine the watercrea talking about love. I glance over my shoulder, suddenly convinced I'm going to see her standing there, watching me with her dark, empty eyes.

I flip forward, passing through time, and stop at an entry from three years ago.

She snuck out again. The guards found her in the gardens, holding hands and giggling with some random maid. They dragged her back kicking and screaming, and now the whole city knows my own daughter doesn't listen to me.

She brought this punishment upon herself. I don't know how to make her understand. My heirs aren't like other people. They can't be.

She's so much like him. She's all feeling and no restraint, like an exposed heart.

I don't think she'll be able to do this.

"What's that?" Ale says over my shoulder.

I jump out of my skin, nearly dropping the journal.

"It's very lewd," I say. "I'll spare your delicate eyes."

Ale gives the red cover a sideways look. Nothing else in this cathedral is red. Not even the wine. The exception, of course, the blood in the underground well, but otherwise it's like the color has been wiped out of existence.

I stand up. "Let's go to the study. You're right. There will probably be more promising things there."

I need to buy myself time to read the rest of this journal. I need to read it all as soon as possible. I can't fully explain why. I just know that I do.

"Are you going to bring that?" Ale says.

"I...yes," I say.

"*You* want to read a *boy's* lewd diary?" he says.

I don't know why he feels the need to emphasize it that way. I don't want to read anyone's lewd diary. I don't depend on other people for my entertainment.

"Yes," I say, and march out the door.

In the parlor, I turn toward the study. But then my eyes fall on the dining room. The doors to the balcony are sitting half-open.

The banner depicting our faces is still hanging out there, telling everyone how dangerous we are. This is a chance for me to give the people of Iris my own message.

I run back to Verene's bedroom and scoop up some of her paints. I rush to the balcony, crawl out to untie the banner, and drag it back into the dining room. For a moment, I just admire the painting of me. I really would hang it in my parlor.

"I think it might be too late to take it down," Ale says. "Everybody in Iris has already seen what we look like."

I turn the banner over.

"But they haven't seen this," I say.

I paint eight circles in a ring. I color one in and label it as Iris. Underneath the picture, I paint the words:

Why is the Heart lying to us?

I step back and admire my handiwork.

"Help me hang it back up," I say.

Ale's face is uneasy.

"Do you really want everyone in Iris to know about the other cities?" he says.

I want Verene's perfect life to be demolished. If her city doesn't trust her, everything will fall apart.

"Fine," I say. "I'll hang it myself."

He doesn't try to stop me. I make sure to bring the journal with me as I work, because he keeps eyeing it. I tie the banner to the railing and unfurl it into the night air. The square below is empty, but in a nearby street, I can see the lanterns of Verene's mob. They start to move in our direction.

The city is small. Once somebody sees what I've drawn, word will spread fast.

"All right." I turn back to lead Ale out of the dining room. "Now we can go to the study—"

We're almost at the doorway when a woman steps in front of us. She's small and bony, but she has deep, intense eyes. She's looking at me like she knows everything that I've ever done wrong in my entire life.

I was wondering where the housekeeper had gone.

"Hello," I say.

I move forward like I fully expect her to get out of my way. She pulls out a knife. I pause.

"I don't want to fight an old woman," I say, very reasonably.

"Well," she says, "you're going to."

"Oh," I say.

"I'm not just a servant, you know," she says. "Their papa has been gone for years, and the way their maman treated them— there's no one else. There's only me."

I assess her. "So you know about their magic?"

"I know that they go into the underground well every day

and come out bleeding," she says. "And I fix them up. I don't ask questions, because they saved this city, and that's all I need to know. And you're not going to ruin that."

So she doesn't know enough to be useful to me. I suppose I am going to fight an old woman, after all.

That's fine. I don't know her. I don't care about her.

I stuff the journal down my front for safekeeping and inch closer. Closer. The housekeeper doesn't take her eyes off me.

"Emanuela," Ale says.

I try to snatch the knife from her hands, and she jabs at me, so I kick her in the knee. She buckles, and I run past her into the parlor. I look around wildly for something I can use to restrain her.

But she's already running at me with the knife. I jump onto the love seat, then leap on top of her. We hit the floor so hard that something in her body crunches.

I've heard that sound before. I scramble off her, certain that it's already over.

She's already back on her feet, limping and grimacing, but still coming at me.

I grab a silver platter off the coffee table and hit her in the head. The clang is resounding. I drop the platter, startled by my own force, and she staggers.

Surely she'll give up now.

She's not giving up.

She slashes at me wildly, and I skitter back. I find a wine bottle on the coffee table and hold it up like a club. She hesitates.

"All right, old woman." I'm breathing hard. "Just stand aside and let us do what we need to do. We'll be out of—"

She slashes at me again. I throw my arm in front my face

instinctively. There's a sharp pain, and then, there's blood. There's more blood than I expected, and for a moment, I'm stunned by the sight of it.

I can't take a light touch with this woman. She's not taking a light touch with me.

I whack her in the face with the wine bottle, and she collapses to the floor. I drop the wine bottle and snatch up her knife instead, then back up to the far side of the room, ready for whatever she's going to try next.

"Emanuela!" Ale is halfway to the front door now. "What are you doing? Let's just go—"

"Not yet," I say.

On the floor, the housekeeper is stirring, and if I don't stop her, she's going to stop me. I have to protect myself. I have to protect Ale.

"We shouldn't stay in here any longer," Ale says. "They're going to come back—"

From the dining room, I hear a door crack open. The door to the underground well.

But the housekeeper is back on her feet. She grabs my abandoned wine bottle and chucks it at me.

It misses. It hits the enormous, beautiful stained-glass window behind me—the one that depicts the white-gloved hands making the water. The bottle goes right through. For a moment, we both stare at the jagged hole.

Then she charges.

It happens so fast. She dives at me like she's going to strangle me, so I push the knife into her as hard as I can. It slips right between two of her ribs, and it feels strangely neat and perfect. Like it's supposed to be there. She makes a faint gurgling noise.

Already, her blood is seeping out of her. It's staining my fingers and her white apron, and for a moment, I just stare at it.

She must have known this would happen if she kept fighting. If she underestimated me, that's not my fault.

Someone is screaming. It's not me. I don't think it's me, at least. I look around, and I catch a glimpse of Verene emerging from the dining room, but then the housekeeper coughs right in my face. Her hot blood splatters my cheek, and for one horrible moment, I meet her eyes.

She doesn't look afraid. She looks completely certain of herself.

I don't understand. I'm the one who's besting her. I'm the one who's supposed to feel confident, because I'm doing exactly what I wanted to do. The housekeeper failed to stop me. She failed to protect her charges. She shouldn't be at peace with that.

I yank the knife out, and it makes a loud, wet noise. The housekeeper groans and doubles over. Blood dribbles out of the wound and stains the black-and-white tile near my feet, and I just stand there, clutching the dirty knife. It occurs to me, then, that this isn't like pushing a woman off a balcony and snapping her neck. If this kills her, it's going to be drawn out and messy. I'm going to have to listen to her ragged breathing and watch her struggle to stay upright and know that she's in pain. I'm going to have to watch the omens crawl across her skin.

So I kick her into the stained-glass window. It doesn't feel like a decision. It feels more like a necessity. I need her out of my sight.

It's spectacular. The whole thing shatters in a spray of blue-and-white glass, and I have to shield my face. When I open my eyes, I can see the black veil and the street below. Tiny pieces at the edge of the window are still breaking loose and falling, like teardrops.

I hear distant screaming from the square. I see even more lantern light coming our way.

I can't believe I stuck a knife in her. I can't believe any of it just happened. It was all so quick.

I turn around. Ale is in the same spot, his face white. At the entrance to the dining room, Theo and Verene are frozen in their tracks. They were running at me. They were trying to stop me.

But they didn't. They couldn't.

I point the knife at Verene. I heard her scream earlier, but now, she looks strangely blank. I don't like it at all. It makes me suddenly aware of the sick feeling of wrongness that's filled up my throat. I want to say something—something pointed and decisive and unconcerned. But if I open my mouth, I'm going to vomit.

This is exactly what needed to happen, I remind myself. Verene needs to know how thoroughly I plan to defeat her.

She needs to know what I'm capable of.

I'm capable of killing someone. I can push them off a balcony, if I have to. But I can also put a knife between their ribs. I can feel their blood all over my hands.

All I want to do is wipe this blood off. It's sticky, and the smell is in my nose and in my throat. But I can't wipe it off. Then I'll look like I'm sorry about this, and I refuse to feel sorry about it. The housekeeper wasn't going to get out of my way. She was an obstacle.

I swallow hard.

"What?" I say to Verene. "If you're going to make this difficult, then so am I."

I'm amazed at how steady my voice is.

Verene and Theo don't move. They look like they still haven't quite figured out what's happening. All at once, I imagine them as the little children in that portrait I saw, in the arms of the woman I just threw out a window. But surely they didn't care that much about her. She was only a housekeeper.

"Well?" I say. "Are you just going to stand here? Because I thought you were—"

"I'll kill you," Verene says.

I can't comprehend the words. Her face is still so blank, like she just said something matter-of-fact. Something that she says a hundred times a day.

"I'll kill you."

She says it again. Her voice is low but unmistakable.

"You'll kill me?" My mouth dry, and I find myself tightening my grip on the knife. "Really?"

"She was innocent," she says. "She never did anything to you."

"Actually, she attacked me," I say. "She said she wanted to protect you. So, really, this is your fault—"

Verene takes a step forward.

She doesn't have a weapon, and I do. She doesn't have any magic that I don't know about. She can't hurt me.

And yet, I feel suddenly outmatched. I've never seen this kind of cold, bone-deep determination in anyone's eyes.

"I'm not going to pretend I know everything about the bizarre way your people worship you," I say. I haven't taken my eyes off her. I'm afraid to even blink. "But I'm pretty sure that if you killed someone, your city would no longer consider you a...good person."

"Sometimes," Verene says, "it's good for people to die."

I notice suddenly the way Theo is looking at his sister. His hand is outstretched, but he's hesitating, like he's not quite sure what's going to happen if he touches her.

I know that the mob is coming for us. I know that if I want any chance of getting Verene under my control, I have to attack her now. But I'm suddenly certain that if I try to fight her, I'm going to lose.

I can't face her like this. I need more. I need more magic.

So I run for the foyer. I push Ale ahead of me, through the short hall with the vase of white roses, and slam the front door.

I have to stop to catch my breath, because I feel like I'm going to faint. My hands are strangely tingly. I just want to get this blood off.

And I can hear footsteps behind the door. They're following us, of course.

I'm about to keep running when my eyes catch on the small statues guarding either side of the door. They're carved to look like Verene, naturally, with her billowing skirts and her graceful neck. They're each holding a large glass lantern with a flame inside. They're so pretty and so perfect.

I lunge at one of the statues and push it over.

The lantern shatters. The flame leaps onto the door and starts to spread, much quicker than I thought it would. Instantly, I feel the heat on my face.

I push over the other statue.

"Emanuela," Ale says.

"What?" I say.

Verene and Theo can escape through their underground well. But they don't deserve to stay in their grandiose hiding place. This is what happens to people who steal from my city and get in my way.

I start down the stairs. But Ale is lingering, wincing at the heat, like he thinks there's anything he can do to stop it.

There's not. There's nothing I could do either, at this point, even if I wanted to. And I don't.

"Ale," I say.

I turn back and grab his hand.

He resists. "I—"

"The mob is coming," I say.

And he follows me, because he has no choice. We race through the dark halls of the cathedral and climb out of the same broken window we used before.

But the moment our feet touch the ground outside, we can't evade the mob. There's too many of them, coming out of every dark street. Three grown men surround me, yanking my arms behind my back and binding my wrists. It's chaos. Everyone is yelling and crowding around, trying to catch a glimpse of the faces of the famed attackers.

I decide not to fight. I let them lead me away. Because a little time in prison has never stopped me before.

FIFTEEN

IN THE DARK HOURS OF THE EARLY MORNING, I PEER OUT OF my cell window and watch Iris burn.

I'm surprised the city has a jail at all, but I suppose even Verene has to lock people up when they commit crimes. It's a tiny hall in the Parliament buildings, and Ale and I are the only occupants. We've been put into two cells across the hall from each other. Mine has a barred window that looks out onto the cathedral, which happens to be a very lively view at the moment.

The banner I made is still hanging on the balcony. Behind it, the cathedral is on fire, bright and smoky against the black veil. For a city absolutely doused in water, they're doing a very bad job of putting it out. People are running every which way with buckets of water and bags of dirt, but it's not enough. In the nearby manors, the nobles are peering out of their windows, watching with grave faces.

I haven't seen Theo or Verene. But every time I think I hear a noise, I jump, certain that it's going to be her. The hall remains empty.

Every so often, I glance over at Ale. At first, he's sitting on his cot, staring at the wall. Then he curls up on his side. I hear his soft little wheezing snores.

Ale thinks that all we need to do to save Occhia is stop the vide. At first, that's what I thought, too. But the more I learn, the more obvious it is to me that we can't rely on anyone else for our water. We can't rely on a capricious spirit in the catacombs or the mysterious rulers of the other six cities. We need something that's all our own.

We need *someone* all our own. We need a savior who's so powerful that no one can ever hurt us again.

I sit down by the bars of my cell. I pull my stolen journal out, angle it to catch the lantern light glowing in the hall, and start at the beginning.

Most of the entries are short and matter-of-fact, and the purpose of the journal is immediately obvious. The Eyes is chronicling the lives of her family. She never talks about herself except in relation to them.

She probably didn't have much else to talk about. She was alive for almost a thousand years, and if she was anything like the watercrea in Occhia, she spent every single day taking scared, unresisting prisoners and turning their blood to water.

I've never thought about what the watercrea's life must have been like. But for the first time, I do. I wonder if she got bored. I wonder if she felt trapped.

She had so much power. She could have done so much more, but she didn't. She just stayed in her tower. The thought almost makes me sad, but I refuse to be sad for her.

I flip through the journal, reading quickly as the Eyes paints a picture of her children growing up. She writes about keeping watch at Theo's bedside when he had a terrible fever that took away his hearing in one ear. She writes about how Verene wouldn't stop making friends with her assigned guards even though she'd been told to keep her distance. She writes about how after his father's death, Theo disappeared into his room and stopped eating. Then the journal is taken over by an exhaustive account of every disobedient thing Verene ever did. She chopped off her own hair. She showed up drunk to her lessons. She lit a fire in her bedroom—though it was hastily smothered by the housekeeper.

At the mention of housekeeper, I skip the rest of the page. I scan and scan, and every so often, I find something that gives me pause.

They're both disappointments. They don't seem to understand how important this is. After a thousand years, I'm going to hand over the city. If they can't handle it, everything will fall apart.

She makes it sound like she was preparing to give her children her magic. As if it's something that could be given. Or something that can be chosen.

Perhaps I should just stay. If the others find out I'm going to turn my city over to an heir, I don't know what they'll do. This isn't what we agreed on.

But it's been so long. And I'm so tired.

I turn the pages faster and faster. Then I reach an entry from two years ago.

Tomorrow morning, I'm going to bring them into the study and tell them everything. It's time for them to do the ritual, and then I'll have my heir.

I just snuck over to check on them. She was in his bedroom, bouncing around and talking his ear off while he tried to read. They've changed so much over the years, but at the same time, they haven't changed at all.

I thought raising them in isolation would be better. My heir doesn't need to worry about the mundane concerns of life in the city—not when they're going to live forever. It's forced them to cling to each other, because they have no one else, especially now that their father is gone. I expected that.

I just didn't expect that it would be so hard for me. I've seen so much worse. I've done so much worse. But they're still my children.

My heir has to be strong. Strong enough to keep a city alive forever. Stronger than I am.

The rest of the journal is blank. For a long moment, I just sit there, staring at it and willing more words to appear.

"Emanuela."

I startle at the voice. Across the hall, Ale is sitting up on his cot, the thin blanket wrapped around his shoulders. He's looking at the book in my hands.

I close it. "What?"

"We need to get out of here," he says.

"I didn't want to wake you," I say.

"I was barely even sleeping," he says. "I can't stop thinking about Occhia. How long have we been gone? Two days? Three days?"

I don't know. Time has lost all meaning for me in this place. All I know is that somewhere across the veil and the catacombs, our people are struggling.

But I'm so close to being able to save them.

"We'll be back there soon," I say.

His eyes are worried. He's probably thinking about his family. Personally, I'm less concerned about them. The House of Morandi had the most water to begin with, and they'll hoard as much as they can.

"So you have a plan?" he says. "Can you just tell me what it is?"

"Does it matter if you know?" I say.

"It's just..." he says. "I want to know if you actually have an idea for how to stop the vide, or if you're going to"—he glances out the window behind me, at the burning cathedral—"destroy more things."

"And what's wrong with destroying things in this city?" I say. "Do you feel bad for them now? The people who stole our city's water for two years? Did they tell you they were going to use the vide to send us to a prison at the very bottom of the catacombs?"

"Well, I don't want that," he says, looking unnerved. "I don't. I just... I wonder what would have happened if we hadn't done it this way. If we had just told them we were in trouble and asked if they might help."

"They would have sent us to their prison at the very bottom of the catacombs," I say, unimpressed.

"Maybe," he says.

"Yes," I say.

He puts down the blanket and runs a nervous hand through his hair, trying to smooth down his bedhead.

"I don't know," he says. "I can't really explain it. I just think maybe they're just doing the best they can in a bad situation. That doesn't make them bad people who need to be totally... ruined."

Apparently, Ale missed the part where Verene looked me in

the face and told me she was going to kill me. I, for one, haven't stopped thinking about it.

"Have I explained how little it matters whether or not you feel like someone is bad?" I say.

"I'm not necessarily saying that they're good people, either," he says. "But they care about their city. And one another. The look on Theo's face when we found you both bleeding—and you should have seen all the work in his study. He did so much to help Verene realize her vision for Iris. I think he'd probably do anything for her." He pauses. "Surely you can understand that."

He looks at me. I look at him. I feel like he's trying to trick me into something, and I don't like it.

"Is there a point to any of this?" I say.

He turns away. If I'm not mistaken, he's a little annoyed.

"Never mind," he says. "It's too late to try and reason with them anyway. It's gone way too far. But you seem happy about that."

"Yes, I am," I say. "I'm happy to fight for our city's water—"

"Are you?" he says. "Or are you just happy to fight her?"

"I—" I stumble on my words, suddenly. "Well—she—"

"You like fighting her," he says. "Because she's powerful. More powerful than you. It gives you a rush to take her down. I know you, Emanuela, and I see the look on your face when you go after her. You're enjoying it."

My ears are very hot. "Should I not enjoy being able to best her at everything?"

"Did you enjoy it when you killed the watercrea?" he says.

I open my mouth. I shut it.

"You did." His voice is trembling. "I was there. I watched you do it. I watched you stare over the balcony and realize that she was dead, and you looked ... you looked so triumphant. You looked like that when you killed the housekeeper, too. It was like you were amazed at what you could do."

I want to tell him that it wasn't like that. I want to tell him that I only did it because I had to.

But that's only half the truth. Maybe when I think about the crunch of the watercrea's bones, and the spray of glass as the housekeeper flew through the window, I also think about how incredible it is that I could put my hands on someone and have that much power over them. Maybe he's not wrong. But it seems like we both know it, so there's not really anything else to say.

"What are we going to do?" he says. "If our city dies? If our families die? Where are we going to live? We can't live here, because now this city is ruined, too."

"Occhia's not going to die," I say.

He bites his lip, like he wants to say something.

"What?" I demand.

"I just ... What if you're wrong?" he says.

"When was the last time I was wrong?" I say.

"Well, there was the time we were about to go into our wedding," he says. "You told me to stop worrying so much. You told me that nothing bad was going to happen."

Silence. Now he's staring at me in a way that looks distinctly accusing, and it gets right under my skin.

"Oh, are you upset about that?" I say.

"Am I upset about watching you get arrested at the altar?" he says. "Am I upset about finding out that you were hiding an omen from me for ten years?"

"Well, are you?" I say.

"Are you serious, Emanuela?" he says. "Of course I am!"

"You didn't do anything about it." Even as I say it, I'm aware that I'm admitting too much. He's supposed to think I didn't want him to help me escape the tower. He's supposed to think I didn't care if he tried to come after me or not.

"What could I possibly have done?" he says.

"Anything," I say. I can't stop myself. "You could have done anything. But you just stood there and let it happen—"

"You could have told me about your omen," he says louder. "It's not like you didn't have plenty of chances. I tell you everything. You know things about me that my family doesn't know. And you couldn't even—"

"I didn't tell you about my omen because it doesn't matter," I say. "It hasn't spread. It won't spread."

"Well, it will spread eventually," he says.

"It won't," I say.

"It will," he says, sounding exasperated. "Why can't you just admit that you're scared of it? You don't have to admit it to everyone else, but you could at least admit it to me."

I draw back.

He's blaming me for everything that's happened. He's blaming me for not wanting to die.

"Why would I admit anything to you?" I say, making sure my voice is as cold as possible.

"Because," he says. "We're..." He trails off.

"What are we?" I say.

He hesitates. But then he draws himself up, his face determined. "We're best friends. We're in this together. We need each other."

"You need me," I say. "I don't need you."

"Oh, I know that's what you think." His cheeks are turning red. "You've made it clear. Many times."

"You can't do anything without me," I say.

"Because you won't let me!" he says. "You don't listen to my ideas. I've had ideas since we've been here, but you haven't listened. You didn't have to attack Verene ten minutes after we met her. You didn't have to tell everyone in Iris about the other cities. You didn't have to set the whole cathedral on fire. And don't tell me it's all in the name of saving Occhia. I want to save Occhia, too, but I don't want to hurt people. I don't want to become someone who lies and who stabs people, and—and I don't think you care about that at all. When there's something you want, you don't care who gets hurt. And if you're planning to do something even worse, if you've found something in that journal, then—"

He stops, breathless. I wait for the rest, but nothing comes. He just looks at me, and I can tell he's afraid of how I'm going to respond.

Good. If he's going to spout nonsense, he should be afraid of the consequences.

"So you think you can save Occhia without me," I say. "That's interesting, because you couldn't even get out of the catacombs without me."

"Well," he says, "if it wasn't for you, Occhia wouldn't even need saving."

My blood roars in my ears.

I killed the watercrea because I had to. I'm changing things in Occhia because they need to be changed. This isn't about quietly putting things back the way they were and hurting no one in the process. This is about me and the moves that only I'm willing to make.

Of course Ale doesn't understand. He's just like everyone else. And if he's not going to listen to me, then he's just another obstacle that needs to be dealt with.

I stand up, and he tenses, like he thinks I'm going to magically fly across the hall and attack him. I reach through the bars of my cell and find the lock keeping me in. Then I pull two pins out of my hair and bend them into position. I reach around, being careful with my bandaged hand. I put the pins in the lock and slowly, painstakingly, start to wiggle them around.

Ale watches me in silence. He knows exactly what I'm doing. I made him go to many parties at the House of Bianchi so that I could break into Chiara's bedroom and snoop around. Sometimes, when Ale wasn't looking, I read her diary, looking for my name. Chiara Bianchi feels strangely far away now. I used to think about her constantly—more often than I even want to admit to myself—but she doesn't seem important anymore.

The lock clicks, and I slide open the door. I step out of my cell and look pointedly at Ale.

"What's taking you so long?" I say.

He presses his lips together.

I make my way down the hall, and I don't look back.

The two constables outside are even easier to get past than I expected. They're watching the cathedral burn and sharing a bottle of wine. I would have been happy to fight them, but in this case, I don't mind being underestimated. It's faster. On my way out, I swipe one of their jackets hanging by the door. It will help hide my rather conspicuously bloodstained dress.

I sneak onto the streets. I keep my head down as I walk, but nobody is paying attention to me. If they're not running toward the cathedral, desperate to help, they're huddling with their neighbors and talking in anxious tones. I keep my ears open. I want to know what rumors are going around.

"Nobody's seen her since they caught the attackers—"

"You don't really think it means that there are other cities, do you? Why would she know about them and not tell us?"

"They're saying her servant put that banner up, and that's why she threw her out the window. But that just doesn't sound like the Heart—"

"I mean, I always did think it was a little strange that she never left the cathedral. She said she was going to be different than—"

I try not to smile. This city has had it good, but now, they're remembering what it's like to have a ruler who keeps secrets. They're remembering what it's like to be afraid. I knew they still had that fear tucked away inside them.

I pick a random manor and sneak into its kitchen, gathering a few supplies and stuffing them into a sack. No one is around. No one bothers me. It's so much easier to get things done in a city in crisis. The servants are too panicked to remember to start on breakfast, and the nobles are too panicked to order them.

Then I find an entrance to the catacombs tucked away in an alley. I push open the door and peer down the dark staircase.

I unwrap my bloodied hand. I wince as I squeeze a few drops out onto the steps.

A moment later, the vide slides up the staircase. It swallows the blood instantly, and my hand tingles. I will it to go into the catacombs and find the person I need.

It doesn't move. It just sits there, like it's waiting.

"Oh," I realize after a moment. "Is that not enough blood to persuade you?"

It's silent. But the silence feels somehow pointed.

"So you're greedy," I say. "Fantastic."

I pull a knife out of my bag—one of the most important supplies, of course. Without giving myself time to dwell on the fact that I probably don't have much blood to lose, I slice my leg and feed the vide even more.

It still doesn't move.

"What's wrong with you?" I say.

It disappears back into the dark.

"Wait—" I say.

I slam the door. I go back to the mouth of the alley and look around the street, highly annoyed. This is exactly why I don't want the vide to be the only thing with the power to save Occhia.

Against my will, my eyes are drawn to the fountain at end of the street. I feel like I can't take two steps in this city without seeing a token or statue of Verene. It would be a waste of my time to run around Iris, destroying every single one. But for a moment, I'm sorely tempted.

Then I realize that there's someone standing in the fountain. He's bent over, digging around in the water. There's a handkerchief over his face, but he's not going to hide from me.

That's why the vide couldn't bring me the person I was looking for. Because he's out here.

The only thing Verene cares about that I haven't yet destroyed.

I sneak around and approach the fountain from behind. For a moment, I'm distracted, trying to figure out what Theo is doing. There's a long hose sitting coiled outside the fountain, and he's hooking it up to something underneath the water.

Oh. He's trying to fight the cathedral fire. How adorable.

I reach into my bag of supplies and pull out the second-most important thing—a heavy iron pan. I climb onto the edge of the fountain and wait, poised. When he straightens up to admire his handiwork, I strike.

The thud is very alarming. The pan vibrates in my hand, and he collapses into the water with a loud splash. I look around to make sure there were no bystanders. Someone's going to come by to refill their firefighting buckets any second. I have to move him.

I have no idea how I manage to drag him out of the fountain. I'm gritting my teeth and sweating as I pull him into the nearest alley. We leave a conspicuous trail of water behind. I prop him up against the wall as best I can, then find a large vase of roses in a nearby window and put it in front of us, which somewhat hides us from view.

Theo shifts and wrinkles his nose. He's starting to wake up and, undoubtedly, feel the pain. I pull out the third-most important thing in my bag—heavy twine. I tie his hands.

He squints at me in the dim light. "Vee? I told you to stay in the gardens."

"Oh, did you?" I say.

The realization hits him all at once. He goes very still. Slowly, he looks down at the bindings around his wrists.

I stand up. I always appreciate the opportunity to have a height advantage.

"I took your sister," I say.

He gives me a long look of disdain. "No, you didn't."

"She's in the prison at the bottom of the catacombs," I say. "I captured her from the gardens and sent her there. With the vide."

I show him my bloodied hand.

"Right," he says skeptically. "So if you're capable of doing that, why are you talking to me? Why don't you just—"

"Oh, I wanted to discuss your map," I say. "And also the journal you keep in the back of your wardrobe."

His face turns stony. "I don't know what you're talking about."

I lean against the wall opposite him. "Please, allow me to clarify. I'm talking about the map of the catacombs and the eight cities. I'm talking about the journal where your maman wrote down every detail of your childhood and discussed at length how disappointed she was to have you as her heirs. Would you like me to describe it page by page?"

He doesn't. That's very obvious.

"How angry would Verene be if she found out you were hiding all this?" I say.

He remains quiet, but there's a muscle twitching in his perfectly chiseled jaw.

"Your sister's entire rule is built on erasing every trace of your maman." I reach into my pocket and pull out the last crucial item I stole—a chocolate that was sitting in a dish on the kitchen counter. I unwrap it slowly. "And yet, you insist on holding on to her things and making secret maps. What a betrayal of dear Vee's trust."

"It's not—" He fumes. "Don't call her that. And it's not a betrayal."

"Oh, do you not know what the word *betrayal* means?" I say through my chocolate. It means—"

"I know what it means," he says. "It's not a betrayal. It's just information. Do you even understand how fragile our cities are? Things can change so quickly, and information is the difference between life and death. We can't just destroy it all because it doesn't fit with our ideals. You can't possibly imagine what it was like when…" He trails off.

"When what?" I say.

"Never mind," he says.

The chocolate has become a little sour in my mouth.

"When the person who makes the water dies, you mean?" I say.

The fact that he refuses to answer is answer enough.

"I can imagine, actually," I say. "People must have panicked. They must have been terrified. And at first…you and your sister had no idea how to save them. How helpless you must have felt."

He's not looking at me.

"You're right," I say. "A city is a fragile thing. It all depends on one person, and no one ever expects that person to disappear."

He's eyeing his bonds like he's desperately calculating a way out of them. I consider him. I consider his painstakingly drawn map of the catacombs and the path connecting each of the underground wells. I consider the puddles of water on the cobblestone between us and the elaborate fountain system all over Iris.

"Are you trying to build something in the catacombs?" I say. "Something that will let you get water from city to city? Why? You have the vide."

"Yes, we do," he says noncommittally.

"But anyone can control the vide." I push away from the wall and pace. "You and Verene share the vide. But Verene doesn't know about this other scheme of yours. Why don't you want her to know?"

"I like having contingency plans," he says. "Is that so wrong?"

"No," I say. "If it was just a contingency plan, you wouldn't go out of your way to keep it from her—"

He tries to leap to his feet and make a daring escape. I dive for my iron pan, but it turns out that my earlier whack is still doing its job. He's so dizzy that all he does is trip over his own feet and fall on his face with a very undignified thump.

I stand over him, the pan in my hands.

"Why do you want to make a way to get water that only you control?" I say.

"You..." He squirms. "You're misinterpreting everything. It's not that I want another way. It's just in case. In case we need it."

"But why would you need it, specifically?" I say.

"Look, you tiny—miscreant—" He finally manages to get back into a sitting position. There's dirt in his curly hair and stuck to his wet clothes. "I just want the city to survive. Is that so hard to understand?"

"Doesn't Verene want the city to survive, too?" I say.

For a long moment, he's quiet.

"Verene wants...more," he says. "It doesn't matter how much she has. She always wants more."

I think I know what Verene would say to that. She would say that she's a good person and that striving to do the most good—more than anyone else has ever done—is exactly what she should be doing.

"How did your maman die?" I say. "Did she really get sick?"

The question catches Theo off guard, and I see something in his eyes that I'm certain he doesn't want me to see. Fear.

That's all I needed to see.

"I'm—" He's stammering, suddenly. "I'm not talking to you any—"

At last, he gets to his feet. I hit him in the head with the pan again.

He staggers but somehow stays upright. I shove him in the direction of the cathedral and herd him quickly through the streets. When he tries to run, I push my knife into his side.

"I know where your sister is," I remind him, urging him along. "I'll tell her everything."

The fire is getting worse. The double doors are open, spewing smoke. People have stopped approaching with their buckets. They're just gathered around the mess, so frantic that I manage to push Theo to the front of the crowd without really being noticed. He's just barely staying on his feet.

"Wait! Don't get any closer!" someone says as I start forward.

I don't listen to them. Slowly, as I advance out of the throng, I feel the people start to recognize me. I feel their confusion. I feel their fear. Things have gone so wrong in this city, so quickly, and they know that it involves me.

I stop halfway up the cathedral steps, which is as close as I dare get. I can feel the heat on my back and the sting of smoke in my eyes. With a little shove, Theo collapses at my feet. I reach down to tie his handkerchief over his mouth. If he stays conscious, I don't want him interfering.

There's a flash of movement at the bottom of the steps. A man in the crowd is running for me. I pull out my knife and point it at him.

"The Heart is in the gardens," I say. "Find her. And bring her to me."

Sixteen

IT DOESN'T TAKE LONG.

I see the crowd near the gardens rippling and parting, and then I see Verene walking my way. Her steps are slow and deliberate as she glides out of the crowd and approaches the base of the cathedral stairs alone.

She's still wearing the same rumpled, bloody clothes. Her face is dirty and exhausted, and her hair is hopelessly disheveled. Even though she's standing with her head held high, I can tell from here how much effort it's costing her.

Her people are uneasy. It's obvious they've never seen their leader like this.

First, Verene looks at her brother, who's barely awake. Then she looks at me. She regards me like I'm the foulest thing she's ever seen.

"Have you not done enough yet?" she says. Her voice carries over the crackling of the flames.

"Why don't you want them to know?" I say.

"We don't want to listen to any more of your lies," she says.

"Why don't you want them to know what you've done for them?" I say. "What you've really done for them?"

"I don't know what you're talking about," she says, stubborn as usual.

"I'm talking about the ritual, of course," I say.

Verene goes very still.

"There's a ritual to get magic," I say. "It's not something you're born with. It's something you choose to do. Your maman chose to do it, long ago. And she wanted you to be like her."

Verene doesn't say anything. She just watches me, her eyes wary.

"But the ritual is violent," I say. "If you want magic, you have to hurt someone else. And your maman pitted you against your brother. She wanted one of you to prove you would be willing to hurt the other. But you chose not to." I pause. "You chose to get rid of your maman instead. Even though you had no water magic of your own. But you decided to lie about that and tell everyone you were better and different. You neglected to mention that, just like her, you're a murderer."

A soft gasp goes through the crowd.

I'm right about her maman. I can see it on Verene's face. I can see it in the fierce set of her jaw.

I knew it. The last time I saw her in her quarters, she looked like someone who could kill. And she is.

"You murdered your old ruler because she was taking your blood," I say. "Now you steal water from the other cities. And you hurt people like me when we try to take it back." I hold up my bloodied hand. "Why pretend that you're a saint? You're powerful, and there's more value in that. You would do anything for your city, wouldn't you?"

Verene casts a frantic look around the square. The people are shifting and drawing back even farther. There's been too many lies and too much chaos in the past day. They don't know what to make of it.

And maybe, they don't know what to do with a girl who's not a saint. They've feared one ruler unconditionally and worshipped the other. Maybe they don't know how to do anything in between.

"I—I would," Verene says. "I would do anything for Iris. I love Iris."

"How much do you love Iris?" I say.

She turns back to me. Her face hardens. "I would do *anything.*"

A chill goes down my spine.

"We'll see about that," I say.

I grab Theo by the hair. I lift the knife.

"No!" She starts to run up the steps.

I press the knife to his throat, and she stops.

"Don't—" Her voice is shaking. "Come down here and fight me yourself."

"I'm going to," I say. "But not without magic."

I watch her face carefully. Her dark eyes are blazing, reflecting the light of the fire, and I see the fear that flashes through them.

"What do you mean?" she says.

"Oh, I'm going to do the ritual on him," I say. "I thought that was obvious."

"You don't know how," she says.

"How do you think I learned everything I know about your maman?" I say.

She's quiet. I can see her thoughts racing.

"Even if you—even if you'd read something of hers, some-how," she says, "she wouldn't have written down how to do the ritual."

I look meaningfully at Theo. He's slowly coming back to his senses, and he tries to struggle away from me. I hold him tighter, digging the knife into his throat.

"Would he have written it down?" I say. "Maybe in the back of a journal of hers? Something he kept without you knowing?"

Verene wants to deny it. I can tell. But she just isn't sure. She looks around, like she can find another way to stop me. But I've taken away her people's unquestioning devotion. I've taken away her sainthood. I've taken away her vide. I've taken away her cathedral. I've taken away her brother. She has nothing.

"So this is what you wanted?" she says. "To destroy me? And now you're going to get magic just so you can kill me?"

"Not quite," I say. "Have you ever been to one of the cities across the veil? Have you ever seen what you've done to us? Our wells are empty, and yours is overflowing. So now, you're going to repay us. I'm going to take all the water you have back to my people. And then, you're going to give me your blood." I look around. "You're all going to give me your blood. And, using a very clever system designed by one of your own"—I shake Theo a little bit—"I'll give that blood to all the other cities. After what you've done to us, we deserve it. I hope you all enjoyed the opu-lence, because it's over now."

The people of Iris are starting to realize what's happening. I see their stricken faces. I hear their terrified gasps. I see some of them turning to run, as if there's anywhere for them to go.

"But don't worry," I say. "The Heart of Iris is still here. She just said she would do anything for you. I'm sure she has a way to save you one more time. She got you into this, after all. I'm sure she can get you out of it."

Verene is looking at her brother. Her hands are clenched and trembling, and there are tears welling in her eyes.

For a moment, I feel a twinge of…something. And it almost feels like regret.

No one's ever fought me like she has. She's so self-righteous and so aggravating and so utterly determined to get what she wants. She made everything about her city better, and it was incredible. She's incredible. And I have the sudden urge to stop everything and make sure she knows that.

But I can't, of course. Because she and Iris are in my way, and so this is what has to happen. There's no mystical way to produce water out of nowhere. Somebody has to give up their blood.

I don't want to do this to her people. Not really. I don't want them to have to go back to the way things used to be.

But my people are dying.

"Well?" I say.

Verene has two choices left. She can surrender. Or she can do absolutely anything to stop me. Maybe she'd even do the one thing she said she would never do. Maybe, if she thinks I know how to get blood magic, she'll get blood magic, too, and then I'll know everything there is to know about magic.

If anyone can make her do this, I think it's me.

As I wait to see what her next move will be, my heart is thrumming.

And when she meets my eyes again, it nearly leaps out of my chest.

She's going to fight.

That's perfect.

I push Theo onto his back. I raise the knife dramatically, like I'm going to hurt him.

I don't know what I'm going to do. I don't know how to do this so-called ritual. But Verene is already sprinting up the steps in my direction, so I just have to pretend until she shows me how.

Then, off to one side, I see an unexpected flash of movement. I turn.

It's Ale. He's running up the steps from the direction of the Parliament buildings. And he looks furious. He looks so furious that I barely recognize him. There's a knife clutched in his hand.

"Emanuela!" he says. "Let them go!"

"Ale," I say. "No—"

He stops a few steps away.

"I know that you know how to stop the vide!" he says. "You were giving it your blood, weren't you? We have everything we need to save Occhia."

He can't be here. I have this all under control, and he can't get in the way.

"Ale." I start in his direction. "Go back."

"I don't want you to hurt them anymore," he says. "I don't want anyone else to get hurt—"

I see Verene running at him. I see her dive and tackle him to the steps. I see a flash of metal as she grabs the knife from his hands. But I don't comprehend any of it.

Not until I hear him scream.

The blade is in his eye. Verene is digging, like she's trying to get it all the way into his brain. He's struggling, prying at her hands and her face, but she won't stop.

She drops the blade. She reaches in and pries the eye out

with her fingers. It trails bloody threads, and she rips them off with a sharp jerk.

I don't know if Ale is screaming anymore. I can't seem to hear. My ears have filled up with a loud ringing sound, and everything around me has faded into white. The only thing I can see is Verene and the eye clutched in her bloody fingers.

She stands up and turns to look at me, all fiery determination, and lifts the eye. I have absolutely no idea what she's about to do with it, but I know without a doubt that this is the ritual, and she's about to finish it. I can't stop watching. I'm rooted to the spot.

Then she hesitates. I watch her take in the bloody thing clutched in her hands, slowly, like she's just realized what it is. She looks around and comprehends just how big her audience is.

She stumbles back. She drops the eye.

All at once, everything becomes very loud. The flames in the cathedral are roaring. The people in the square are screaming and running away. And Verene is staring at her bloody hands.

"I…" she says. "No. I'm not…I'm not like her. I would never—"

She looks at me. The fury on her face makes me lose my breath.

"You," she says, and her voice is shaking. "You did this. You—you ruined everything. You ruined me. What did you do to me?"

The last words are more like a sob. Behind her, Ale is sobbing, too. He turns on his side, clutching his face, and I catch a glimpse of the bloody, gaping hole where his eye used to be.

And then, it feels like I don't even have control over my body anymore. I just attack Verene with everything I have. We fall to the steps. And then we're tumbling down, and I'm driving the knife into her soft body. And I'm doing it again. And again.

When we hit the bottom of the steps, the knife falls out of my hands. I realize, all at once, that Verene has stopped fighting me. I see the blood all over her and back away and for a moment, I just stand there, staring at her as she lies helplessly on the ground, struggling to breathe.

I don't know if I meant to do that to her. I don't know if I wanted it to happen. I just did it. She hurt Ale, so I hurt her, because that's what she gets.

Ale. I look for him and realize that he's crawled down the steps, dripping blood. He reaches the cathedral square and tries to look around. He's looking for me. I run to him, and when I touch his shoulders, he makes a terrified little noise and squirms away.

"Ale," I say, and my own voice sounds odd and distant. "Ale. It's me."

I pull him away from the steps. I've forgotten what I was even trying to do in this city. Right now, I just want to get him out. But we only make it a couple of feet before he collapses. I kneel down at his side. I take off my jacket and wad it up to press it over the hole in his face.

But the bleeding won't stop. I watch it soak into the fabric, dizzyingly fast.

I hear noises and look around vaguely to see that Theo is scrambling down the steps toward us. Toward his sister. Somehow, he got the bindings off his wrists. He reaches for Verene and pulls her into his lap. She's still taking those horrible, rattling breaths. Theo touches something on her forehead, gingerly, like he's not sure it's real.

I recognize the red smudge the moment I see it. It's an omen. A moment later, another one appears right next to it.

She's dying.

Verene tries to say something and chokes. She coughs up blood.

"Theo—" she says. "You have to—the city."

"What?" He barely whispers it.

"The city," she says again. She curls her fingers into the front of his shirt. "Theo, you have to make sure they see me. They have to know that I died for them. For the good of Iris."

Theo lifts his head to look around the square. It's emptied out. Maybe people are watching from the windows of their manors. Or maybe we're all alone with a burning cathedral.

"I'm not scared," Verene says. "But they have to know. They have to know what I did for them. You can't let me just disappear without—"

She's clutching his shirt so tightly. She is scared.

There's a strange expression on Theo's face. He's no longer looking at his sister. All his attention is focused on something clutched in his hand, and he's just staring at it, like he can't decide what to do with it.

It's the eye. Ale's eye.

And then Verene notices it, too. She recoils. She tries to squirm away.

"No," she says. "No. I won't—"

"Verene," Theo says. "You already did."

She's trying to get away. But he's already shoving the eye into her mouth.

All I can do is watch, strangely mesmerized, as Verene gags. Theo covers her mouth and forces her to chew. And chew. And chew. It takes so long, and she fights it the whole time, but he doesn't let up. When it's finally done, she goes limp.

She's crying, and it's a small, broken noise. He takes his hand off her mouth and pushes her hair away from her face, gently. He's watching her like he's waiting for something to happen.

So I watch her, too. I watch her shuddering breaths. I watch her seeping wounds. I watch the omens crawl down her face and onto her neck.

And then, the omens stop in their tracks. They disappear. Every last one.

Her wounds stop bleeding.

Verene goes still. Then, all at once, she wrenches herself away from her brother. She scrambles back on her hands and knees. She's moving like she doesn't feel any pain at all, but her face is gray and terrified.

She blinks once, twice, and something happens behind her eyes. Even from here, I can see it. In an instant, they're darker.

Colder.

"No," she says, her voice hushed. "No—"

I know what I'm looking at. I've seen it before.

Magic. Blood magic. The most powerful magic a person can have.

I have to get out of this city. I have to get back to my home.

I stand up and scoop up my knife off the cobblestone. Somehow, I get Ale on his feet. His arm is around my shoulder, leaning on me heavily, as we stumble into the nearest street. I look around wildly for an entrance to the catacombs. I see dark manors and terrified faces peeking out of the windows. I see bubbling fountains and beautiful white rose gardens. I can't remember if

I've been on this particular street before, and I want to scream. I don't have time to be lost. Ale doesn't have time to be lost.

At last, I spot a familiar door in an alley. I drag Ale onto the first step. Instantly, a few drops of his blood fall. A moment later, the vide is there, swallowing it up.

I pull the blood-soaked jacket off Ale's face. I wring it out onto the vide, and its shadowy form gets darker. The air gets colder as the splatters of blood disappear.

"Ale," I say. "Tell it to take us back to Occhia. It will listen to you."

Ale sways, and all at once, he's collapsing down the steps. I chase him. He's landed in a crumpled pile on the catacomb floor, barely conscious. His one remaining eye is fluttering, but really, all I can see is the gaping, bloody hole in his face.

"Ale." I grab his shoulder and shake him. "Tell the vide to take us home. Now."

"It hurts," he whispers.

"I know," I say.

"Why?" he says. "Why did she do this to me?"

His voice is so small and helpless, and for a second, I completely lose my nerve. For a second, I'm convinced that I can't do this. We can't do this. We're never going to be able to make it back to Occhia, and we're going to die right here on the floor of the catacombs.

But then I shake myself. Ale needs me. He needs his best friend—the one who can and will do anything for him.

I press my knife against my unblemished hand. I hold my breath and slice, quick and decisive. I squeeze it out over the floor again. And again. And again.

"Listen up, you gluttonous thing," I say to the shadow

underneath me. "We've given you more than enough, so you'd better—"

The floor opens up beneath us.

And everything goes black.

I'm flying through the air, and I have no idea which way is up until I hit the ground, hard.

I struggle to suck in a breath, suddenly desperate for air. Traveling inside the vide was quick but deeply disorienting. I felt like I was dragged into a black room and tossed onto its floor like a doll. All I wanted to do was get up and look around, but I couldn't. My body wasn't listening to me.

I wonder if being dead feels anything like that.

There's a heavy thump beside me, and I turn to see Ale, lying with his back to me. I sit up and reach for him. I shake his shoulders, and he doesn't move.

"Ale?" I say. It comes out as more of a whimper.

He's passed out. He's lost so much blood, and it's still seeping out of his face.

This is my fault. I was supposed to be with him the whole time. I was supposed to protect him.

Then I realize that the shadow is still hovering next to him. It's quietly sucking up the blood pooling below his empty eye socket.

"Stop it," I hiss at the vide, suddenly furious.

We're lying at the foot of a staircase that looks just like the one we left. Up above, a door is cracked open to reveal the red light of the veil.

If we're not really back in Occhia, I don't know what I'm going to do.

I start dragging Ale up the stairs. The vide follows us.

"Stop!" I say, aware that it's probably not going to do any good. "Leave him alone."

I reach the door and shove it open.

We're back in our city. The manors all around me are dark and quiet underneath the glowing red veil of midday. The narrow cobblestone streets are empty. Everything looks so dry and deserted and . . . dead.

Maybe it is. Maybe they're gone, and this was all for nothing. Maybe I'm going to have to sit here alone and watch Ale bleed to death.

No. If there's anyone still here, they're going to find us, and they're going to help him right now.

"Hello!" I yell.

It echoes. For a moment, everything is still.

Then I hear footsteps. I spot a flash of movement at the end of the street, and three guards in red coats are barreling toward me. They grab me, knocking the knife out of my hands. In an instant, there are chains around my wrists. One of them notices Ale and moves for him.

"I stabbed him," I say. "He wasn't loyal to me. Perhaps you can still save him. Perhaps not."

The guards mutter to one another. One of them wrestles Ale into his arms. He runs off down the street, much faster than I'd ever have been able to, and my head spins in relief.

One of the guards grabs the end of my chain and pulls me forward.

"How long has it been?" I say.

"Three days," he says.

"Is the water gone?" I say. "Has anyone died?"

"Oh, people have died, all right," he says. "Some because of the water. Some because of the riots. I suppose you're happy about that."

I don't know why I'd be happy about that. It's not like I just woke up one day and decided it would be hilarious to kill the watercrea.

"I know how to get us water," I say.

"Sure you do," he says.

Fine. He can put me in a jail cell if it makes him feel better. He'll realize the error of his ways soon enough.

After the dazzling white streets of Iris, my city feels so dark. I immediately see what the guard meant when he said there were riots. The black manors have broken windows and boarded-up doors. The cobblestone is littered with debris and abandoned clothes. People died right here, in the street, fighting over the few drops we had left.

A dark anger simmers low in my belly. If Verene hadn't stolen from our underground well, this wouldn't have happened. We could have lasted three days while I found an answer for us.

I was right to destroy her city the way I did. I won't feel bad about it.

"Murderer!"

The voice comes from somewhere over my head. I crane my neck to see a woman leaning out the top window of the nearest manor.

"Murderer!" she says again.

And I realize she's talking to me.

"You've killed us all!"

This voice comes from the other side of the street.

"Push her off the top of the tower! It's what she deserves."

That's from a man in the nearest doorway.

The guard picks up the pace, but the yelling only gets louder. It's coming from everywhere. It's a little terrifying, but it's also, somehow, a little exhilarating. My people never protested what the watercrea did. They always just stood by and let it happen. It's nice to see them finally getting angry about how bad things are.

We turn a corner, and my blood runs cold. We're in front of the House of Morandi. The watercrea's red silk gown is still lying in the street, right where she died. It's surrounded by roses and flickering prayer candles.

They're mourning her like she was special.

She wasn't special.

Then we pass my family's house, and I wish we hadn't. The door is barely hanging on by a single hinge. The windows are all shattered.

"Where are they?" I ask the guard.

"Why do you care?" he says.

Because they're my family. I have to save them. I have to show them that I'm the best of us.

We reach the cathedral, and the guard starts to pull me around the side, along a path that's entirely too familiar.

No. We're not supposed to be going this way.

"Oh good," I say. "I was afraid you were going to put me in a jail cell. But we're going back to the tower. That makes things easier for me."

He ignores me.

"Because I already know how to break out of it," I add.

Nothing.

The silent black tower is getting closer and closer.

He can't put me back in there. There's no point. There's no watercrea.

"Well, good luck explaining this to the lords in Parliament," I say. "You finally caught the dastardly Emanuela Ragno, and in your most brilliant move ever, you...put her in the exact same place, and she escaped. Again."

"You're not going to escape this time," the guard says without looking back. "And half the lords in Parliament are gone, so don't expect an old-fashioned trial. More likely than not, they're going to assemble what's left of the city in the cathedral, drop you at the front, and let the mob have its way with you. We'll see how mouthy you are then."

Half of Parliament is gone after just three days. That's more than I expected. That's too many.

We reach the door of the watercrea's tower. It's hanging open. The guard tries to drag me inside, and I dig in my heels without even really deciding to. He yanks, and I tumble over the threshold. As soon as the sickly smell of blood hits me, I retch all down my front.

"Oh, don't try and make me feel sorry for you," he says.

I can't be in here. I'd rather be in the jail. I'd rather be thrown to a mob. This tower is where I die.

Two more guards appear from the staircase. They're carrying chains. Lots of chains. They wrap my arms and my legs until I'm so useless that I can't even walk. One of them throws me over his shoulder and carries me up the stairs. They open one of the small, round cell doors and stuff me inside. It slams shut.

I lie there with my face pressed into the cold floor. The guards mutter to one another and thump back down the stairs, and the tower door shuts, and the minutes stretch on, but I can't seem to move.

I have this under control, I remind myself. I just have to wait until Ale is better. Ale will get me out of here. And then I'll bring our water back. I can still bring our water back.

And then they'll see. They'll all see.

SEVENTEEN

"EMANUELA. EMANUELA."

There's a soft voice calling my name. I scramble up, awkward in my chains.

"Ale?" I say. "Are you—"

There's a shadowy figure peering through the bars of my cell. It's not Ale. It's a man in a crisp black suit. His eyes are sharp, glinting even in the darkness of the tower.

"Papá?" I whisper.

He moves in closer. His face is gaunt, and his mustache has grown unkempt. For a moment, we just stare at each other, like we're trying to make sure the other is really alive.

"The family," I say. "Is everyone—"

"They're alive," he says.

"What about Paola?" I say.

"Who?" he says.

"My nursemaid," I say.

"The nursemaid who was helping you hide your omen, you

mean?" he says. "I don't know. We dismissed her right after you went to the tower."

My skin gets very cold. When I saw Paola, she didn't mention that. She acted like she was fine.

"Have you—have you heard anything about Ale?" I say. "Is he—"

"I've heard that he has a giant hole in his face," he says slowly. "And the guards are saying it was you. He's not saying a word to anyone."

Ale is awake. All of a sudden, I can breathe again.

"I'll explain it later," I say. "But first—I know how to save the city."

He gives me a sideways look. "You do?"

"There's something else out there, Papá," I say. "There are other cities under the veil."

"There are?" he says, and his disbelief is plain.

"Yes," I say. "And one of them was stealing our water. So we can steal it back."

"How?" he says.

"I can do it," I say. "You just have to let me out."

"And what are you going to do?" he says.

"I'll show you when I get out," I say.

"You can't get out, little spider," he says, like the mere thought is ridiculous. "You can't leave the tower."

My heart drops to my feet. "What?"

"Not yet," he says. "This situation is very delicate. The people are clamoring for your head. It won't be safe for you to come out until the water is back."

"So you just want me to tell you how to save the city?" I say. "That's why you're here?"

"Isn't the important thing that the city is saved?" he says.

I don't understand. We're a team. We can save the city together.

"So?" he says.

"So?" I echo.

"What do we need to do to get the water?" he says.

I draw back. "Why don't you figure it out yourself?"

"Don't be unreasonable," he says.

"I'm being very reasonable," I say. "I'm the one who found the answers. I fought for them. Why should you be the one who gets to—"

"Think about this logically, Emanuela," he says. "You have to do what's best for the whole family. A mob chased us out of our home, you know. Mamma and your brothers... they're wasting away. All the cousins—they're so weak. Do you want to make things even worse for them?"

"Of course not," I say. "I'm not going to make things worse. I'm going to save us."

"Well, you turned the entire city upside down," he says. "It's a mess out here. I can't even begin to describe to you how unruly things have gotten. But we can fix it. Once the House of Ragno saves the city, we'll start repairing your reputation. It will be grueling, but it can be done. I have some ideas for where to start."

This is how it always is. He always has ideas. We always work together.

But as long as I'm in these chains, we're not working together.

"We'll repair my reputation," I say slowly.

"Yes," he says.

"And what?" I say. "I'll go back to the exact same life I had before? The life you set up for me?"

"Is that not what you want?" he says.

"I...I don't know." I'm realizing it as I say the words. "I don't know if I want to spend all of my days in Parliament with a bunch of old men and their laws."

"You have the mind for it," he says.

"I have the mind for many things," I say. "And Ale and I— we're best friends. That's what's always mattered. Not whether or not we were married."

Something flickers in my papá's eyes.

"The Morandi boy would be the most valuable husband in the city," he says. "We can still find a way to—"

"And the watercrea..." I say.

If I hadn't killed the watercrea, I would have spent the rest of my life afraid of the moment she discovered me. I had to stop her. I'm doing exactly what I need to do. Right now, I'm more certain of it than ever.

"Emanuela," my papá says. "Your old life was perfect. You don't have to lose it all just because you..." He pauses. "We can fix all this. Together. What else could you possibly want?"

He doesn't understand. I'm not just going to bring the water back. I'm going to save us. I'm going to protect us. I'm going to make sure I'm doing absolutely everything I can for us. There are six other cities across the veil that I haven't gotten to see yet. There's a girl in a white gown I still have to defeat—a girl who just got magic and whose next move is now, thrillingly, impossible for me to predict.

"More," I say.

My papá is quiet. But he understands. He must. I got my ambition from him.

"Well?" I say. "Can I come out now?"

"There really are other cities?" he says. "There's a city that has our water?"

"Yes," I say breathlessly.

He hesitates. I wait for him to start picking the lock on my cell.

"And how do we get the water back?" he says.

"I—" I falter. "I told you. I can show you. There's a way to—"

"Just tell me how, and I'll do it," he says as calm as ever.

"No," I say, automatically. "I have to show you—"

He sighs and stands up. "Clearly, you can get to the other cities through the catacombs, since that's where you came from. So I'll send another search party down there."

"Wait," I say. "It won't be that simple. There's a—" I cut myself off.

"There's what?" he says.

I can't tell him about the vide. Until I'm out of this cell, I can't tell him anything.

He sighs. "I don't enjoy seeing you in here, Emanuela. I want you out. I do. But things are getting very dire for Occhia. If you can't control your hysterics for long enough to comprehend my very sensible plan, I'll do it without you."

He starts to turn away, but then he pauses.

"You'll thank me later," he says.

As if he gets to decide that. As if he gets to decide anything at all about me.

I throw myself at the bars, and when I hit them, the clang is tremendous. My papá flinches and stumbles back.

"I can do this without you," I say.

His eyes flicker to the chains wrapped around my whole body. "It doesn't look like it."

Then he's gone, slipping away down the stairs. The tower door creaks open and slams shut.

I sink down to the floor of my cell. I don't understand what just happened. I don't understand why he's not proud of me. I don't understand why he doesn't want me at his side.

I've never seen him flinch the way he flinched when I threw myself at him. He looked... terrified.

Last time, the tower was mostly silent, but that was nothing compared to the quiet now. There's not even the faintest suggestion of breath or movement from the other prisoners. They must have all wasted away and disappeared. There are no guards thumping up and down the stairs. Outside, the cathedral bells aren't even ringing.

I feel like I'm the only person in the whole city. All I can do is remind myself that I'm not. I have to be patient.

But when I'm lying here, alone in the dark, I have nothing to do but relive it all again. The watercrea's needle in my neck. The cold, sick feeling of my blood being sucked out of me. The quiet defeat of the other prisoners—the sound of a hundred people dying without a fight.

I turn over and shut my eyes, desperate to block it out. But I can't. This place is crawling all over my skin and into my ears. It's telling me I only managed to escape it for three days. It's telling me that being able to run from my omen for ten years was just luck, and I can't run forever.

I know it's lying. But the longer it talks, the harder it is to fight off.

Hours later, when I hear the tower door creak open, I sit up and press my face to the bars. I don't care if it's an angry mob. I just need to talk to someone.

"Hello?" I say. My voice sounds so small in the empty stairwell.

I hear his soft steps and see his long shadow on the floor, and then Ale comes into view. He stops in front of my cell. He doesn't say anything. He just looks at me.

He's changed clothes. It's good to see him in familiar Occhian attire, dark and drab as it is. His missing eye is covered with gauze, bandages wrapped around his head to hold it in place. His hair is matted with dried blood. Apparently, even at the illustrious House of Morandi, he didn't have enough water to clean himself properly.

I want to ask if the wound hurts. I want to ask if he's all right. But they seem like such silly questions. The important thing is that I get him the water he needs. Then I'm going to make sure he rests, because he looks like he really needs to lie down.

"Did the guards see you?" I say.

He hesitates. Then he shakes his head. He gingerly touches the bandage around his head, like he's making sure it's in place.

"Verene is going to pay for what she did to you," I say. "I'll make sure of it."

"I know," he mutters.

He looks miserable. It's not that I expect him to look overjoyed, but we are about to save our city. That's not something to be miserable about.

But maybe he's remembering the way the two of us fought in the jail in Iris. We've never fought like that before.

"Ale," I say. "What happened in Iris…"

He turns back to me.

We won't fight like that again. From now on, he's going to

listen to me. He's learned, unfortunately, what happens if he doesn't.

"It's behind us now," I say. "Let's go save Occhia."

He doesn't move.

"I can teach you how to pick a lock," I say impatiently. "It's not that hard. Just reach in here and get some of the pins from my hair. We're going to have to be quick, because my papá was acting very strange, and he might be—"

"I thought you were dead."

Ale barely whispers the words. I stop, certain I've misheard.

"What?" I say.

"When the watercrea took you away," he says. "I thought you were dead. I thought your omens were going to spread in hours. My papá didn't even say goodbye when he got his, you know. He ran straight to the tower, because he wanted to give up as much blood as he could. He wanted to set an example for everyone else. The next day, the guards brought us back his clothes and his wedding ring. It was… it was just so quick."

Ale hasn't said a word about his papá since he died. The elder Signor Morandi was loud and gregarious and very unlike his son, but he doted on Ale, dragging him to meetings and showing him off at parties and telling everyone that one day he was going to be a wonderful head of Parliament. At the time, it made Ale miserable. He endured as little of it as possible before slipping off to a corner to read. But he loved his papá.

I should have tried to talk to him about it sooner. That's what a good best friend would have done. I just didn't know what to say. And right now, I can see the pain on Ale's face, and it looks as fresh as if it all happened last night.

"After you left, I sat and stared out my window all night,"

he continues. "I kept expecting to see you on your balcony. In the morning, I was so sure I was going to get one of your letters. But by that evening, I was married to Valentina. And her maids were carrying all her things into my room, making a mess of my books, and she was just sitting there, staring at me like I was the last person she'd ever wanted to marry. I had no idea what to talk to her about. And I realized you were really gone. I realized I had absolutely no idea how to live without you."

His voice is broken, and all at once, I'm no longer angry at him for leaving me in the tower. He didn't know better. But he does now. That's what he's going to say next.

"When I saw you again, it was like..." He hesitates. "I don't know. I was scared for you, but at the same time, it was like everything had suddenly become right again."

I'm smiling. "So let's—"

"But then..." he says. "Then...this happened."

"What happened?" I say.

"This," he insists. "All of this."

"We got rid of the watercrea and saved Occhia?" I say.

"How are you going to save Occhia?" he says. "Are you going to steal the water back from Iris? Are you going to turn the vide against them? Or are you going to...get the blood magic?"

I open my mouth.

"You don't have to answer," he says. "I know you will. I was in the crowd when you were giving that speech in Iris. I heard everything you said. And I saw the look in your eyes. You looked..." He trails off, like he's too unsettled by the memory to finish his sentence.

The blood magic will make me unstoppable. The blood magic will get rid of my omens. He doesn't know what it's like to have an omen on his skin, taunting him every second of every day. He doesn't understand.

"Occhia needs a savior," I say. "It needs someone powerful enough to fight for it. And who would you rather have fighting for you than me?"

Ale steps back.

"Ale—" I say.

"I love you," he says softly.

I have no idea how to respond. He's never said that to me before. I assumed he thought it only belonged in a *real* marriage.

"Do you love me?" he says.

Of course I do. But right now, I'm in a cell, and he's making no effort to help me.

"I—" I say.

"Stop," he says. "I can see you thinking. I'm not asking you to say the thing that will convince me to let you out. I'm asking you what you feel. What you really feel."

He waits. His fists are clenched, like he's braced for me to say something horrible. As if I didn't break out of the watercrea's tower and immediately run for his house. As if I wouldn't kill anyone who hurts him. As if we're not going to change our city together.

"You're my best friend," I say. "Of course I love you."

For some reason, the words pain him. I can see it on his face.

"I know," he says. "I know. I do. But too many people have gotten hurt, and—I'm afraid, Emanuela. I'm afraid of how much worse it could get. So it has to stop."

He turns away.

Like he's going to leave.

"Ale," I say.

He starts down the stairs.

"Ale—" I throw myself against the bars. "You don't have what it takes to save Occhia."

He doesn't look back

"I can do it," I say. "Just let me—"

All I can see of him is his shadow.

"Ale," I say. "You can't just leave me in here—"

He hasn't stopped.

"Ale!"

The scream rips itself out of my throat, and at last, his shadow hesitates. He's listening. But I'm shaking and gasping for breath and I can barely find any words.

"If I—if I die, it will be your fault," I choke out. "But if I live... I'll break out of here, and I'll find you, and I'll—"

I stop. It looks like his shadow has turned around.

He's coming back. He must be.

"That's all you have to say to me?" he says. "Threats?"

"Ale," I say. "I'm going to die in here. You're not really going to let me—"

I'm not able to put the words together anymore. All I can do is stare at his shadow.

He doesn't move. For a long moment, he doesn't even speak.

"You've always told me I can't do anything without you," he says. "But I've never even tried. Maybe I can."

He turns away. He starts back down the steps, and his shadow disappears.

No.

I try to call out to him, but all I can manage is a sob. I have to make him understand. He needs me. I need him.

The tower door creaks open, then shuts.

And I'm alone.

I'm lying on my side, surrounded by darkness, when I feel it. Something invisible and foreign comes out of nowhere and pokes me in the hip, gentle but insistent.

The hand of God.

I don't have to look to know what it is.

A second omen has blossomed on my skin. Right next to the first.

They'll spread eventually. I can't outrun them forever.

But I will.

I have to.

Eighteen

There's someone on the stairs.

I've been sitting up for hours, staring blearily at the same spot. I'm desperate for the unthinking oblivion of sleep, but I can't shake the feeling that if I let myself close my eyes, my omens are going to spread in an instant. So I've decided that I'll simply never sleep again.

My head is pounding, and my vision has gone blurry. That's why it takes me a long moment to process a new presence. I can hear their footsteps. I can see their shadow coming closer and closer.

"Ale?" I whisper, and I hear how helpless I sound, but I can't make myself care.

But it's not Ale, I realize a moment later. It's a guard. He unlocks the cell and starts to pull me out.

"What—" I say.

"Your people want to see you," he says.

It sounds a little mocking. I suppose it's time for my trial by angry mob.

I'm dizzy from blood loss and covered in chains, so the guard has to scoop me up in his arms. I can barely keep my head up, but I look around at the empty cells we pass. I try to find an opportunity to escape. I don't see one.

We're already in the foyer of the tower somehow.

I struggle.

"Don't bother," the guard says.

No. There has to be something I can do. I can't face my people like this. I have to look like someone who can save them.

The guard opens the door to the tower. He stops short.

"Signor Ragno," the guard says, a little wary.

My papá is just outside. He's straightening the collar of his suit and looking very grim.

"Let me carry her," he says.

The guard is silent for a moment. "I'm the head guard," he says finally, like this is a position that means anything anymore.

"I don't recall you being the head guard," my papá says.

"Well, I am now," he says.

"She's my only daughter," my papá says. "If your daughter had done something terrible—"

"My daughter would never do something like this," the guard says.

"—she would still be your daughter, wouldn't she? Please. Don't deny me the chance to hold her one last time."

There's a brokenness in my papá's voice that I've never heard before. For a moment, I'm terrified. He really thinks I'm about to die helplessly at the hands of a mob. He really thinks he's about to lose me forever.

Then I see the glint in his brown eyes.

I knew it. I knew my papá would still help me. I knew someone would help me.

"I don't want to go with him," I say. "I don't care about any of you."

That, apparently, is the persuasion that the guard needs.

"Fine," he says. "You take her, and I'll walk behind—"

He shifts me into my papá's arms like they're trading a sack of potatoes. My papá isn't a big man, and he wavers for a second, undoubtedly surprised by how heavy I am with all the chains. He still smells like our family's house—a scent I didn't even realize I knew until this moment. I'd never left for long enough to miss it.

He turns to face the long side of the cathedral.

But then he sprints in the other direction, into the city streets.

The guard swears and chases after us. In spite of myself, I laugh. My papá isn't big, but he's fast.

"Just get to the catacombs," I say. "I'll take care of the guard."

"He won't follow us in there," my papá says. "Most of the other guards are gone because they went in and never came out—"

My papá knows exactly where to go. He's obviously planned for this. In moments, we're pushing through a door and stumbling down dusty steps into the darkness of the catacombs. He sets me on the ground and starts to say something.

But then a shadow blocks out the light from the top of the stairs. The guard has followed us. He hesitates for a second. Then he squares his shoulders, touches something in his breast pocket—a superstitious herb blend that he thinks will protect him, no doubt—and descends.

Frantically, I turn onto my side. I press my bloody leg into the floor, hoping I can still get something out of the wound I made in Iris.

Nothing happens. For a second, none of it feels like it was even real—the white city across the veil, the shadow creature roaming around the catacombs, and the girl with the blazing eyes who I almost destroyed. But then, I feel the stone underneath me grow cold.

The guard reaches the bottom step and starts to lunge at my papá. But a second later, the floor opens up beneath the guard, and he's gone.

For a long moment, my papá just stares at the empty space where the guard used to be. When he turns back to me, his face is white.

"What…" he says. "What did you just do?"

"Do you have something to break me out of these chains?" I say.

My papá doesn't say anything.

"Oh," I say. "Maybe the guard has keys. I can bring him back—"

"Emanuela," my papá says. "Do you know what they were about to do to you? In the cathedral?"

I hesitate. "They…they were going to—"

"They were going to kill you," he says. "The city is almost dead. They think that sacrificing you—the watercrea's murderer— is our only chance. We have no other way to save ourselves." He pauses. "But you have a way."

"Yes," I say. "Just help me get out of these chains."

"There's no time," he says. "More people will come looking for us. Just tell me what to do."

The realization creeps across my skin, slow and cold. I thought he was here because he wanted to save me. But he only wants to save himself.

The vide is lingering by my leg, waiting for more blood. I feed it. I ask it, tentatively, if it has a way to break my chains. I'm not sure what it's capable of, but I have to try.

I feel something cold on my thigh. I look down.

There's a faint, shadowy hand extending out of the darkness. It's creeping across my skirt.

It takes everything I have to hold still. I watch the thin fingers slide up, reaching for my bindings.

The chains get very cold. And then they shatter.

My papá startles back.

I leap to my feet and shake myself free. I have no idea what just happened, and the vide just looks like a formless shadow again. But it's a formless shadow that's hovering very attentively by my feet.

I think it wants payment. It occurs to me then that if I don't give it payment, it could eat me up before I make it out of the catacombs. This is its domain. I'm just a visitor.

I swallow hard and turn to my papá. There's a loose rock in his hand now. He's holding it close to his side, like he doesn't want me to see it.

"Go back up to the city, Papá," I say. "I'll be there soon."

"How did you do that?" he says.

"I told you," I say. "I know how to save us."

"Emanuela." He advances on me. "Tell me how you did that, or I'll—"

I take a step forward. He stops.

"You don't have a plan," I say. "Your only plan was to

manipulate me into helping you and taking all the credit. You just wanted me to be your accessory."

He looks around the dark catacombs. He's shaking and desperately trying to gather himself. I've never seen him look so rattled.

"Emanuela," he says, softer. "You're not my accessory. You're my daughter. We have to save the city. We can't let ourselves die. I just—"

"We're not going to die," I say.

"My little spider," he tries again. "I—"

I look at the rock in his hands. He tightens his grip, ever so slightly.

"You're afraid of me," I say.

"You're—" He's stumbling over his words. "You're just a little girl. You're my little girl. I could never—"

"You thought you could put me in charge of Parliament and tell me what to do," I say. "You thought I would never question you. You thought you could control me. But do you really think you're powerful enough to do that? After what you've seen me do?"

I step closer, and he flinches. Again.

"I killed the watercrea," I say. "That makes me the most powerful person in the city."

He swings the rock at my head.

And then I'm on my hands and knees. There's a searing pain in my head. I'm so dizzy. I can't make sense of the dark shapes in front of me.

He hit me.

I didn't think he would actually hit me.

I touch my forehead and find blood. Like an instinct, I smear it on the floor.

I look up and find my papá, standing over me. He's clutching the rock in both hands, and his eyes are dark and cold.

He doesn't even look sorry.

"Don't make me do this," he says.

And then the vide has swallowed him up.

In the silence, I manage to get to my feet. I brace myself on the wall and try to breathe.

I don't have time to think about what just happened. I need to save Occhia. I need the magic.

The vide is at my feet. There are two men trapped inside it right now. I could use either one for my purposes. It doesn't matter.

I look down at my hands. My fingers are already stained with my own blood. I curl them into fists.

It does matter.

I back away from the vide. I wait.

It opens up again, and the moment my papá appears on the floor, I strike.

I know exactly what I have to do. My hands are so quick and decisive that he has no chance of stopping them.

I wasn't prepared for the sound of his screams. I wasn't prepared for how slippery it would be. But I dig my fingers into his eye, gouging deeper and deeper, and I pull.

Somehow, it's free, and it's in my grip, hot and wet and mangled. There are threads keeping it attached, and I can't manage to tear them off with my hands. So I tear them off with my teeth, and then the whole eye is in my mouth, because I can't hesitate now. I've come too far.

It's salty. It slides around and squishes between my teeth, and I'm chewing and chewing, desperately. I think about Verene, struggling in her brother's arms and gagging, and in spite of myself, I feel a little sorry for her.

I press my hands to my mouth and force myself to swallow the last of it down. I stumble to my feet and brace myself on the wall, and I turn to face my papá.

He's crumpled on the floor, letting out horrible, gurgling sobs. I squint at the blood all over his face and try to get it to bend to my will, but it doesn't.

I clench my fists and try harder.

I refuse to believe that it didn't work. It has to work. I saw it happen. It saved Verene's life. It turned her into something magical. Something immortal.

But nothing is happening. I don't feel any different.

Maybe I just need more.

My papá was barely able to put up a fight the first time. The second time, he's even weaker. The last of his eye goes down my throat, and I nearly choke on it. I wait to feel my new powers.

And still, nothing is happening.

No.

This *will* work.

I have to get magic. I have to get rid of the omens on my skin. They can't spread any farther. They won't.

I march out of the catacombs and look around the streets. They're silent and desolate. Everyone who's left must be in the cathedral already, waiting for me.

I walk desperately. I can barely stay on my feet, and my stomach is churning, but I have to stay on my feet.

I turn a corner, and then I spot a flash of something in an alley. A person.

I run for them. I don't care who they are. I need their eyes.

I lunge into the alley, grabbing for the shadowy figure. They yelp, startled, and try to pull away.

I stop short.

"Paola?" I whisper.

She's no longer wearing the gray servant's uniform of the House of Ragno. Her clothes are rumpled and dirty, and even after only three days, she looks shrunken and gaunt. But I'd recognize my nursemaid anywhere, of course.

Her eyes are wide. It takes me a long moment to realize that she doesn't seem to recognize me.

"Em-Emanuela?" she says.

"They dismissed you," I say. "My family."

She's looking at my dress. She's looking at the blood all over my hands.

"How did you survive?" I say.

A servant like her—fired in disgrace—would have nowhere to go. Servants are born into the house they serve, and anyway, no one would want a servant who helped her charge defy the watercrea's laws.

"That's..." she says. "That's not important. Is that...is that your blood?"

I try to explain. I find that I can't. I find that, all of a sudden, I'm swaying on my feet.

Paola takes my shoulders. She pulls me deeper into the alley, and I sink down to the cobblestone. I lean back against the wall and close my eyes.

"It didn't work," I whisper.

She's produced a handkerchief out of nowhere. She's wiping at the blood on my face, as if one little handkerchief is going to make any difference.

"You shouldn't even be near me." I don't open my eyes. "Everyone else in the city wants me dead."

"Well," she says, "everyone else is useless. I've heard what they're saying about you. They're saying that you're going to destroy the city. They're saying that you found a demon in the catacombs and made a pact with it. And they're saying that you're the one who hurt Alessandro, which is obviously just nonsense. It's just the panicked lies of terrified people."

"So what's the truth, then?" I say.

She stops wiping my face. She reaches out and strokes my hair, without hesitation, like she doesn't notice all the blood and grime.

"You're a girl who wants to live," she says.

She's right. I want to do more. Be more. And I want to live. I want to live forever.

And everyone else keeps trying to stop me.

Paola sighs. "You know, it's a blessing to make it as long as I have. But I've lost so many to the tower. When the water-crea died, for a moment, I thought—I thought about how amazing it would be if we could find another way. If we could make things better. And I thought if anyone could do it, it was you. I know how hard you tried. Even if it seems like no one else knows, I do."

She hesitates. I feel her plucking at my wet gown.

"Where..." she says. "Where is this blood coming from?"

I open my eyes.

"I'll try again," I say.

"What?" she says. "How?"

I turn to her. She's so pale. She looks tired and thirsty, and I open my mouth to explain.

And then I blink.

And I don't see Paola anymore. All I see is blood.

I see the spiderwebbing veins in her head. I see the blood flowing to her brain and her eyes and her nose. I see her pulse thrumming in her neck. It's horrifying. It's beautiful.

The ritual did work.

It actually worked.

And then, every single one of Paola's veins burst open. I blink again, and I can barely see. There's blood in my eyes. It's all over my face and in my mouth.

Paola's head is gone. It's just...gone. Her body collapses in a heap, and a moment later, it's gone, too. I'm left sitting next to a crumpled dress in a pool of blood.

No.

I pick up the dress. It's soaked and dripping. I can't quite make myself understand what it means.

I didn't do that. It was the magic.

The magic.

I drop the gray dress, and I scramble to pull up my skirts and look at my hip. They're gone. My omens are gone. For the first time in ten years, I'm unmarked.

I'm free. I'm alive.

I leap to my feet. But then I look at the spot that used to be Paola.

I did this to her. The magic and I did this together.

I retch and cover my mouth, but I force myself to swallow it back down. Paola believed in me. She wouldn't want me to stop just because she was reduced to ... this.

So I won't stop. I'll control the magic better next time. I know I can.

I turn away. I pick up my skirts and run across the cobblestone.

I have a city to save.

Nineteen

THE STREETS ARE EMPTY AND THE BLACK MANORS ARE silent as I run to the House of Morandi. The watercrea's gown is still lying there, a splash of red on the dark stone. I kick aside the prayer candles to reach it. I strip off my clothes and pull on hers, barely even noticing the dark blood dried on the back. The silk is soft and luxurious. It still smells like her rosy perfume, but that doesn't bother me. She can't touch me now.

The skirts are dreadfully long, of course, so I tie them off to one side in an artful knot. Everyone can enjoy the sight of my legs. I have nothing to hide.

I make my way down the street. I run up the steps to the cathedral and barge through the doors.

The whole city is supposed to be here, but it feels so empty. The only Occhians left are clustered in the front pews, buzzing and chattering and ready for the trial. At the crack of the chamber doors, they startle and turn around. When they see me coming, unchained and wearing her red gown, their rage and despair turns into fear. It's so strong I can taste it.

I blink, and the shadowy people disappear. The only thing I can see is their blood. I blink again, and the people come back.

I can control it, I tell myself.

"You all look surprised to see me like this," I say loudly. "You shouldn't be. It's just like I told you. I'm untouchable, and with the watercrea gone, you're going to be free."

I let silence reign as I glide to the altar. I whirl around.

"You're welcome," I say.

I turn my gaze to the red carpet that stretches down the aisle. The last time I was here, someone else used her magic to drag me across it. That will never happen again.

I can't tell if the rest of my family is here. Everybody is hunched and terrified. They're slowly sinking down to hide behind their pews.

"Look at me," I snap.

They freeze. For some reason, I notice suddenly, they've filled the wooden benches with bundles of things. There are bags of clothes and rolled-up tapestries and even old, precious paintings—the type of family heirlooms an Occhian family would never remove from their home.

"I..." I falter for a moment, bewildered. "I'm going to bring back our water. Come with me to the underground well and—"

"No."

The voice comes from the first pew. And then its owner is stepping into the aisle.

Ale.

I don't know why I'm so surprised to see him. Everyone else left in Occhia is here, after all.

There's a fresh bandage around his eye. He's wearing an

enormous dark jacket with ivy leaves embroidered on the collar that I recognize instantly as his papá's. There's a sack over Ale's shoulder. It looks like it's full of books.

"No?" I say.

Ale lifts his chin. He swallows hard. "We're leaving." He says it so quietly I almost miss it.

"I'm not going anywhere, Ale," I say. "Not until I—"

"*We're* leaving," he says. "All of us here. We're going…"

He hesitates. He glances into the pew at his mamma. She nods encouragingly.

"We're going to another city," he says.

I have no idea what to say. I can't comprehend the fact that Ale is standing in front of me and speaking for the whole of our people.

"You're going to Iris?" I say.

"No," he says. "Somewhere else. We're going to ask them for help. There's so few of us now. We won't be a burden."

It takes me a long moment to understand what he means.

"You're just going to submit to life in another city," I say. "With another watercrea. You're going to give up your blood to her."

"It's—it's better than dying," he whispers.

"How are you going to get through the catacombs?" I say. "They're dangerous."

He reaches into his pocket and holds something up. His hands are shaking.

It's the map of the eight cities and the paths between them. I'm supposed to have the map. It was in my pocket.

It only takes a moment for me to figure out exactly when he took it. After Verene and I fought in the catacombs, and I passed out, I woke up in his lap. I thought that was because he was taking care of me.

I blink furiously, and I see his blood.

I look away quickly. My eyes sweep the silent faces gathered in front of me.

"So you all want to go back to the way it was," I say. "You want to never have quite enough water for comfort. You want to live your whole lives in fear of your first omen. You want to die before you even get to see your children grow up. Is that what you want?"

Silence.

"No," I say. "You want things to be worse. Think about it. No one has crossed between the eight cities in a thousand years. Do you really think the people on the other side will accept you? Do you think you'll be able to get a home just like the one you have here? The people across the veil don't know you. They don't care about you. They don't have a place for you. But they'll certainly want to take your blood."

Nobody is even looking at me. Ale is staring determinedly at his feet.

"Are you really going to follow him?" I gesture at Ale. "Look at him. He can't defend you. He's not even defending you now."

"Emanuela," Ale whispers to the floor.

"What?" I say.

"Just…" he says.

Everybody is looking at him now. Ale hates it when everyone looks at him. He's trembling so hard that I can see it from here.

"What, Alessandro?" I say. "Tell them why I'm wrong. Tell them why they should trust you."

He tries to say something, but he can't get the words out. There are tears welling up in his eye.

He's terrified. He can't do this. He knows he can't do this. And I can see the way people are watching at him. Like maybe they're starting to doubt.

I'm burning up inside with something ugly and victorious. This is who Ale is without me. This is going to be what the rest of his life is like—small and pitiful and meaningless.

"Anyway," I say, "I'm going to bring back our water. And then, I'm going to bring us more. Forever. And I'm going to do it without ever putting any of you in a tower again."

The silence is profound. I can tell that no one believes me. But they will.

I start forward. "Come with me to the—"

"We're not going anywhere with you."

I stop. Ale's mamma has joined him in the aisle. She faces me and draws herself up to her full, impressive height. Even in the dim cathedral light, her face pale and drained, she's very beautiful. Once or twice in my life, I've looked at her and imagined my children having her elegant cheekbones.

"You shameful, vile creature," she says. "You've destroyed our whole city. And you've destroyed him."

"Mamma—" Ale whispers.

"I never wanted him to marry you," she says. "Never. Not from the moment that slimy father of yours approached us."

At the mention of my papá, my stomach turns, sudden and violent.

"Alessandro was so devoted to you," his mamma says. "He has so much love in his heart. And you... you have nothing at all."

I blink, and I see her blood.

"This is how you repay him for giving his life to you?" she says. "You drag him into the catacombs and—and mutilate him? Look at him. He's ruined."

I glance back to see Ale's hand dart to the bandage over his eye. The hurt on his face is unmistakable.

"Are you done?" I say. "Because I'd like to move on to saving us all—"

"Do not speak to me that way," she says, advancing on me. "You're not our ruler."

"Don't come any closer," I say.

"You will never be our ruler," she says. "You don't have any power. You don't have any magic. You're just a soulless coward who thinks she's an exception to every—"

I blink.

And the cathedral is full of screams.

I stumble back, blinking frantically.

Ale's mamma is no longer standing in front of me. She no longer exists. She's just blood and guts and skin, splattered all over the aisle and everyone nearby.

No. I was just going to control her blood. Just a little bit. I was going to show everyone why they should listen to me.

I look at Ale, and he looks at me. Her blood is all over his face.

And then people are pouring out of the pews. They fill up the aisle and scramble for the chamber doors.

They're running away.

They don't realize what they're doing. I'm going to save them. They need me.

I race after them. I catch up to a woman and grab the back of her dress.

And then, all I see is blood.

The woman is gone. I don't know where she went. I try to find someone else, and I can't find anything but blood.

There's so much blood.

There's too much blood.

And then there's nothing at all.

I open my eyes, and I see the arches of the cathedral ceiling high above. I sit up, and my head spins. There's a sore spot on the back. I think I fainted.

It smells sickly and sweet. It's so dark and so quiet. I don't know where everyone is, but I vaguely remember them running away from me. It seems my encounter with them didn't go quite as I'd hoped.

Ale.

I leap to my feet.

They must be following Ale out to the catacombs. I have to stop them. I have to show them that I really can bring back the water.

I turn around, and I trip over something.

It's a pair of pants, soaked in blood and almost unrecognizable as clothing. I follow the blood down the aisle, trying to find the place where it ends. But it's not ending. It's stretching on and on and on.

Slowly, I lift my eyes.

The double doors at the front of the cathedral are still closed.

Scattered all over the aisle and in the pews are piles of bloody, abandoned clothes.

For a very long moment, I can't make myself comprehend it. My people were running away from me. It almost looks like they all died in here. But that's not possible.

I didn't mean to kill them. So they can't be dead.

Then I taste the blood in the air, and it hits me all at once.

I run, bursting out the cathedral doors. I stumble down the steps.

Everyone in my city was in there. Ale was in there. They can't be dead.

I was going to save them.

I'm alone in the cathedral square, underneath the bright red veil. All around me, the black manors are empty and silent. I've never heard a silence like this. It makes even my breath seem so loud. Too loud. It's coming so fast, but I can't seem to get any of it into my lungs.

They can't be dead. This is my city. These are my people. One little dose of magic can't possibly be enough to kill them all so quickly.

I hear a noise behind me and turn, but everything goes black. I scream.

"Emanuela! Emanuela!"

Somebody is wrestling with me.

"It's a blindfold," he says. "I'm just blindfolding you. That's all."

I break out of his grip and stumble back. I touch the fabric over my eyes.

"Ale," I whisper.

He's still here. I can't see him, but I can feel his presence.

I don't know how he could have possibly survived.

"Ale," I say. "I…"

The truth of it is sinking in, all at once.

"I can't control it," I say. "Why can't I control it?"

Nothing. But he's still there. I know he is. I can feel him looking at me.

"Ale," I say.

"I'm going to touch you again," he says.

"All—all right," I stammer.

And a moment later, I'm in his arms. We're moving, but I don't know where we're going. I don't know what's happening. But I don't have it in me to worry about it. There's only one thing I can think about.

I can't control it.

I wanted the most powerful magic I could have. But it's more powerful than me.

I smell the catacombs when we descend into them—dust and stale air. Ale gently sets me on the ground. I lie there on my side, curled up. The taste of blood is all in my mouth and throat, and I don't know if it's ever going to come out.

I know Ale is still nearby, and it's the only thing that brings me comfort. Right now, I feel like I could lie here forever, hiding. All I want to do is hide.

Then the ground underneath me turns cold.

I sit up.

"Ale," I say. "What's happening? Is that…is that the—"

My throat fills up with panic, and I can't finish. For a long moment, Ale doesn't say anything.

"I don't know what else to do with you," he whispers finally.

The ground disappears.

And I'm falling.

I hit the floor hard. I rip off my blindfold and scramble to my feet, looking around wildly.

But I see nothing. It's pitch-black. I wait for my eyes to adjust, and they don't.

I drop to my hands and knees, expecting to find the stone floor of the catacombs, but instead, I touch smooth metal. Iron, maybe. It smells like iron. I feel my way across the floor and bump into an iron wall.

There's absolutely no light. I have no idea where I am, and it's too quiet, and it's freezing, and my best friend is nowhere to be found, and I didn't mean for this to happen.

I just wanted to save my city.

I back up frantically. I run into something solid but strangely soft. It smells disconcertingly sweet, like flowery perfume.

I know that perfume. But by the time I realize it, Verene is already screaming and shoving me away.

Twenty

VERENE AND I DON'T SPEAK. WE SIT ON OPPOSITE SIDES OF our small prison at the bottom of the catacombs, and we do nothing.

Time passes—hours, or maybe days. I don't know. All I know is that we're inside a very deep cell. It's the blankest place I've ever been. It's so dark that my eyes never adjust. There are never any new sounds, and there are certainly never any visitors.

Except for the bundles of food and water. They fall from above every so often, carefully packed so that nothing breaks. At first, I don't eat. I can't eat. The taste of blood is still too strong in my throat, and everything I put in my mouth makes me retch. But eventually, I get so hungry that the instinct comes back. I don't have the will to do anything else, but somewhere deep inside, I suppose my body still has the will to survive.

The food is all from Theo, who must still be in Iris. I can tell by the bread. It's still fluffy in the middle and crunchy on the outside, like bread should be, but it's just not the same as Occhian bread.

Of course it's not Occhian bread. There's no one in Occhia to make bread. I'll never have Occhian bread again.

The bundles are mostly basic—fruit and loaves that can be easily wrapped—but there are always a few treats. There are chocolate bonbons and candies I've never had, sticky and chewy, tasting like everything from sweet orange to sharp licorice.

Verene never takes any of the candies. So either her brother is purposely sending her things she doesn't like, or they're all her favorites, and she's trying to take some sort of righteous stand in front of no audience.

There's no food coming from Ale. Apparently, he doesn't care if I live or die in this prison.

I have no idea where Ale is. He had a map of the catacombs, and he knows how to communicate with the vide. He has nowhere to go. He could have gone anywhere.

Time stretches on and on, and still, I refuse to speak to Verene. I don't want to have to explain the details of how I ended up being banished to a pitch-black cell at the bottom of the catacombs. I don't want to talk about all the terrible things I did to her in Iris. I don't want to listen to her preaching at me about how I ruined her, blaming me for why her life is in shambles.

She probably thinks I'm so quiet because I'm scheming. I'm not. The cell is too tall to climb out of, and it has no weak points in its walls. The iron keeps the vide from being able to reach us, apparently. It can toss the food inside, but we can't offer it any of our blood.

And even if I did get out, I'm just a girl with no city and magic she can't control. I might as well stay in here and lie curled up on the cold floor, alone.

I have no idea how long it's been when I hear a voice from the other side of the cell.

"Aren't you wondering how we found out about this place?" Verene says.

I realize that I've sort of forgotten how to speak. I struggle to answer her.

"I'm going to tell you whether you want to hear it or not," she says. "I miss the sound of my own voice."

"Of course you do," I mutter, surprising myself a little.

"After our maman died—" she says.

"After you killed her," I say.

"—we went into the catacombs," she says, pointedly ignoring me. "We knew there were other cities. She'd told us that much. And we knew, of course, that it would be dangerous to try and cross the other rulers. But we needed water, and I was so sure that we could find a better way. Something that none of them had found before."

She pauses.

"We got lost," she says. "The only reason we survived is because Theo had this ridiculous bag of supplies that would have lasted six months. Somehow we ended up at the very bottom of the catacombs. And we found this strange iron circle in the ground. I realized it looked like a door. So I opened it."

"Oh, always a smart move," I say. "What did you think you were going to find at the bottom of the catacombs? Do your people not have terrifying superstitions about what lives down here?"

I'm acting like I wouldn't have opened the door, too. But I would have done it in a smart way, with a weapon poised. Verene probably just flung it open without even warning her brother.

"We have plenty of superstitions," she says. "But... thinking about what was going to happen to Iris without water was scarier than any of that. And I thought…" She pauses again.

"What?" I say.

"Never mind," she says. "You're going to mock me again."

"I'm going to mock you regardless," I say.

"I thought it looked like a well," she says. "I don't know why there would have been a well down here. But that's what I thought. Anyway, I opened it before Theo even realized what was happening—"

I knew it.

"He pulled me back," she says. "I fell, and I accidentally cut my hand. I left blood on the floor. We looked down through the door, and we saw…this. It was empty. But then I noticed that my blood was gone. And there was a shadow in its place."

I'm quiet for a moment.

"So…" I say. "The vide was a prisoner."

"It was very weak at first," Verene says. "But I think it's getting stronger. Sometimes…sometimes I would test it. To see how much it could do. It could do more than I expected."

I think about the way it shattered my chains. I know what she means.

"All of this is your fault," I say. "All of it."

She doesn't say anything.

"This all happened because you decided to play around with a thing from the catacombs that you don't even understand," I say. "Because you decided to steal from my city until it was so thirsty that our ruler was— She was desperate for prisoners. And it's because of you that—"

"I know," she snaps.

I'm thrown for a moment. I didn't expect her to admit it.

"I know it wasn't right to steal from you," she says. "But until I met you, I'd never seen anyone from another city. I could almost believe that you weren't real. I don't feel good about what I did. Do you think I feel good about it?" Her voice is trembling. "But my people needed water. And I couldn't put them in a tower. I just couldn't. I couldn't be like..." She trails off.

"Tell me about what happened," I say. "When you did it."

"Did what?" she says stubbornly.

"When you killed her," I say.

At first, I think she's not going to answer me. It's too dark to see her, but I can imagine her huddled against the far wall of our cell, starved and weak with blood on her clothes but still insufferably determined to be perfect.

"She brought us into her study," she says quietly. "We thought it was for our lessons. But then she told us that it was time for her to choose her heir. We'd always thought we were going to rule together. But she told us how to do the ritual, and she told us that whoever did it to the other would be the heir, and I realized she had planned it that way all along."

Her voice has become strangely flat.

"We tried to run," she says. "But she stopped us. I knew she wanted him to win. He was always her favorite. He was smarter than me, and better at everything, and he had *control* over his emotions. She was always talking about how important it was to keep control. But she still didn't understand him. He would never have done that to me. I realized that if we didn't do what she wanted, she was going to kill us both. She didn't care. She would just try again, with new heirs. So...I killed her."

"How?" I say.

"Does it matter?" she says.

I think about the crack of the watercrea's bones on the cobblestone. I think about Verene's housekeeper, dribbling blood onto the floor. I think about my papá, standing over me with a rock in his hand, looking at me like I was just an obstacle in his path.

"I want to know," I say.

"She had this big glass jar on her desk," she says. "She would put blood in it and show us her magic. When we were children, we thought it was...I don't know. Interesting. We didn't understand. I grabbed the jar, and I hit her. She fell down, and I kept hitting her until the jar broke. I got one of the shards, and I stabbed her until she was dead." She pauses. "Until she had disappeared, actually. I didn't notice it at first. I just kept stabbing at the floor."

I shiver a little bit, imagining the sound of it. The feel of it.

"I said I would never do the ritual on anyone," Verene whispers. "I was so sure about that. But then...you threatened me. Just like she did. And I would have done anything to stop you."

She takes in a shuddering breath.

"I'll never be able to learn to control the magic," she says. "I'll hurt people. I deserve to be in here."

I go still.

"We can learn to control it?" I say.

"Our maman said it's always hard to control at first," she says. "She said she was going to train her heir for years."

So it's not just me.

"But I don't want to learn," Verene insists. "I don't want to go back to Iris and become the Eyes. Theo is bringing them water now. He was prepared to do it without me. He told me—" She chokes on a sob. "He told me that he always knew I'd go too far, and that he'd have to pick up the pieces."

She sobs again. "I just wanted to do something good for my city," she whispers.

She sounds broken, and I'm surprised by how much it hurts me. The pang in my chest is extremely disconcerting.

I don't want her to feel so helpless. I don't want her to give up and let herself wither away. She deserves better than that.

"No," I say. "It's not that you went too far. It's that you didn't go far enough."

"What?" she whispers.

"What is your brother doing in Iris?" I say. "Stealing water from the other cities, just like you were doing before? That's not the answer. You tried everything you could to change Iris for the better, and you couldn't. But it wasn't your fault."

"What was it, then?" she says.

"It's these cities," I say. "In these cities, we can't get water unless we feed on blood. The person who makes the water can't do it unless they feed on eyes. Of course you couldn't truly change your city for the better, because your city is broken. They all are. And who made them this way? Who's been around for a thousand years? Who told everyone that this was how things were always going to be?"

"The rulers," Verene says. "All of them."

I'm on my feet. I haven't been on my feet in so long, and it's dizzying.

"How do we know they're right?" I say. "They kept so much

from us. The Eyes was your maman, and she barely told you anything."

"She said we would learn everything once we had our magic," Verene says. "But I don't even know if that's true. She said she was going to pass her power on, but she liked having power. She was so secretive about it. My—" She stammers a little bit. "My papa didn't even know the truth about where she got her magic. He felt sorry for her. He thought she was trapped. If he'd known…"

"Of course she liked having power," I say. "Who doesn't like it? Who doesn't want to be the most powerful person in the whole city?"

I hear Verene rustling. She's on her feet, too.

"But if we can get out of here, we'll be just as powerful as the other rulers," she says. "No—we'll be more powerful. Because there's two of us."

"Yes," I say.

"We can use the power for good," she says. "We can find out what the other rulers are hiding. We can find out why they're keeping things this way."

"And then we can stop it." I'm rushing forward in my excitement. "Really stop it. And then we'll be—"

I bump into her and stop short, startled. I didn't realize she was so close to me.

But she is. I can smell her, sweet and fresh underneath all the grime. My hand seems to have gotten tangled in something soft—her shirt. Beneath, I can feel the warmth of her body. I can feel her stomach rising and falling as she breathes.

And then her fingers are on mine. She's no longer wearing gloves. I feel the rough gauze of the bandage around her wounded palm, and her long, delicate fingers. They curl around mine, and I tighten my grip without even thinking.

She shoves my hand away.

"No," she says.

She backs up.

"No," she repeats. "I'm not—I'm not working with you. What am I even saying? We could never be a team. You'll just use me and betray me, because you don't care about doing good. All you care about is yourself."

My fingers are still clutching empty air. My heart is pounding in my throat.

"I'm not going to forget what you did to me and my city," she says. "I'm never going to forget. You can pretend that you want to find something better, but I know just what sort of person you are."

I back up until I hit the cold wall. It brings me abruptly back to myself.

I know what sort of person I am, too. I'm a girl who's going to save the cities that still need to be saved. I'm a girl who's going to turn them upside down and change the things that need to be changed. I'm a girl who's going to live forever.

I cross my arms. Obviously, Verene can't see me, but I need to know that I look effortless and completely unaffected by her and her sweet-smelling shirt.

"Fine," I say. "It's not like I need you and your sanctimonious, bothersome prattling. You'll slow me down. In fact, I'd rather we didn't work together."

"Fine," she says.

"I'll just figure out how to break out of this prison on my own," I say.

For a long moment, she's quiet, and the challenge hangs in the air.

"Not if I figure it out first," she says.

I have no way of knowing for sure, but I swear I can hear her smiling.

And that's...perfect.

Epilogue

The city of Iris is quiet.

Overhead, the veil is the blazing red of midday, and clustered below are the white manors. The beautiful plants the Circles of Iris used to display on the sides of their houses—each family quietly judging and trying to outdo the other—are gone. Now, the city is blank and dry.

But the streets are full. The people have all emerged. There are groups in every intersection, huddled around the white marble fountains. There are vases and buckets and jugs clutched in their hands. They're waiting.

For almost a thousand years, the people of Iris had a mysterious ruler who put them in a tower and took their blood. Then, in a two-year daze that doesn't feel real to anyone anymore, they had a girl in a white gown who gave them everything they ever wanted.

Now, they have this. Every day, at noon, the fountains turn on, just like they used to. But this time, they only run for five minutes.

They don't know how it's happening. It's been a whole month, and no one has seen the girl in the white gown. Sometimes people claim that they saw someone who looks suspiciously like her brother. A lady in the Circle du Tasse insists that she peeked out her window at night and spotted him lurking around one of the fountains. A kitchen maid in the Circle du Richard is pretty sure he was the one who snuck in and stole the bread she'd just finished baking. But they haven't made an effort to chase him down. They don't want to get too close to the son of the Eyes. After all, he and his sister hardly ever left the cathedral, and no one has any idea what went on in there.

The cathedral has been reduced to a crumbling charred ruin. The banner that was hanging from the balcony, showing a drawing of the eight cities that nobody really understood, has turned to ash.

Some bold people went into the catacombs, looking for answers. None of them ever returned. The rest decided to stay in their homes. They decided to survive, the way they always have. They don't have much, but at least they have water.

And right now, they're just waiting for it.

It's almost time. The people standing around the empty fountains start to jostle one another, subtly. They pretend that there's an order to things. Each family is allowed a certain number of people at the front. But really, the moment the water appears, it's chaos.

The people of Iris are so busy waiting that they don't notice what's happening up above.

The brilliant red of the veil is shifting and growing. It almost seems like the veil is getting closer to the city. And closer.

Then it stops. And everything is still, like it never even happened.

With a rush and a gurgle, the fountains of Iris come to life. No one was looking at the veil. No one saw.

And far below the cities, at the very bottom of the catacombs, a girl has just climbed out of a prison.

ACKNOWLEDGMENTS

I have no one to acknowledge. I did this all myself, and frankly, you all should acknowledge me for letting you read it.

That's what Emanuela would say if given the chance to write this section. I, her author, am extremely humble, and in my humbleness, I need to thank all of the following:

Thank you to my agent, Carrie Pestritto. You saw something in this gremlin of a book that no one else did, and for that, I am forever grateful. Thanks also to Samantha Fabien, Elana Roth Parker, Laura Dail, and Tamar Rydzinski for your support and behind-the-scenes work through the wild ride that has been taking this story from "Word document hiding on my computer" to "actual book on the shelves."

Thank you to my editor, Alexandra Hightower, for taking me on with such poise and enthusiasm. I can sleep at night knowing I've landed in such great hands. Thank you also to the whole team at Little, Brown, including but not limited to: Alvina Ling, Katie Boni, Bill Grace, Savannah Kennelly, Victoria Stapleton, and Sasha Illingworth. I'm so grateful for your hard work and so happy to be a part of the LBYR family. And thank you to Billelis for the coolest cover I've ever laid eyes on.

To Patrice Caldwell: thank you for being the "yes" that every author dreams of. To Hannah Allaman: thank you for understanding this book better than I do. I've been so fortunate to have so many champions, and it was an honor to work with you both. Thank you also to the other members of the Disney team who saw this book early in life, especially Jody Corbett, for making sure I described eyeballs correctly, and Tyler Nevins, for the beautiful designs.

A thousand thanks go out to my unruly coven of writer friends. When I first met you over the Internet, I was skeptical. So far, none of you have turned out to be catfishes. But there's still time. Thanks to Maddy Colis, Ashley Burdin, Alexis Castellanos, Kat Cho, Amanda Foody, Tara Sim, Claribel Ortega, Melody Simpson, Ella Dyson, Meg Kohlmann, Axie Oh, Amanda Haas, Erin Bay, Akshaya Raman, Katy Rose Pool, Janella Angeles, and Christine Lynn Herman. To Ella, Meg, and Amanda: your early enthusiasm kept me going. I drank it up like a vampire. To Christine and Tara: thanks for the memes—I mean, emotional support. To Erin: thanks for the emojis. To Katy: thanks for arguing with me about pedantic things and feeding my Ravenclaw soul. To Janella: thanks for the solidarity and *Shrek* memes (the two food groups). To Akshaya: thanks for enduring the text meltdowns and for the formal Skype interview that led me to this group in the first place. I'm so glad I picked up that call.

And thanks to all of you for teaching me how to use a gas stove.

To Jessica Rubinkowski, Julie C. Dao, Rebecca Caprara, Kati

Gardner, Kevin van Whye, Austin Gilkeson, Heather Kaczynski, Jordan Villegas—thank you for the emails and so much more. No author should go through publishing alone. Thank you for making sure I didn't.

So many thanks also to Christine Calella, Malika Maya, Emily A. Duncan, Isabel Sterling, Sadie Blach, Kalyn Josephson, and Rosiee Thor. Thank you for your support. You are all shining stars. That sounded fake. It's not.

Thanks to my family, and especially my parents, for gamely going along with…all of this. Also, thanks for giving me the *Little Shop of Horrors* soundtrack at a formative age. Virtmo.

And finally, thanks to you, the reader. The author is only part of it. We all bring a little bit of ourselves to the books we read. Thank you for being here.

Turn the page for a sneak preview of the
darkly delightful sequel

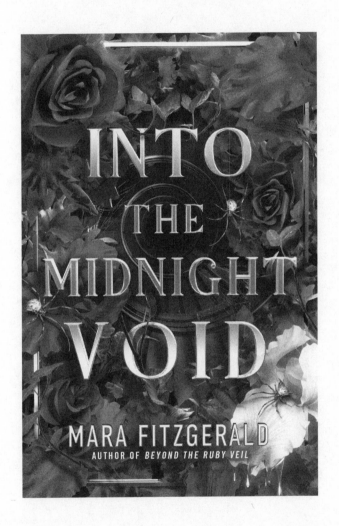

AVAILABLE JANUARY 2022

ONE

I'VE BROKEN HIM.

And I haven't even done anything yet.

All I did was stand here, waiting quietly as the man was dragged before me. My guards dropped him unceremoniously at the foot of the cathedral steps. He lifted his eyes, beheld my form, and in an instant, he was sobbing like a baby.

It's been going on for about ten seconds. But it already feels like an hour.

"I didn't mean it, Highest Lady Emanuela," the man manages to choke out. "I didn't mean it."

"Oh, so you're not even going to try and deny it?" I say. "Good. We can get this over with quickly."

"I didn't mean to insult you," he insists. "I simply had too much wine at the party, and I mixed up my words."

"And what were your words again, exactly?" I say.

The man hesitates, trembling, his eyes on the stairs. "I didn't mean it—"

"What were your words?" I say, sharper.

The man's bottom lip wobbles treacherously. He looks around at the assembled crowd. They're huddled at the edges of the cathedral square, watching the proceedings in wide-eyed silence.

All of my prisoners have this exact same moment of desperation. They hope that, against all odds, someone is going to leap out of the safety of the throng and help them. This man's clothing is finely stitched, his jacket a rich shade of green and the gold buttons polished within an inch of their lives. He thinks people will care about him because he's wealthy. If not that, then surely his mother, or his best friend, or paramour will come to his defense.

They're not coming. They never do.

"I didn't mean it—" the man tries again.

"Guard?" I say.

One of my guards, who's standing stiffly at the man's side, unfolds a sheet of paper and begins to read.

"All I'm saying is that it's strange. Our old ruler lived for a thousand years, and now she's just gone? What gives this girl the right to take over and change everything? Why does she hide behind all those veils? And why is she so short? If you ask me, she's nothing but an ugly child pretending to have magic. She can't actually make us any water. It will dry up soon, and she'll be unmasked as the murdering fraud she is. You'll see."

Silence.

The man kneeling on the ground has gone extremely still.

"Anything else you'd like to add?" I say.

Apparently not.

I gesture at the guards, and they pick the prisoner up.

"Wait!" The man comes back to life, flailing uselessly in

their grasp. "Please, Highest Lady Emanuela. I'm sorry. I'm sorry. I don't want to die."

"Well, you should have considered that before you disrespected me," I say.

And then he's gone. The guards drag him, sniveling and pleading, around to the back of the cathedral. Another guard in a red coat approaches from the edge of the crowd and bows to me.

"That was the last of them, Highest Lady Emanuela," he says.

The entire crowd holds their breath, waiting for me to declare that I'm satisfied. For one long, delicious moment, I stay silent and let them imagine what could happen if I'm not.

"Very well," I say finally.

I turn and march up the cathedral steps, my long red cloak streaming behind me. The people gathered around the square don't move. They won't move until I pull the double doors shut. Then, they'll go back to their lives, and they'll wait for the next appearance of the mysterious Highest Lady Emanuela. And, if they're smart, they won't go around telling people that I'm an ugly child.

I proceed through the dim foyer of the cathedral. Two guards are poised at the entrance to the inner chamber, waiting for me on either side of the tall arched doorway.

"The prisoners are ready, Highest Lady Emanuela," one of them says.

I sweep past them without a word of acknowledgment. This building used to be the center of life in the city called Auge. They had worship and weddings and every single holiday celebration here. They spent almost as much time in it as they did their own houses. But now, the cathedral belongs to me.

The room has been emptied out. In the center, sitting alone on the black-and-white tile floor, is an enormous glass tank shaped like a dome. The prisoners of the day—about twenty in total—are trapped inside. As always, they're scrambling for freedom, clawing at the door the guards have bolted shut. The man I just had arrested is kicking futilely at the thick wall. When they see me coming for them, the frenzy only intensifies.

As I stop before the tank, my guards shut the doors to the inner chamber with a dull thud. Highest Lady Emanuela always does her magic in private.

I say nothing to my prisoners. I simply reach up and start to pull aside the veils covering my face.

All the clamor inside the tank stops. The prisoners turn to watch, transfixed in spite of their terror. I haven't looked in a mirror in a long time, but I know I'm very pretty, with tiny sharp features and chin-length hair that I cut to perfection myself. And then, of course, there's the thing everyone notices first—my viciously dark eyes.

Things used to be different in these cities. People died for something they couldn't control. They got a silly little mark on their skin, called an omen, and they were forced to hand themselves over to their ruler. She locked them in her tower and killed them slowly, draining their blood through a little needle in their neck. They wasted away for days, feeling every drop of life being squeezed out of their body.

I changed all of that. I control who lives and dies now. People who respect me are rewarded. People who don't are shoved into this glass dome for execution. I'm not like their old leader. I don't put them through long, agonizing deaths alone in a cell.

I allow them to die on their feet, surrounded by their fellow misguided citizens.

And as a little treat, the last thing they ever see is my face.

I blink, and my magic floods into my eyes, cold and hungry. My new vision strips away everything else about the people in front of me, leaving the only piece of them it wants—their blood. Just like that, the prisoners have become nothing but intricate, pulsating webs of veins.

They barely even have time to scream. A moment later, they're all gone, exploded out of their skins, and the inside of the dome is soaked with blood.

"That's what you get," I inform them.

And then I'm gone, waltzing through a side door without looking back.

I make my way through a familiar maze of narrow halls, winding up pitch-black staircases. The veil outside is approaching the dark red of evening, but I don't bother to light any lanterns. I'm used to the dark.

The cathedral has four spires, one at each corner. I've claimed the one at the top right as my personal quarters. It's a small, unassuming space—aggressively neat, the way I prefer it. On one side of the round room is a small red love seat. In the middle is my sewing table, draped in swathes of vivid red fabric, a half-completed gown on a mannequin. And over by the window is my desk.

This doesn't look like a living space that could sustain a normal human, with all their normal human needs. Because it's not.

I approach my desk, pulling off my crown and depositing it

carefully in my tank of pet spiders. I let them weave fresh webs among the thorns each night to achieve that perfect, shimmery effect. Then I sit down, and for a moment, against my will, my eyes go to the darkening veil outside. It's hard to ignore. At the top of this spire, the noise of the streets below is far away, and there's nothing but the two of us—the girl that looms over the city, and the veil that looms over the girl.

To everyone else, the veil is a presence as constant and inevitable as air. It stretches above our heads, surrounding our manors with a glowing presence that turns red in the day and black at night. My people used to say it's where our souls dwell before we're born, and it's where they return when we die. Everyone in every city believes, more or less, the same thing. We live our little lives until the veil puts omens on our skin. When the omens cover us, we die, and we have no control over any of it.

When I took over, I told people that we weren't going to let our omens have so much power over us. I told them that the first mark isn't the death sentence they used to believe, and that some people live for years before their omens spread and kill them—a fact their previous ruler conveniently glossed over so she could terrify everyone into giving themselves up to her tower. The people were uneasy at first, but a few months later, they'd all seen the truth of it for themselves. My favored citizens—the ones who are wise enough to show me respect—see this for the gift it is. Now, in Auge, they happily walk around with omens exposed, even going out of their way to show them off if they're feeling bold. The old wives have come up with ways to divulge meaning from their location—they claim people who get marked on the face first are the luckiest, and so on and so on. When someone's omens do spread, as they always will, they're in their own homes, going out on their own terms.

I've made things so much better for so many people. Right now, somewhere in the streets below, there could be a little girl sitting on her bed, staring at the red mark that just appeared on her skin for no reason at all. Now that I'm here, she doesn't have to die.

And the best part is that I'm just getting started. The old rulers devoted themselves to keeping things exactly the same for a thousand years. Their lack of vision was tragic—not to mention dull—but fortunately, that's all over with, and a much worthier successor has taken their place.

I finally light my lantern, and I turn my attention to the map on my desk. It shows the eight cities, arranged in a ring, barely overlapping with their neighbors. In the center of the cities is the veil. Outside of the cities is the veil. Everything except us is the veil.

There are two cities I've left unlabeled. I never look at them. I only bother with the six I control. I make a little tick mark next to Auge to indicate today's successful visit.

As I set down my pen, I become aware that the hairs on the back of my neck are standing on end. Someone else is in the room. And they're right behind me.

There's only one person in the six cities who can sneak up on me like this. It takes skill to move through the darkness as easily as I do.

I hastily fiddle with my outfit, making sure it's perfect. When I stand up and turn around, I make a show of being casual about it, but my heart is thrumming.

"Fancy seeing you here," I say.

"Oh, believe me," the intruder says. "I don't fancy it."

There's one very important thing that sets me apart as the ruler of the six cities. I have magic, and it makes me dangerous and immortal and untouchable. It creates water from blood and keeps my people alive. It's a power that no one else has.

No one else, that is, except the girl in front of me.

Beneath my veils, I smile. It's always nice to see an old enemy.

Mara Fitzgerald

writes young adult fantasy about unlikable female characters who ruin everything. She is a biologist by day and spends entirely too much time looking at insects under a microscope. She was born near Disney World and now lives near Graceland, which is almost as good. *Beyond the Ruby Veil* is her debut novel.